Invitation from the Author

My "day job" is as a writer/producer of music. Therefore, I couldn't imagine ILLUMINATED without a musical accompaniment. I called on some of my closest and most talented friends in the industry to help out. I hope you'll enjoy listening to this soundtrack as much as I enjoyed writing the novel to it!

The soundtrack is available totally free at Mattbronleewe.com.

Advance Acclaim for *Illuminated*

Matt Bronleewe has crafted a seat-of-your-pants thrill ride into a world of cryptic messages within ancient documents. *Illuminated* is what *The Da Vinci Code* should have been. The characters are more endearing, the twists more believable, the story more satisfying. And don't even get me started about that nasty she-villain! *Illuminated* is sure to be a welcome addition to any suspense fan's library.

—Robert Liparulo, author of *Deadfall, Germ,* and *Comes a Horseman*

If you turned *National Treasure* into *International Treasure*, traded Da Vinci codes for Gutenberg Bibles, married it to Indiana Jones, and finally added the pacing of *24* you'd be in the neighborhood of *Illuminated*. Make sure you have plenty of time when you pick this up because you may not easily put it down. Better known as one of the founding members of the band Jars of Clay, Bronleewe has struck gold with his first novel. This one goes to eleven.

—Mark Parolini, *Aspiring Retail*

I think we're going to have to invent a new genre to describe Matt Bronleewe's "theological thriller," *Illuminated*. Obsessively detailed and so fast-paced it could outrun a freight train, Bronleewe's debut is a taut, intelligent ride that will induce finger cramps from how tightly you'll be clutching the pages.

—Robin Parrish, author of *Relentless* and *Fearless*

Matt Bronleewe bursts onto the scene with a spirited thriller. I always love authors who can mix history and suspense, and Bronleewe does so with doses of fact, sprinkles of laughter, and bucket-loads of action. Reading *Illuminated* is like watching a big-budget summer movie played out on the pages.

—Eric Wilson, author of *A Shred of Truth*

Matt Bronleewe's ability to take something and turn it into an opportunity for innovative expression is one of the very reasons I choose to work with him so often and respect him so much. And *Illuminated* is no different. I was educated while I was entertained. This is not your every day read, but such an intelligent escape from it. Loved it.

—Tiffany Arbuckle Lee a.k.a. Plumb, Songwriter and Curb Records recording artist

Illuminated is a riveting debut from a fresh new voice in thriller fiction.

—Chris Well, author of *Tribulation House*

Illuminated is a wonderful work that shows Matt Bronlewee is simply warming up.

—Dan Haseltine (reader of some books, and writer of essays) Jars of Clay

Multi-talented is a vast understatement when used to describe Matt Bronleewe! I have worked with Matt in his song-writing and producing capacity for many years now and have long been impressed with his creativity. Now we add novelist to the list! This book reads like a movie. With drama and realism combined, Matt takes his readers on an unforgettable and thought-provoking journey. Rock on Matt!

—Rebecca St. James

ILLUMINATED

matt bronleewe

THOMAS NELSON
Since 1798

NASHVILLE   DALLAS   MEXICO CITY   RIO DE JANEIRO   BEIJING

Published in Nashville, Tennessee, by Thomas Nelson. Thomas Nelson is a trademark of Thomas Nelson, Inc.

Author is represented by the literary agency of Alive Communications, Inc., 7680 Goddard Street, Suite 200, Colorado Springs, CO 80920, www.alivecommunications.com

Thomas Nelson books may be purchased in bulk for educational, business, fund-raising, or sales promotional use. For information, please e-mail SpecialMarkets@ThomasNelson.com.

Scripture quotations are from the King James Version of the Bible.

Publisher's Note: This novel is a work of fiction. Names, characters, places, and incidents are either products of the author's imagination or used fictitiously. All characters are fictional, and any similarity to people living or dead is purely coincidental.

Library of Congress Cataloging-in-Publication Data

Bronleewe, Matt.
  Illuminated / Matt Bronleewe.
    p. cm.
  ISBN: 978-1-59554-249-6
  1. Manuscripts, Medieval–Fiction. I. Title.
PS3602.R64266I45 2007
813'.6–dc22

2007015670

Printed in the United States of America
07 08 09 10 11 QW 7 6 5 4 3

For Karin.
Your love has illuminated the path of my life.

Truth is captive in a small number of little manuscripts that guard the common treasures. Let us break the seal that binds these holy things, let us give wings to truth that it might fly.

JOHANNES GUTENBERG

illuminated prologue illuminated

AD 1415
KONSTANZ, GERMANY

The storm clouds unleashed their torrent of rain upon the people gathered by the street. None scattered for cover. All were waiting for the heretic to pass by. All were waiting for the opportunity to spit in his face, throw a rock at his feet, mock his defiance of the Holy Roman Empire. Their hatred grew as they jostled for a better view, a front-row view of the hellfire in the devil worshipper's eyes. Seventeen-year-old Johannes Gutenberg struggled through the confusion, his own eyes fixed on his father.

"Try to keep up," his father said. "The metallurgist won't wait forever."

"Coming," Johannes said. But he stopped for a moment to glance at the spectacle on the street. A block ahead he saw a man draped in heavy rusted chains, walking toward him. A small battalion circled the man, swinging their swords to keep the raucous crowd at bay.

"Johannes!" his father said. But the boy lost sight of him, lost among the growing throng. Pushed to the ground, Johannes crawled to the edge of the street. He stood as the chained man approached. Johannes squinted up, seeing that the heretic wore a tall, pointed hat—a miter—the same hat a priest wore. Only this one bore a terrifying image of the devil and a mocking title: Ringleader of Heretics.

The chained man staggered to the ground. Without thinking about the implications, Johannes leaped to his side to help him. A soldier pointed his sword at Johannes's neck. "Leave him alone, boy!"

He ignored the soldier and gazed into the heretic's eyes. Despite the man's state of distress, there was not a shred of malice in them. In that moment, Johannes sensed a peace so deep and so profound that the howling of the crowd around him faded to a whisper. The man murmured something, motioning him closer. Johannes leaned in.

"Boy, get away, or you will burn at the stake with this devil worshipper!" the soldier barked. "Do you hear me?"

The heretic reached out and placed a small object in Johannes's hand. "What is it?" he asked, fingering a small metal disc. But the heretic did not reply.

A sharp pain stabbed Johannes's shoulder, the point of a sword digging into his skin. He felt himself lifted and shoved back into the crowd. The press of bodies prevented him from falling, and he slipped the object into his pocket. He turned to watch the heretic shuffle down the road, the angry mob still swirling about him. Had this all really happened? Had his encounter been nothing more than a strange dream?

His father's strong hand yanked him to his senses. "Where on earth have you been? There is no doubt I will be late now. Your mother will not be proud to hear that her son has caused such disgrace."

"Sorry," he said. He followed his father down a side street, away from the crowd, fingering the hidden disc. "What will become of that man?"

"That's no business of ours," his father said. They walked for many blocks in silence. His father studied a map, and before long they stopped before a small green door.

After two knocks, the door opened and a face appeared, broad and ruddy, with wisps of hair sticking out from his head like shocks of bleached wheat. "Can I help you?"

"It's Gutenberg. And son, for that matter."

"Gutenberg? Yes, yes, come in," the metallurgist said, ushering them inside. "I've been expecting you. Didn't know if you would make it with all the quarreling going on."

"We almost didn't," the father said, glaring at his son. "Where is the machine I have traveled so far to see?"

Johannes's cheeks flamed. The metallurgist pointed toward the adjacent room. "Go ahead," he directed the elder Gutenberg. "I think you'll be more than pleased with the progress we've made. It can stamp nearly twice as many coins as the last machine." Johannes, not invited to see the device, hung back. He thrust his hand into his pocket and drew the metal piece out into the light, as if seeing it with his own two eyes might confirm that it was real. It was a coin.

"May I take a look?" the metallurgist asked. He took the coin and bit it between his yellow teeth. "Tin," he pronounced, flipping it back to Johannes. "Where did you find that?" he asked, his voice as much accusing as curious.

Johannes held up the coin and watched the light dance on its edges. "A man in the street gave it to me. The one they were calling a heretic."

The metallurgist looked over his shoulder, then back at Johannes. "That man will die today. And his death will mark the beginning of a new age." He pointed to an image on the coin: a woman's face. "Do you see this?" he said, voice quivering. "It is the mark of the coming revolution."

"And what about this?" Johannes asked, indicating an impression on the flip side.

The metallurgist smiled. "That you will have to discover for yourself."

The occupants of Flight 1213 weren't surprised when the lights went out. They had been flickering for the last ten minutes, so it was no shock when the blackness hit. It was more surprising, however, when the airplane dropped from the heavens like a bird shot in midair.

August Adams could hear the scream from first class over the deafening roar of the engines. A drink cart raced down the aisle, narrowly missing a curious youngster who retracted his head just in time. The plane leveled out for a brief moment, then dipped sharply to the left. A suitcase toppled out of an overhead storage unit, striking an old man two rows up on the forehead. He slumped forward. The child next to him began to wail.

At the window in seat 24F, August flipped open his seat buckle and jumped to his feet. He climbed directly over the row in front of him, angering the businessmen parked there. "Watch it, buddy!" one of them said as August put a foot on his shoulder.

August thrust his body over the next set of seats. The boy looked up at him and shrieked, "What's wrong with Grandpa?"

"Don't worry. It's going to be okay," August said to him, grabbing a scarf held out by a woman in the next row. A steady stream of blood oozed from the gash. The man appeared to be unconscious. August rummaged through his mental files, calling up a first-aid manual he'd read during a CPR class. "What's your grandpa's name?"

"I think it's Ford," the boy said.

August tied the scarf around the grandfather's head, pressing to stop the bleeding. He instructed the businessman behind him to apply pressure to the wound. The businessman shook his head. "I'm staying right where I am," he said. Bathed in the red emergency lights that illuminated the cabin, the businessman bore the distinct expression of a man who had just wet his pants.

"This guy might die if you don't help me."

The speakers crackled above them, probably the captain trying to tell them to remain calm. *Too late*, thought August.

"Why don't you do it?" the businessman asked, voice quivering.

"Because I need to find a first-aid kit," August said. "C'mon, man! Just loosen your belt and lean forward. Wrap your hands around the top of the seat. I'll help you."

"I can't," said the businessman. "I'm sorry."

The two men next to him had their heads tucked firmly between their legs, their arms crossed protectively over their necks. They weren't going to be any help either.

"Someone get a first-aid kit for this man!" August said, slamming a fist down on the seat. The plane shook again, and he anchored his hand to the armrest like a bull rider.

The lights came back on. August felt a tap on his side. "Is my grandpa going to be okay?" The boy was only a couple of years younger than his own son. August weighed his answer. "I hope so," he said.

A flight attendant rushed down the aisle with the first-aid kit. She cracked it open and pulled out a wad of bandages, which she immediately placed over the old man's wound.

"Is there a flashlight in there?" August asked, pointing to the kit.

"I think so," she said, rifling through it. The plane dipped, and the contents spilled to the floor.

August reached down and retrieved a small penlight. He pried open the old man's left eye and shone the light in it. He then repeated the process for the right eye.

"You're checking for a concussion?"

"If the injury caused his brain to swell, there could be dangerous tissue compression inside his cranium. That compression would put pressure on his optic nerves, and his pupils would react strangely to the light." August stepped into the aisle and had her take a look at the old man's eyes. "You should check him every fifteen minutes."

"Are you a doctor?"

"I wish. You should ask for one on board. I just never forget a word I read."

"Lucky for him."

"Yeah, well, let me know if he's okay," August said, turning to go back to his seat. Down the aisle this time. "The kid too. He looked pretty frightened."

"He's not the only one," she said.

"Sorry about that, folks," the captain said, his amplified voice clear now. "Please keep your seat belts fastened, as we might be experiencing a few more bumps before we reach New York."

"If that was just a bump, I'd hate to see what a real problem looks like," the attractive occupant of 24D said to August as he squeezed past. "Not that you wouldn't be able to handle it, Superman."

"Just trying to help out," August said, sitting down. "I have a boy about the same age."

"And I'll bet he gets his casual good looks from you." She laughed. "You're married?" she asked, glancing at his ringless fingers.

August wondered if the question implied anything more. "Divorced. One year and counting," August said. He put out his hand. "August Adams."

"Xandria Muro," the woman said, returning the handshake with a confident grip. A memorable name to go with the memorable face. "We've got almost seven hours left to fly, so I apologize in advance if I end up telling you my life story."

August got the impression from her crisp business attire that her life story would be less than thrilling. "Actually, if you don't mind, I was thinking that I might—"

"Get some sleep?" Xandria asked. "Sorry."

"No, it's okay," August said, not sure why he felt bad about try-ing to avoid conversation. Her embarrassed blush highlighted her round cheekbones, which seemed lifted in a perpetual smile. "I probably couldn't sleep right now anyway. After all the commotion."

She accepted the invitation by tucking a gold strand of hair behind her ear and tilting her head. "You were quite the superhero, weren't you? So what do you do when you're not saving the elderly?" Xandria asked.

August laughed. "If I'm a superhero, then we're in trouble," he said. "I collect and sell rare books. Emphasis on the *sell* part."

"How'd you get into that?"

"I thought you were supposed to tell me *your* life's story," August said, restraining a smile. "But to answer your question, I used to be an archaeobibliologist."

Her full lips rounded into an *O*. "You studied Bibles?"

"Bibles are a primary focus, but an archaeobibliologist examines all kinds of texts."

"Examines them for what?"

"Clues. Historical and cultural references, mainly, but also for information about ancient secret societies, lost treasures . . . you know, real-life Indiana Jones-type stuff."

"Sounds amazing. Why did you quit?"

"I didn't quit," August said. "I just got tired of sitting in a room, reading about adventure. I wanted to make some of my own."

"Is that why you were in Germany?" She pointed to a book on the seat between them about art confiscated by the Third Reich. August had dumped it there when he bolted up.

"I spent a month there tracking down a book. Now I'm going to New York to deliver it to the buyer."

"Must be a pretty important book."

"My buyer thinks so," August said. "It's a Gutenberg Bible. Dates back to about 1457. It was originally commissioned by a guy named Prince Hunyadi, who wanted to commemorate his victory at the Siege of Belgrade. After Hunyadi died, some of his subjects hid the book. No one knew where it was until about a year ago, when I was contacted by my buyer. He had a tip on where the book was buried. Turned out he was right."

"I guess that's not something you'd just send him in the mail."

August chuckled. "Insurance wouldn't cover it. Plus, I want to be there to pick up his check in person."

Xandria smiled. "Must be a big one."

"Enough to get me back on my feet, hopefully," August said. "I've got to start saving up if I plan to get my son into college."

"You don't look old enough to have a kid in college," Xandria said.

She was definitely flirting. He slapped on his Nicolas Cage smile again and ran a hand over his high hairline. "I'm not. Charlie is only eight."

"Does he live with you?"

"No," August said. "He lives with my ex. To be honest, it's probably for the best. Business keeps me on the road constantly."

Xandria fetched her purse from under the seat in front of her and pulled out a plastic sleeve full of pictures. "I've got two," she said. "A girl and a boy." She handed the pictures to August. "That's Eric. And that's Samantha. It's driving me crazy not to be with them."

"I know what you mean," August said, glancing through the photos. The beach. The zoo. The carnival. August couldn't help but feel guilty for not having similar pictures of Charlie. He handed them back to her. "Makes you think about what's really important in life."

A muffled ring came from Xandria's purse. She excused herself from the conversation and answered the call. "Hello? Yeah. Everything's great. We hit some turbulence, but hopefully it'll be smooth sailing from here." She placed a slender finger on her lips while she listened. "Okay. Yes. I will. Yes. See you soon." She hung up. "Sorry. My horrible boss is always checking on me."

"You get coverage up here?" August asked.

"It's a sat-phone," Xandria said, showing it to him. "Brand-new. A prototype. I work for the provider. I can talk to anyone in the world, crystal clear." She smoothed out a wrinkle in her black skirt. "You watch, everyone will have one a year from now."

"I should get one of those," August said. "I could talk to my son everywhere I travel. He'd get a kick out of that."

"Now you're making me feel guilty." Xandria held out the phone, her clear eyes dancing. "You want to talk to your son?"

August held up both hands. "I wasn't trying to imply anything."

"I know you weren't. But I know how it is, being away from home and everything. Here. I insist."

August looked at his watch. Charlie lived in Washington DC. There, it was only late afternoon. The timing was perfect. April, his ex, wouldn't be home for another few hours, meaning he could avoid an argument with her. "I'm sure it's a really expensive call," he said, as weak an argument as he could present.

"No problem. It's a company phone," Xandria said, placing the sleek device in August's hands. "I can tell you miss him. Believe me, I understand. You should call him."

August's calls to Charlie were far too infrequent. Traveling around the world, he would often forget what time it was back in DC and end up calling at three in the morning. Only a couple weeks ago, April answered, voice groggy, and immediately hung up on him after looking at a clock. "Hey, thanks for this," he said, dialing the number. It only rang once before someone answered.

"Adams residence. Charlie speaking."

His voice sounded younger than August remembered. "Hi, buddy," August said.

"Dad? Where are you? Are you in DC?"

"No, afraid I'm not," August said. "But I wish I was." In the background, he heard the sound of the television. Probably PBS, the only thing April allowed him to watch.

"I wish you were here too," Charlie said. "Hey, Dad, I made a new friend at school today. His name is Nicholas. He likes *Power Rangers* just like me."

"Your mom lets you watch *Power Rangers?*"

"No."

"Are you watching it now?"

"Yes," Charlie said, his slow response telling August the rest of the story.

"It'll be our little secret," August said. "Where's Grandma Rose?"

"She's talking in the other room with somebody."

"Who?"

"I don't know. But I think I heard him say something about the FBI when I was spying on him earlier."

The FBI? What could they want with Grandma Rose? "You playing Superspy today?" Xandria gave August a knowing smile and raised her eyebrows as she returned her photos to her purse. She had the prettiest—

"Oh, yeah! Mom got me a cool Sonic Sleuth for my straight-A report card. It's got a range of three hundred feet, Dad. Grandma Rose and I tested it. You'll have to check it out."

"You know I want to, buddy. Can you go find out who the guy is?" August asked. "I don't like the idea of a stranger in the house."

"Sure, Dad. Be back in a minute," Charlie said.

"But don't let him see you, okay?"

"Dad. Of course they won't see me. I'm a superspy." There was a clonk as Charlie set the phone down on the floor and pattered away.

August turned to Xandria, wondering if he had overstayed his welcome on her phone. "Sorry. I swear I'll be off in a minute."

"Don't worry about it," Xandria said, waving him away. "But you're going to owe me."

"I hear this airline has an amazing wine list."

"Perfect," Xandria said.

August listened as Charlie's phone rattled around on the floor. A few seconds later, he picked it up, wheezing. He kept repeating something, but August couldn't make out what he was saying.

"Slow down," August said. "What is it? What's going on?"

". . . g . . . gu . . ."

"Son, you've got to breathe," August said, remembering a handful of late-night trips to the emergency room with Charlie when the boy was younger. Two years had passed without incident, as far as he knew anyway, and August wondered what would cause the problem to come back. "Breathe with me. In. And out. In. And out. Just like when you were little."

Charlie's wheezing relaxed as he followed his father's instruction. Then it worsened again. August heard the phone rattling. Was he running? No. *Crawling*. Crawling where? Why?

"Dad . . ."

August felt a lump in his throat. Something was horribly wrong. "Hey, Superspy. Give me your report. Is Grandma Rose okay?"

"Dad . . . please help," Charlie said, trying to calm down. He was being as brave as he could. "The guy tied up Grandma Rose, and he's holding a gun to her head."

August sighed, then shook his head. He'd almost bought it, hook, line, and sinker. It wasn't the first time Charlie had dreamed up something disastrous. Once, when he was four, he claimed a polar bear was trapped in the refrigerator. Only a few days before the divorce was finalized, he'd declared the backyard a nuclear war zone full of flesh-eating zombies. Maybe April was right to limit his television intake.

"Son, you know better than that," August said. "Guns are not a joke."

He turned to Xandria and gave her a you-know-boys shake of his head. Her clear blue eyes had darkened to gray.

"What if the boy isn't joking?" she whispered.

August froze, his mind unable to grasp what was taking place. *What if the boy isn't joking?* How could she know what was going on? He kept eye contact with her. "Charlie, listen to me. I want you to hang up and call 9-1-1 right now."

Xandria pushed up the armrests, slid into the middle seat, and grabbed the phone. August could smell her perfume. "Charlie, don't hang up. Don't move a single muscle, or we'll have to hurt your grandmother," she said, as calmly as if she were reading him a bedtime story. She handed the phone back to August and put her lips near his ear. "We'll kill her, actually. And him too, if you don't cooperate."

August recoiled. "Cooperate?" he mouthed. He heard Charlie calling to him and placed the receiver back against his ear.

"Dad?" Charlie's voice shook. "What do I do?"

"Stay where you are," August said. "Everything's going to be okay. Just sit tight." Across the aisle, he saw a teenager, eyes closed, bobbing his head to the beat of whatever was blaring through his headphones. Next to him was someone August guessed to be his younger sister, thoroughly engaged in a book. To her right was a man, asleep, mouth wide open, wearing a T-shirt that acknowledged his status as the world's biggest windbag. And none of them had noticed a single thing that had just transpired. He put his hand over the receiver. "What do you want?"

She took the phone and ended the transmission with the touch of a button. "Once, when I was a child, I stole a cookie from the jar that sat in the middle of our dining room table. After supper that night, my father took out a Bible, excused everyone else from the room, and read to me from Proverbs 23. Are you familiar with it?"

August knew most of the proverbs, having studied them extensively with the Bible's other wisdom literature, but he sensed she didn't care to know that. He shook his head.

"It says: 'When thou sittest to eat with a ruler, consider diligently what is before thee: And put a knife to thy throat, if thou be a man given to appetite. Be not desirous of his dainties: for they are deceitful meat.'" Xandria pushed up the right sleeve of her pink silk blouse. "Do you know what he did to me after he read that?"

Silence. August didn't want to know.

"He took a knife, and he did this," Xandria said, showing August a long, jagged cross-shaped scar on the inside of her forearm. "I never stole from the table again," she said.

"Don't hurt my son. He hasn't done anything," August said, the voice of his frightened little boy echoing in his ears. "Please, just tell me what you want."

"It's simple, really. You took something that doesn't belong to you, and I want it back," Xandria said and pulled down her sleeve, covering the scar. "If you do exactly as I instruct, if you follow my directions precisely to the letter, then no harm will come to your son. My father didn't know the meaning of the word *compassion.* But I do." She rebuttoned her cuff. "All I want is your hundred-million-dollar book."

two

The ornate ceiling of the Great Hall stretched like a dark sky above the heads of the twelve fifth graders. They followed their guide, resident archaeobibliologist April Adams, who gently pressed a finger to her lips, signaling to the children to remain quiet as they marveled at the illustrious paintings covering the walls of the main grotto, the Greek statuettes standing guard at each entrance, and the books—there was simply no end to the books. The faint, musty-leather smell of them permeated the air.

April's cell phone rang and several kids tittered. She pretended to be embarrassed—they loved that—and pulled the phone out of a lightweight messenger bag at her hip. She'd opted for a comfortable but presentable outfit in exchange for her usual business suit today because of the school tours. Two came through earlier, and this was her last. She was never more grateful than she was now for stylish athletic shoes, cotton-spandex pantsuits, and hands-free accessories.

Unless the call was from home, she wouldn't answer. Unknown number. She silenced the ringer, tucked the phone away next to her wallet, which she never left at her desk, and used the ID badge around her neck to gain entry to an adjoining room. April ushered the class inside and lined them up in a semicircle around her. "Okay, kids. We can talk in here," she said, adjusting her glasses.

They exhaled in unison.

April smiled. "You guys are doing great. Before we finish our tour of the Library of Congress, do any of you have any questions?"

A girl with unruly red curls raised her hand. "How many books do you have?"

"There's over twenty-nine million," April said. The kids looked impressed. "This is the largest library in the entire world. If you took all the bookshelves here and put them end to end, they would stretch all the way to New York City and back again."

"That's as far as the moon!" said a boy with a bad crew cut.

"Not quite," April said. "But we've got plenty of books you could read about the moon. We've got books on just about everything."

The children's teacher piped up from behind them. "Ms. Adams, would you mind telling the children a little more about what you do?"

"Sure," she said. "Kids, have you ever seen a really old book?"

The red-haired girl raised her hand again. "My mom still has books she read when she was my age. They're really old."

"I'm talking about books a lot older than that," April said.

"Hundreds of years older, in fact. Books written before America was even discovered."

"You mean books from those days are still around?" Crew Cut said, voicing the wide-eyed surprise of the other kids.

April continued. "My job here at the Library of Congress is to study those old books and find clues."

"Clues about what?"

"History . . . society . . . all sorts of things, really," April said. She turned and motioned the children to follow her toward one of two gold display cases set in the middle of the room. "Maybe I can show you better than I can tell you."

The children surrounded the display case and peered through the glass. The book inside was incandescent, radiating with a warm glow that seemed to come from within it. "Is that a magical book?" asked a little African-American girl in braids.

"I know what you mean," April said. She had entertained the same possibility the first time she saw it herself. The colorful images on the pages seemed to dance, an illusion both strange and beautiful.

"Could you tell us a little more about this book?" asked the teacher, as enthralled as her students by the book's hypnotic glow.

"It's a Gutenberg Bible, the rarest book in existence today," April said. "We're very lucky to have one here at the library. It's the reason I came to work here. For someone in my field, there's no greater joy than to study a book like this."

"Is this the only one there is in the whole world?" asked the red-haired girl.

"No. *Rare* means more than just 'uncommon.' It means a lot of people out there would love to have one but can't. Only a few lucky people do. Of the one hundred eighty original copies of the

Gutenberg Bible that are out there, only forty-eight copies exist today. And only a few of those are here in America. Most are in other parts of the world."

"You mean like Texas?"

April laughed and gently motioned for a girl to stop leaning against the case. "Well, Texas *does* have a copy! But I'm really talking about places farther away, like France, Germany, and even Japan."

"Why do so many people want one?"

"Because of how important it is. The Gutenberg Bible is not just a book; it's one of the great marks in human achievement. It might even be more important than the Great Wall of China or the pyramids in Egypt."

"The pyramids are cooler," one boy chimed in, letting his boredom be known.

"Jeremy!" scolded the teacher. "That's enough."

"It's okay," April said. "Some people need more than dusty old pages." She looked around at the children's faces. "But there's always a few that understand the magic."

"Children, let's all give our guide a big thank-you before we go," the teacher said.

"Thank you!" came the obligatory chorus. The teacher thanked April as well, then paraded the children out of the room. As they left, April noticed a man standing next to the exit. His thin, Asian face was familiar, but April couldn't remember why. He was staring at her.

"Can I help you?" she asked.

"Sorry," he said. "I didn't want to cause any unnecessary alarm to the children. Very interesting tour."

That's why she knew his face. He had been following the group at a distance. But he was not obvious about it, always turned away, always with an open book in his hands. The book was gone now. "Thank you for the compliment, but you might find the regular tour more interesting. If you'd like, I could—"

"No," he said, walking toward her. "I didn't come here for a tour. I came here to talk to you."

"About what?"

"About the Gutenberg," he said, pointing toward the display case. "Has anyone contacted you about it recently?"

People were always contacting her about the Gutenberg. It was a milestone in history, marking a pivotal shift in the power structure of the world. It was the launchpad for both the Renaissance and the Reformation. These qualities, when united with its gape-jawed splendor and bank-breaking rarity, resulted in a slew of research requests from historians, scientists, archaeologists, bibliophiles, and even religious fanatics. But none of their wishes were ever granted. The Gutenberg was off-limits to everyone. Except her.

She placed a protective hand on the display case. "You need to tell me who you are before we talk about the Gutenberg."

He opened his jacket and flashed a badge. "FBI. Name's Meng. What can you tell me about a man named Alex Pierson?"

April hadn't heard that name since she and August had divorced. Years ago, Alex and August were bitter rivals in the rare-book industry. Everything changed when Alex accepted the prestigious title of head curator at the Morgan Library and Museum in New York. After that, Alex and August became inseparable, brought together by the library's massive collection of rare manuscripts. "He's a friend of my ex-husband's," she explained. "I never knew him well myself."

"Late last night, two men forced him to open the book vault at the Morgan Library. It contains hundreds of priceless items, but when police searched it this morning, only one book was missing."

April was afraid she knew which book it was. "A Gutenberg Bible," she said.

"The vellum copy."

"What happened to Alex? Is he okay?" April asked, remembering his wife and three children.

"I'm afraid not. Shot twice in the back."

"That's terrible," April said, putting a hand over her mouth and sensing where all the questioning was leading. "You think they might be coming here next?"

Meng answered hesitantly. "Maybe."

"We should move the Gutenberg to a security vault on the basement level right away." April approached a red phone attached to the wall and picked it up.

Meng raised a hand. "No need to call."

April hung up the phone. "Why not?"

"Because we're about to arrest the person responsible."

"Who?"

"You, Ms. Adams," he said, snapping handcuffs around her wrists.

Disbelief stunned April into momentary silence. She fumbled for an articulate response.

"What are you talking about? I would never do anything to jeopardize the Gutenberg!"

Meng got in her face. "We've got e-mails, phone calls, text messages, everything we could ever need to put you away for a very long time." He grabbed the chain between the cuffs and directed her toward the exit.

Officer Norman Briggs came blustering into the room. "What's going on in here?"

Meng held out his ID, keeping one hand firmly on April. "FBI," he said. "This woman is being arrested for conspiring with known felons."

"Norman, help me," April pleaded. "They think I'm trying to steal the Gutenberg."

"That's nonsense," Norman said. He turned to Meng. "Does she really look like a thief?"

"I don't base my investigations on looks."

"I'm just saying that I think you've got the wrong man," Norman said. "Er . . . I mean . . . the wrong *woman.* I've known April since her first day here, and I can vouch for her dedication to the Library of Congress. I'd bet my life on the fact she's innocent."

"I'd take you up on that bet," Meng said. "But it just seems wrong to gamble on a person's life." He continued moving her toward the door.

Norman followed them. "What do you want me to do, April?"

"I don't know," she said, looking back, flustered. She'd never had so much as a speeding ticket, and now here she was, being dragged away by the FBI for conspiring to steal a national treasure. "Just make sure no one takes the Gutenberg."

Two more men whom April presumed to be agents came in just as she and Meng reached the door. They took hold of April's arms from either side. She looked Norman directly in the eye. "Please help me."

He stared at her. An understanding passed between them; then he turned to Meng. "I never would have believed it," he said, shaking his head. "She seemed so loyal."

"The best ones always do," Meng said, pushing open the door.

The agents guided April down the mammoth steps of the Library of Congress toward a black SUV parked at the curb. Meng opened the rear door, and she stepped inside. The agents got in as well, one sliding in next to her, the other hopping into the front passenger seat. Meng shut the door and returned to the library.

Behind the steering wheel sat a large Samoan man, whose multiple ear-piercings and long, bushy hair did not fit her preconceived notions of the FBI's usual neat-freak tendencies.

"Where are we going?" April asked.

No one replied. The door locks clicked shut, punctuating the silence. The Samoan threw the SUV into drive, and they darted away from the library.

"Isn't anyone going to answer me?"

"No," said the agent sitting next to her.

"I need to talk to my family," April said. "I need to let them know what's going on."

"They're fine," said the agent in the passenger seat.

"How would you know?"

The Samoan stared at her in the rearview mirror. His eyes were bloodshot, as if he'd been up all night or was high on crack. April couldn't see his mouth, but his eyes were grinning. And she knew why.

She was trapped.

three

Grandma Rose fought hard not to gag. The rag was shoved too far down her throat. She wondered if she would die choking on her own vomit. Not exactly a great epitaph, she thought: DIED CHOKING ON VOMIT.

She still couldn't believe she had gotten herself into this mess. He looked harmless enough: brown suit, dark-orange tie, expensive loafers, nice hair. Excellent hair. He was very good-looking. Pleasant smile. Excellent smile.

"Mind if I come in?" he'd asked.

"I'm sorry, I don't usually just let people in," she replied, trying to sound exasperated with the situation.

"I'm sure you don't," he said. "My name is Ben Anderson. I'm with the FBI."

"FBI? Is there a problem?"

"I'm afraid there is," he said. He pulled out his badge and showed it to her. "May I come in?"

"I don't think so," Grandma Rose said, her voice thick with suspicion. "For all I know, you may have bought that badge on eBay. Good-bye!"

"Ma'am," Ben said, putting a hand against the door. "If you don't let me in, you'll be charged with impeding a criminal investigation by the FBI."

"I don't care if you're IRS, CIA, or CSI, I'm not letting you in," Grandma Rose said. She never let people in the house while she was watching Charlie. Repairmen of all types were sent away on a regular basis, much to her daughter's frustration. She even sent away a respected senator one time. A rule was a rule.

"It's about your daughter."

"April?"

"She's been taken in for questioning."

"I don't understand."

Ben took a document out of his inner jacket pocket and stuck it through under the chain of the barely open door. "I have a warrant."

Grandma Rose opened it. "How do I know you didn't make this at Kinko's?"

Ben sighed. "Listen, I know this must be a little scary, but your daughter is in real trouble. I just need to take a look around and see if she left something here. If it's not here, then I'll leave."

"And if I don't let you in?"

"Then I'll be back in an hour with two other agents who will be a lot less patient."

"Do you have a gun?"

Ben paused. "Yes. I do."

"You're going to have to leave it in your car. I have a young, impressionable boy in here. Guns are strictly off-limits."

"Fair enough. I'll be right back."

She watched through the crack in the door as Ben jogged over to his car and deposited his gun between the seats. He locked the door and returned to his position on the front porch. "Open your jacket," Grandma Rose said.

"Lady, you are hard-core." Ben showed her the empty holster under his arm.

"Ankles too."

He pulled up his pant legs. "Satisfied?"

She closed the door.

"Hey!" came a muffled cry.

She slid the chain out of the lock and opened the door. She would leave it open just in case she needed to scream for help.

"I'll be out of your hair in a minute," Ben said. "Just point me to your daughter's bedroom. I'd like to start there."

"It's right over there," Grandma Rose said, directing Ben past the dining room. "I'll wait here for you, if you don't mind." She stood positioned between Ben and the stairs that led up to Charlie's room.

"Thanks. Be right back."

Grandma Rose looked at her watch. Ten minutes. That's all she was going to give him. She heard the television come on upstairs, loud at first, then quieter and quieter. Even at low volume, she could discern the sound of fighting and explosions. What was

Charlie watching? *Power Danger? Danger Badgers?* She could never remember the names of all the programs on April's do-not-let-Charlie-watch-these-shows list. She turned to walk up the stairs and caught her breath. There was a man standing in the front entry. At first, Grandma Rose thought he might be an associate of Ben's. Until she noticed the gun he was pointing at her face.

He put a finger up to his lips. *Quiet.*

Grandma Rose froze, one foot on the bottom stair. The gunman shut the door. Could she have made it any easier for him to walk in? How could she have been so foolish?

Behind her, she heard Ben exiting April's room. "Didn't find anything in there. I just need to check—"

"Don't move," said the gunman.

"What's going on here?"

"I was hoping this might be a friend of yours," Grandma Rose said. "Some kind of misunderstanding?"

"No," Ben said. "What do you want?" he asked the gunman.

"Where's the boy?"

"He's not here," Grandma Rose said.

"Shut up," the gunman said. "I didn't ask you. Where's the boy?"

"He's not here," said Ben calmly.

There was a noise from upstairs. The gunman's gaze lifted. "You sure you don't know where he is?" he asked again.

Ben's face was a question mark.

"Then I guess you're no good to me," he said. Three silent rounds flew from the silenced barrel of his gun, each lodging directly in Ben's chest.

Grandma Rose began to tremble as his body tumbled to the ground. There was blood everywhere. "Please, please, please—"

A rope came out of the gunman's pocket. "Grab a chair," he said.

Not knowing what else to do, she took a chair from the dining room and brought it back to the gunman. Her mind raced. Where was the phone? Was it in the kitchen? When was April coming home? She couldn't remember anything.

"Sit down," said the gunman.

Grandma Rose hesitated. "Why are you doing this?" she asked, wondering if she could reason with him. "If you want money, I'll give you everything we have."

The gunman pushed her into the chair. "I don't want your money," he said.

Grandma Rose closed her eyes. She felt the rope twist around her arms, her legs, her torso, her neck. She listened to the short, shallow breathing of the gunman, his face only inches away. She sensed his adrenaline rise to dangerous levels. One wrong move and he would kill her, just like he had killed Ben.

"Look at me," said the gunman.

She opened her eyes. He held the gun in one hand, a dirty rag in the other.

"Is the boy upstairs?" he asked. "I thought I heard something up there."

"No. He's not here," she said. "Went to a friend's house."

He aimed the gun at her forehead. "I've been watching the house since you brought him home. Now, is he upstairs or not?"

"You wouldn't have seen him go. He left through the back door." The tip of the pistol pressed into the flesh of her cheek. It was still hot. She clenched her teeth.

The phone rang. Once. Twice.

"Where's the phone?" the gunman asked.

"I don't know. It's cordless."

The ringing stopped after three rings.

"Just a wrong number," Grandma Rose said. "Happens all the time."

The gunman raised his head, his attention caught by the sounds coming from upstairs: the metallic purr of the television, the pitter-patter of small feet on the hardwood floors. "Or someone upstairs just answered the call," he said, smiling.

"Hide, Charlie!" Grandma Rose shouted. Her courage cracked, and the tears streamed down her face.

"Why do you women have to be so difficult?" the gunman asked. He wrapped his arm around her head and shoved the rag down her throat. "Don't worry," he said. "I'll be nice to the boy."

Grandma Rose watched through blurred vision as the gunman pulled out his cell phone, placed a brief call in hushed tones, then crept up the stairs. She struggled against the ropes, but they held tight. She coughed hard, hoping to dislodge the rag. Nothing worked. She couldn't even stomp her foot in anger. She prayed that Charlie had heard her warning.

Boards creaked above her head. The gunman was working his way through the rooms upstairs. Charlie had numerous hiding places, but he was only eight. It would only be a matter of time before the gunman found him.

Why was this happening? Why was a dead FBI agent lying on the floor in front of her? Why was a man with a gun hunting for her grandson? There had to be a reason. She thought through the possibilities.

One: Charlie had done something. The child spent most of his time at either school or home, which limited his opportunities to meddle with criminals. April monitored his time on the computer, so he hadn't stumbled into trouble online. And he never went over to friends' house unsupervised. No, Charlie was out of the equation.

Two: April had done something. Unless she was living a double life, it was hard to imagine that she had anything to do with this. She held a government job and socialized with powerful people, but her workplace was a glorified library, not the White House. Still, an FBI agent had just arrived looking for something of hers. And now that FBI agent was dead. His death must have been a terrible error, a horrific coincidence. The real blame lay elsewhere.

Three: August had done something. Of course he had. Grandma Rose fought her instinct to blame him, but he was certainly a prime candidate. Danger not only followed him; it seemed to envelop him like a fog. He bartered with scoundrels. He peddled to billionaires. If she had to wager a bet, her chips would land squarely on August.

She mentally scrolled through the recent conversations she'd overheard between April and August. Her eavesdropping was purely accidental, the result of picking the phone up at the wrong time. Most were heated battles over the lack of time August spent with Charlie. *It's not my fault,* he would explain. *My work requires me to travel, and without my work I wouldn't be able to send you child support.* April parried with a battery of questions. *Child support? Is not spending time with your son called* support? *Is not sending a check for two months called* support? *Be patient with me,* he always said. *I'm working on something big.*

Something big. Had she heard what that something big was? Nothing came to mind. She remembered her daughter saying that August was in Germany. *He's book hunting again,* she griped.

Grandma Rose would just laugh at her. She remembered a time when August's exploits were a drug to her daughter, a love-inducing elixir that sustained her during the weeks that he was away. Grandma Rose had warned her that heartbreak was in her future, but she wouldn't listen. She was young. And, for a genius, she wasn't always the brightest when it came to real-life matters like love.

Grandma Rose heard a noise upstairs. The collapsible ladder to the attic dropped and hit the floor in Charlie's room. The attic was Charlie's favorite place to hide—a complicated maze of rotting boxes and forgotten junk. Grandma Rose wished it wasn't. Once, when digging through a pile of old clothes, she'd found a dead rat. She showed the grisly find to Charlie and warned him to stop poking around the attic unless he wanted to get rabies. A week later, she caught him trying to sneak leftovers from the kitchen to feed the little beasts.

Grandma Rose struggled against the ropes, her neck burning as the cords rubbed against her windpipe. She pushed harder. The ropes wouldn't budge. She stopped to catch her breath and to listen. Quiet swallowed the house.

E veryone was talking. Cheery voices discussed the usual topics: politics, family, weather. It really didn't matter what the subject was. The passengers simply needed their minds diverted from the fact that they were soaring high above the earth in a hollow tube, probably en route to another storm, possibly en route to their own demise. It was not an easy thing to ignore, but they managed.

August envied them. He wished it were merely his own life on the line, and not Charlie's. "How do I know he's okay?"

"Because I'm telling you he is," said Xandria. She stared at the laptop she'd set up on her tray, her long, light fingers like feathers dusting the keyboard. The satellite signal allowed her to log in to an e-mail account and download a large batch of files waiting for her. She stopped the mouse clicking for a moment. "If I say he's okay, then he's okay. You're just going to have to trust me."

"Trust the woman holding my child hostage. I don't think so," August whispered.

Xandria didn't bother turning from the computer. "Don't make this harder than it has to be."

August grimaced. The situation was already worse than Xandria knew. The check waiting for him in New York was going to do more than just make him rich; it was going to lift him out of the deep pit he'd dug for himself.

He was broke. He was in trouble. He had stopped answering the phone months ago, there were so many lenders hell-bent on getting his money. There were seven credit cards in his wallet, and every single one of them was maxed out. His car had been repossessed. His landlord was threatening to evict him. After selling everything he could on eBay, he was still too short on cash to pay child support.

But the Gutenberg Bible was supposed to change all that. It was going to turn the tide in his favor. He would finally have the resources to be the father Charlie needed. He wouldn't quit working entirely, but for the first time he would be completely available. Maybe he'd get a house in DC. Or maybe he would buy Charlie one of those lifetime air-travel passes so that he could join August on adventures. Whatever the kid wanted, August would give him.

But now the expectation was evaporating like a dream upon waking.

Unfortunately, financial ruin had just become the least of his worries. The buyer waiting for him in New York was Leo Kahn, a criminal so high above the law he was claimed to have put a hit out on his own mother. Had it not been for the substantial cash Kahn was willing to lay out, August never would have gotten involved with him. Failing to deliver the book to such a maniac would surely result in more than a few broken bones. The gruesome possibilities piled up in his mind like kindling for a fire.

"Listen, I know I'm not in a position to make demands," August said. "But you may want to rethink taking the book."

Xandria was still in the process of downloading files and sorting them. "After months of planning, I believe you're wrong."

"Ever hear of a guy named Leo Kahn?"

Xandria paused. "Unfortunately, yes."

"Leo Kahn is my buyer. If I don't put that book in his hands, he'll kill me."

"And that matters to me because . . . ?" Xandria asked, making her indifference as clear as possible.

"Because if you take his book, you'll be next in line for a visit from Leo's pals," August said. "But maybe there's a way to work this out. You don't want the book. You want the money. You want the hundred million dollars. So let me take the book to Leo and get the money. Then I'll turn around and give the money to you." It was a reasonable request. Surely Xandria would understand that it was in her best interest.

"No," she said. The word fell like the gun hammers of a firing squad.

"But Leo will kill you," August said.

"You really thought Leo was going to give you that much money?" Xandria asked.

The thought had run through his mind a multitude of times.

"You are every bit the sucker I was told you are," Xandria said.

"I'm not taking the Gutenberg for the money." She clicked the mouse a few more times, then stopped and stretched her fingers. "I need it for a far greater reason."

"I don't understand. You have a buyer who's willing to pay more?"

Xandria closed the laptop and folded her hands on top of it. "There was a story my father used to tell me: A king gave a portion of land to his son. He instructed his son to work the soil there, and said if he did an excellent job the yield would be plentiful. But the son was lazy. Instead of heeding the wise words of his father, he borrowed money against the land. Night after night he threw elaborate parties, and before long, the money was gone. Eventually a collector came, and when the son could not provide him with enough to settle his debts, the collector demanded the deed to the land. The son could do nothing but hand over the land that his father had entrusted to him. A few days later, the son went crawling back to his father. He explained the whole story and begged for forgiveness. The king frowned. 'I told you to work the soil,' he said. 'Did you not do as I instructed?' 'No,' replied the son. 'I squandered what you gave me. But I have returned to beg for your mercy!' The king stood, enraged. 'You fool! My treasure was buried in that land! You have handed over the kingdom to a mere peasant!' The son was immediately taken by the king's guards and—at his own father's command—executed."

August shook his head, then said, "You're a prime candidate for some psychotherapy."

Xandria shook her head. "You don't get it, do you? The Gutenberg Bible holds the key to a treasure that's been hidden for over half a millennium. Men have given their lives to keep that information from falling into the wrong hands. And you were about to hand it over to a common criminal."

August couldn't decide whether Xandria was being dramatic or believed what she was saying. In some ways, he hoped Xandria was right. Riddles had surrounded the Gutenberg Bible for hundreds of years. If Xandria spoke the truth, then perhaps the veil of questions would be lifted.

August had become reacquainted with the mystery during his month in Germany. There he met a Russian archaeobibliologist named Nikolai Arsov. According to Nikolai, very little truth was known about Gutenberg's life, including a period from 1443 to 1448 when he vanished from history.

It was this five-year disappearance that led Nikolai to believe Gutenberg had been in the possession of something exceptionally dangerous and went to great lengths to hide it. He confirmed this opinion with a story from a priest at the Cathédrale Notre-Dame in Strasbourg: In the winter of 1438, an associate of Gutenberg's named Andres Dritzehen died unexpectedly. When Gutenberg heard the news, he sent a message to Dritzehen's home: *Destroy everything.* A few days later, Gutenberg showed up to ensure his command had been carried out. To his horror, the object of their secret collaboration had disappeared. What the project was and why Gutenberg was so concerned about its discovery was still unknown.

Did Xandria have the answer?

"Leo Kahn is a saint compared to you," August said. "I really don't care who ends up with the book. Just as long as my son is safe."

"And he will be, if you do exactly what I say." Xandria held up her cell phone. "Every sixty minutes, I will receive a call from the man detaining your son. He will ask me if he should kill the boy. If I tell him no, then Charlie lives to see another day. But if I tell him yes . . ."

August envisioned a gun pressed against Charlie's head and shuddered. "I already told you I'd give you the book."

"I'm glad to hear it. But that's not all you will do."

August let his head tip back against the headrest. Xandria could ask him to strip down to his socks, and he'd have to do it. "One hundred million dollars goes a long way these days. What more could you want?"

"I'll explain when the time comes," Xandria said. She looked as if she had more to say but was cut short by the ringing of her phone. She held the device by the antenna like she was holding a dead mouse. She snuggled her shoulder against his. "What do you think I should do?"

August wanted to choke the life from her body. "Just answer it," he said.

Xandria flipped open the phone. "Then we have a deal?"

Without hesitating, August answered, "Of course we do."

"Good," Xandria said. She whispered a few words into the receiver. After a short discussion, she hung up. "My associate tells me your son is a troublemaker. But it sounds like he isn't half as irritating as your mother-in-law."

"*Ex*-mother-in-law," August said. As much as he disliked Grandma Rose, he was glad she was with Charlie. He remembered one time at a theme park a man accidentally flicked some cigarette ashes on Charlie's head. Before he could react, Grandma Rose had taken the cigarette out of the man's hand and extinguished it on his forehead. Over the sounds of his screaming, Grandma Rose proceeded to give him a lecture on the dangers of smoking.

"That phone call means we're ready for step two," Xandria said. "I'm afraid you're not going to like it."

"What a surprise."

Xandria opened the laptop and double-clicked on one of the files she had downloaded. "I want you to look at this," she said, turning the screen toward August.

August peered at the computer and instantly recognized the image as a page from a Gutenberg Bible. "I'm assuming this isn't a photo you got off the Internet. Where did you get it?"

"From the Morgan Library. A friend of yours helped us."

August only knew one person who worked there. "Alex Pierson? I don't believe you."

"Just like you, he didn't have a choice. But things didn't go as well for him." Xandria pressed a button on the computer and another picture appeared. It was a photo of Alex, facedown on the pavement, his limbs at odd angles. His tweed jacket was marred in the middle of the back by two ragged holes. "Somehow he set off a remote alarm system. We didn't want to harm him, but he forced our hand."

August's anger boiled just beneath the surface. "Alex is one of the nicest people I've ever known. You didn't have to shoot him."

"We needed to send a message. And I'm gauging from your response that it's coming through," Xandria said, closing the laptop. "You're a book man, so it's probably hard for you to comprehend the idea that strong words don't get you very far in this life. It's action that speaks. And it's well-planned action that speaks the loudest. Which leads me back to step two. Have you ever heard of the term *ranging*?"

"No."

"It's what makes GPS systems work, the process of using multiple points of reference to locate a target between them. But it's not merely a geophysical term. It can also refer to other things . . . tri-angulating coded information, for instance."

"I don't follow."

"Gutenberg was smart enough not to bury all of his secrets in the same grave. He spread them out. In order to put the pieces of his puzzle together, we need at least three sources."

August scoffed at Xandria's bravado. Three Gutenberg Bibles! No one person could obtain multiple copies of such a rare work. And yet, she had already managed to get her hands on two of them. But where was the third copy coming from?

"You know where all this is leading," she said.

The answer coiled around August's mind like a snake. "April," he said. "She has the third copy."

Xandria swept her honey-colored hair over the opposite shoulder. "My associates don't realize it yet, but they're going to need your wife's assistance. You need to convince her to help them get the Bible. I'm sure you'll have no trouble doing that, given the situation."

April would be completely unaware that Charlie was in any danger. The thought of calling her and trying to explain what had happened gave August an instant ulcer. "You're asking for the impossible," he said. "The Library of Congress is a fortress. Their copy of the Gutenberg is untouchable."

"To everyone but your ex-wife," Xandria said. "She has an impressively high security clearance."

August had hoped she didn't know about that. Xandria had obviously done her homework. But she didn't know April like August did. The most dangerous thing April had ever done was read a book without her glasses. Stealing a priceless treasure from under the watchful gaze of the government would be too much for her. August shook his head. "There's no way she can do it."

"Something tells me she'll figure it out," Xandria said, holding out the phone.

August took it and dialed April's number. He closed his eyes and took a deep breath, casting about for the words to say. The phone rang a few times before going through to her voice mail. August was both relieved and alarmed. What if he couldn't get in touch with her? "I'm going to have to leave a message," he told Xandria.

"Tell her it's urgent," she said.

teðilluminatedfiveilluminatedillu

The SUV crawled like a black beetle through the hazards of DC traffic. April's phone rang, and the eyes of the agent next to her warned her not to pick up. Not that she could have with her cuffed hands. She looked out the heavily tinted window and watched as the cars floated by, filled with people happy to be headed home, tapping their steering wheels, singing their favorite songs. Their worry-free existence was only a stone's throw away, but it was still too great a distance for April to bridge.

A boy in the backseat of a car stared directly into April's eyes. For a moment, she thought he had seen her through the opaque glass, until he began to make funny faces and stick out his tongue. He was playing games with his reflection.

"They can't see you, so don't try anything," said the man next to her, named Millar. He looked like an ex–hockey player who had taken too many hits.

"You've got the wrong person," April said. "If the Gutenberg is in danger of being stolen, then you should be at the library protecting it."

"Meng's overseeing that," said the man in the front passenger seat. His name was Prichard, and April had identified him as the person in charge of the operation. Even when speaking, he seemed to be contemplating his next move. He removed his round, wire-rimmed spectacles and cleaned them with the edge of his jacket. "I can assure you we have everything well under control," he said, positioning his undersized spectacles delicately back on his W. C. Fields nose.

"Miss Adams, before we reach headquarters, I want to ask you a few questions," Millar said. "What do you know about a crime organization known as the Orphans?"

April turned to look at her seatmate and felt a chill creep up her spine. "The Orphans? I've never heard of them."

Millar studied her face. He seemed concerned with her reaction. "You've never heard of them?"

"No."

"That's odd, because we have acquired information that suggests you've been working for them for almost a year now."

"I don't know what information you found," April said, "but it's wrong. Just call the library and ask for Dr. Winter. He'll explain to you that there's no way I could be involved in some plot to take the

Gutenberg." She felt certain Dr. Winter would defend her case. As the head of the archaeobibliology department, he was her boss, but somehow, despite his reputation for being eccentric, he had become more to her than that: a mentor and, occasionally, a friend. It was amazing, really, considering where their relationship started.

She was sitting in the lobby of his office, waiting for him to interview her for a job at the library, when a man walked in and sat down next to her. He was in his mid-fifties, African-American, with a graying shock of hair on top of his head. He reached into his tattered jacket and pulled out a pipe, which he immediately lit. A plume of blue smoke swirled about his head. "Do you mind if I smoke?" he asked.

April smiled. "I don't mind, but I'm guessing they don't allow it in here."

"I'm sure they don't," he said, taking a deep puff. "But I'm an old friend of Dr. Winter's, so I can get away with things most people can't."

"You know Dr. Winter?" April asked.

"Sure do. Since high school," the man said, removing his pipe. "He was the class president, and I was the class clown. Somehow we got to be good pals."

"What's he like?" April asked, unable to help herself from digging for some facts that might help her in her interview.

"Oh, he's a tough critter," the man said, crinkling his face as if to warn her. "Very serious. Always was. Reads a book a day. Always has. I suppose I was put into his life to impose some balance. I took him to parties. Introduced him to girls. Eventually his wife too. If it wasn't for me, he'd probably be hunched in a chair somewhere, making his way through a pile of Dostoyevskys, living life inside the pages of a book."

"That doesn't sound so bad to me," she said, only half serious.

"If that's how you feel, then I can tell you right now that this interview won't go well," the man said. He took a couple quick puffs. "Sorry. I shouldn't have said that. I've got a bad habit of speaking my mind."

"No," April said. "You're probably right. My ex-husband used to accuse me of being trapped inside my books."

"That's an awful thing to say to a person."

"You just said it yourself," April said.

The man grinned.

A door on the other side of the room opened, and a tall man in a well-tailored suit entered. "You can come in," he said, motioning to April.

She rose. "Just in time."

"Come with me," he said, holding the door open. "I hope my friend hasn't been causing you too much trouble."

She turned to the man with the pipe. "None at all," she said, hoping she sounded confident. She exited the lobby and walked down a narrow hallway leading to Dr. Winter's office. Upon entering, her eye was caught by the walls, which were covered in black-and-white photographs. They featured settings that spanned the globe: the Parthenon in Greece, the Machu Picchu in Peru, the Angkor Wat in Cambodia, and a hundred other exotic locales. April marveled at the pictures, noticing that the man with the pipe was in every one of them. "He must be a really good friend of yours," she said, pointing to the man.

"I just met him this morning," the man in the suit said.

"I'm sorry?"

"I'm a psychologist. I'm here to do your final evaluation," he said. "Dr. Winter was the gentleman you met a few minutes ago. The man with the pipe."

April gasped. She'd made a fool of herself. "I should just leave now," she said, completely embarrassed.

"Don't go," said the psychologist. "Dr. Winter said he would only let you see me if he was confident you were perfect for the job. And here you are."

April dropped into a chair. "Here I am."

Dr. Winter had become no less mysterious since that meeting a year ago. He would probably laugh after hearing that April had been accused of a crime. He might even be proud.

"We've already talked with Dr. Winter," Prichard said. "He was in support of us taking you into custody."

April snapped back to the moment. Dr. Winter must have been misinformed. Did he really believe she had anything to do with this? Her head began to spin. "I think I'm going to be sick," she said.

"Millar, reach under your seat. I think there's a plastic bag."

The agent retrieved the bag and held it out to April, who just looked at it, her hands cuffed behind her back. Not about to hold the bag for her, he unlocked her cuffs and resecured her hands in front of her. She closed her eyes against a wave of nausea. "What if the real criminals are at the library right now?" she asked, thinking of Meng.

"We've got the real criminal," Prichard said.

"You don't understand," April said. "The Gutenberg Bible is my responsibility. If it disappears, then everything I've ever worked for disappears too. My entire life is wrapped up in that book."

"Then why don't you tell us more about the Orphans?"

April heaved. "I told you, I don't know anything about them."

"We'll see if you have the same answer in the interrogation room," Millar said.

April's mind raced. She had to get back to the library to protect the Gutenberg. Once they reached headquarters, her chances of escaping would be less than zero. She had to do it now.

She retched into the bag.

Both Millar and Prichard looked away, disgusted, which gave April a short window of opportunity. She dropped the bag to the floor.

"Are you done?" Millar asked.

"No," she said, raising her arms.

Before he could react, April reached forward and slipped the chain of her handcuffs over the Samoan's head. She yanked back with all her might and listened as the big man wheezed against the constriction. He reached up to save his neck, and the SUV careened into oncoming traffic.

Prichard and Millar shouted as the SUV slammed head-on into a metro bus filled with commuters. Air bags exploded and an acrid, gunpowder-smelling smoke filled the cabin. The entire world came to a deafening halt.

April shook her head and tried to get her bearings. She looked in the rearview mirror and saw that the Samoan was unconscious, a thin trail of crimson trickling from the corner of his mouth. Millar was out as well, the window next to him cracked and spiderwebbed from the spot his head had smashed. In the front passenger seat, Prichard was motionless.

Damaged in the crash, the SUV's horn blared nonstop, exacerbating the screams emanating from the metro bus. April struggled to remove her seat belt, watching as Prichard stirred to life. He turned, blood dripping from a gash in his forehead. A lens in his glasses had popped out. "Where do you think you're going?"

"I have to get back to the library," April said, fumbling to unlock her door.

"You're not going anywhere," Prichard said. He pushed the air bag away and with an agonized growl rose to his knees on his seat. He reached into his suit and withdrew a pistol, which he stuck in April's face. "Don't move, and let me see your hands."

April put her bound palms in the air. "Why are you doing this?" she asked. "I'm completely innocent."

Prichard frowned. "You know too much to be innocent."

Too much? Clearly Prichard believed she knew more than she actually did. She decided to play along to see if she could get some information out of him. "They forced me to cooperate," she said. "I didn't know what else to do."

Prichard's eyes widened as if he hadn't expected a confession. "The Orphans will do anything to get their hands on that Gutenberg."

The Orphans. Why did he keep mentioning them? Hadn't they disappeared over five hundred years ago? She was trying to recall everything she had read about them, when suddenly she saw a figure standing outside the window.

Prichard followed her eyes and swiveled his head to the left just as the passenger-side glass exploded in his face. There was the loud crack of bone snapping as the tip of a policeman's billy club hit him in the face. An arm reached in through the smashed glass and opened the door. Prichard's body slumped out, and Officer Norman Briggs leaned in. He held out his hand to April. "Are you all right?" he asked.

April reached for Norman's strong hand. "I've never been worse," she said. "But it's good to see you."

Norman pulled her over the seat, and the two of them exited the SUV. People were milling about. The undulating din of police sirens could be heard approaching from behind them. Though Norman was advanced in years, he was spry and strong. He pulled her in the direction of his waiting car and freed her wrists.

"I didn't think you believed me," April said.

"Honestly, I didn't know what to think," Norman said. "But the whole thing felt out of whack. So I followed you and made a call over to a friend of mine at the FBI. Asked him if he knew anything about bringing in someone from the library for questioning."

"And?"

"He had nothing on record. Which means that either these guys aren't FBI, or they're acting independently. Either way, it's bad news."

"We need to go back to the library to see Dr. Winter. I have a few questions for him."

"Can you trust him?" Norman asked.

"We'll have to take that chance," April said, throwing herself onto the front seat and slamming the door. "He may be the only person who has information about the Orphans."

"The Orphans?" Norman asked. "Weren't those the kids Peter Pan used to hang out with?"

"No. That was the Lost Boys."

"Oh. Why did I think it was the Orphans?"

"The Orphans were a secret society formed after the martyrdom of a man named John Huss," April said. "Not Peter Pan."

Norman was deep in thought. "Ah!" he finally said. "*Little Orphan Annie!* That's what I was thinking of! I had a Little Orphan Annie decoder ring as a kid. Sorry, April. What were you saying?"

"John Huss was an early church reformer," April said. "That doesn't sound dangerous today, but back in the 1400s it was enough to get Huss burned at the stake. The order was given by an emperor named Sigismund, who was trying to protect the power held by the Holy Roman Empire."

"Ouch," Norman said. "So where do the Lost Boys come in?"

"Orphans."

"Right."

"The name was literal," April explained. "After Huss was killed, his legion of militant followers gave themselves the name Orphans because they were left behind."

"Did you say *militant* followers?" Norman asked, leaning the car around a sharp curve. His hard-core nerves, strung during his youth as a marine, clearly took control as they flew down the streets at an interstate pace. "I thought church guys in those days were monks."

April put her hands against the dashboard for support. "These were more fierce, led by the general Jan Žižka, and bent on changing the world through a bloody holy war. I remember reading the lyrics to a song they would sing on the battlefield: 'We are the warriors of God, and we've come to slay, slay, slay them, every one.' And slay them they did. They developed a number of revolutionary techniques on the battlefield."

"Wait! That sounds familiar," Norman said. "I think they were the creators of the first tank."

"You're right," April said. "The most famous invention of the Orphan army was an armored wagon. They built hundreds of them to defend their stronghold, the city of Tábor; it's part of the Czech Republic now. But how did you know about that?"

"I watch a lot of the Military Channel."

"Why does that not surprise me?" April said. They hit a pothole, and April nearly hit the roof of the car. She wondered if they'd arrive at the library alive.

"So what do these warrior monks have to do with the Gutenberg?" Norman asked.

"I've read that Gutenberg was an ally of the Orphans. But beyond that, I'm not sure." She felt that the answer was lost inside her, waiting for the right moment to find its way into the light. But it would be worth nothing if the great book were stolen. "We can't let anything happen to the Gutenberg."

Norman took his eyes off the road for several seconds. "I've never seen you like this," he said.

April stared at her reflection in the window next to her. She didn't recognize herself, seeing the fear and excitement burning in her eyes. "Sorry," she said. "The thought of someone trying to steal the Gutenberg makes me furious."

"Good," Norman said. "You're going to need that anger if we run into trouble."

April pulled out her cell phone. "I should call home to make sure everything's okay," she said. She saw that there was a voice mail waiting for her. She decided to listen to it in the event it was from Grandma Rose.

Norman revved the engine as they bounced through a red light. Horns blared. Norman waved back at the scowling motorists in a mock gesture of politeness. They rounded a corner and saw the Library of Congress looming only a few blocks away.

"Oh, great," April said, listening to the voice mail. "It's from August." Her irritation morphed to disbelief in the space of ten seconds. *Someone has Charlie. Don't call police. Call this number.* She hung up and frantically dialed, tears rolling down her cheeks.

"Hello?" It was a voice April didn't recognize, a woman's voice. Did August have a girlfriend? "I must have the wrong number," she said. "I'm looking for August Adams."

"You have the right number, April."

April got the sense that her name had been added to the end of the sentence purposefully, almost playfully. "I'm sorry? Do I know you?" she asked.

"Hang on," the voice said. "Here he is."

Norman put a hand on April's shoulder. "What's going on?" They rolled into a parking space a block away from the library.

"April?" The voice belonged to August. "I'm so sorry about this."

April erupted. "You're sorry? Tell that to our little boy!"

"Please . . . I . . ."

"Shut up. Just shut up," April said. "It's one thing when you put your own life on the line. It's another when you involve the rest of us."

April spied a black FBI van parked about twenty yards in front of them.

"We don't have time to fight about it right now," August said. "I need your help. Charlie needs your help."

April had never heard him ask for help. Especially from her. When they were first married, it had been wonderful to depend on his confidence and self-reliance. But over the years, April had begun to feel like there was no place in his life for her. "What am I supposed to do about this?" she asked.

The reply didn't come quickly, as if he was contemplating any other possibility before delivering the inevitable conclusion. "You have to steal the Gutenberg Bible."

tedilluminatedsixilluminatedillu

J oe Radford stared at the drop-down ladder leading up to the attic. He knew the boy was up there somewhere. It wouldn't be long before he spoke with Xandria again, and there was no chance she'd believe his lies twice. If the boy wasn't in his hands, he might be relieved of his duty. Permanently.

The first step creaked as he placed his foot on it, a good reminder that he should hit the gym after all this was over. He'd spent a little too much time doing Xandria's dirty work behind a desk, and the baby fat was beginning to show. When he'd accepted her invitation to join the Orphans, he'd been promised a life of danger. But until today, the most danger he'd ever seen was accidentally slicing his finger with a pair of scissors while clipping newspaper articles about the Gutenberg Bible.

The next few steps groaned as Joe climbed. He wished the ascent were quieter, but it probably didn't matter. The kid was trapped, probably huddled behind a box, scared out of his mind. He wondered if it was even necessary to have his gun out. Joe thought about the expression the kid would have when he pointed the weapon in his face. Yeah, he'd keep the gun out.

Joe's eyes broke the plane of the attic floor. He stared at a sea of dilapidated boxes. What a mess. It was odd, because the rest of the house was spotless, without even so much as a picture frame off-kilter. Even the boy's room, which he'd passed through to get to the attic ladder, was neat and tidy. Poor kid. His mother must be a nightmare.

The darkness was penetrated by a few pencil-sized streams of dusky light from some tiny cracks in the opposite wall. In the dimness, he could see dust stirring in the air, which could only mean that the boy had recently been crawling around. He was close.

"Why don't you just come on out?" Joe asked, wondering if the kid would be dumb enough to stick his head up out of the box he was in. "Your grandma is really worried about you, and she wants to see you right away." He listened and heard some movement from the left rear corner. He raised his gun and began to trudge through the assembly of boxes toward the sound.

"No fooling around, okay? Just come on out and everything will be all right. Understand?" He squinted and spied a large box quivering about ten feet away. "Do you *understand*?" he asked, raising his voice, trying to panic the kid out of his cardboard cave.

Joe raised his gun, pointed it at the box, and squeezed the trigger.

A mouse scurried out from the torn paper. Joe fired again, and the mouse was instantly splattered among the old baby toys stuffed inside the box. The death of the tiny creature did nothing to absolve the frustration building inside him like a tsunami. Where was the boy? It would take serious self-control not to wring the life from his body when Joe finally found him.

A metallic screech sprang up behind him. Joe bolted for the trapdoor, too late. He watched in dismay as the ladder snapped up into the floor. "No!" he said, slamming his fists down on the ladder, which was fixed to a section of plywood that sealed off the room below. He heard the patter of small feet running away beneath him.

A grim awareness engulfed him: the ladder had been thrown shut by the boy.

And then a second one: there was no escape.

✠

Charlie leaped down the stairs three at a time. His heart was like a hummingbird trapped in his rib cage. He wondered if it was possible for his heart to explode. Hadn't he read that somewhere? Or seen it on TV? He slowed down just in case.

He hit the bottom of the steps. Across the room was Grandma Rose, strapped tightly to a chair. Charlie ran to her. He yanked the rag out of her mouth and began to fight against her ropes.

"Get out of here now," Grandma Rose croaked. "Don't worry about me, Charlie. I'm going to be fine."

Charlie knew she was lying. He'd seen that look before, a year earlier, when she came to live at his house. When she lied to him the first time.

He remembered it was a Saturday.

He always woke early on Saturdays to catch some questionably violent cartoons before his mom got up and turned them off. If he was up at six, he could catch his favorite: *RapidFire*, code name for the heavily armed ex-military brat who declared, on every show, "Heroes always help! No matter what!" But that morning she didn't turn them off, even though it was nearly ten o'clock. She walked right through his room, in the middle of *Harry's House of Horrible Heroes*, her least favorite show in the entire world. She stared at the screen for a minute and then just smiled at him and kept on walking. He felt so guilty he turned off the TV anyway.

Grandma Rose arrived a little after lunch. He was on his second peanut-butter-and-jelly sandwich, another thing his mom usually prohibited, when Grandma Rose walked in the front door. He remembered her coming over to him and rubbing his head for a very long time as she talked to his mom. His mom was crying.

Grandma Rose sat down next to him and waited until he finished his lunch, saying nothing to him, just watching.

"Charlie, would you like to get some ice cream?" she asked after he'd stripped away the last morsel from the crust.

"Not really," he said. "I'm kind of full."

"Why don't we get some ice cream?" she said, getting up and pulling his chair away from the table. "I think you'll be hungry for it by the time we get there."

"Then we better be going to Taipei, because we're going to have to go that far before I'll be hungry again."

"Taipei? Where's that?"

"Taiwan."

"Charlie, Taiwan is very far away."

"Why do you keep saying my name?"

"What?"

"You start every sentence with my name. Why are you doing that?"

"Charlie . . . ," Grandma Rose said, stopping as she heard her own voice. She sighed. "Come with me."

They drove to Bob's Famous Ice Cream, a small parlor in the Glover Park neighborhood. They walked in and were warmly greeted by a man behind the counter. Minutes later, Charlie found himself staring at a chocolate sundae as big as his head. He plunged in his spoon, wondering how on earth he could eat the whole thing. He would at least have to give it a try.

"Charlie, do you know why I'm in town?" Grandma Rose asked.

"You're doing it again."

"Ch—" She started over. "I'm in town because I'm going to be staying with you for a while."

"Are you sick?" he asked, steadily working his way through the baseball-sized glob of ice cream stuck to his spoon.

"No."

"My friend Derrick's grandma came to stay with him after she got sick with cancer. She died last Christmas."

"I'm sorry to hear that, but I don't have cancer," she said. "I'm coming to stay with you because your mother is going through a hard time."

He was horrified. "Does my mom have cancer?" he asked around a mouthful.

"No."

"Does she have Marfan syndrome?"

"Mar*what*?"

"Marfan syndrome," he said. "I saw it on PBS."

"Your mom isn't sick," she said. "But she is really sad."

That bite of ice cream hit his stomach like a boxer. Grandma Rose was acting strange, and it made him feel nervous, more nervous than the time he had to play piano in front of the whole school. "What's she sad about?"

"Your father."

"You mean *Dad*?" He didn't understand what she meant. What was there to be sad about? He always brought home gifts. He always told the funniest jokes and had the most amazing stories about his travels around the world. Dad was amazing. Charlie didn't know why, but he felt like he was going to cry.

Grandma Rose scooted her chair around the table and put her arm around him. "Before I say anything else, I want you to understand that this isn't your fault."

He stabbed his spoon into his half-empty bowl and rubbed his watering eyes with the palms of his hands. He knew what Grandma Rose was going to say next. He'd talked to enough friends at school to know what *it's not your fault* meant. He pulled out his inhaler and gave his mouth a shot, breathing in deeply. "Mom and Dad are getting a divorce, aren't they?"

"Yes," she said softly. "They are." She tucked him under her arm and felt him tremble.

"I think I'm going to be sick," he said, rising from his chair and running to the restroom. He opened the door and barely made it to the stall in time. He fell to the floor and curled up, wailing. Why was he crying? He hadn't broken anything, had he?

"I'm so sorry," Grandma Rose said, coming to his aid. She helped him up from the floor and wiped off his mouth with a white linen handkerchief. "Let's go back home."

"You're not supposed to be in here," he said, limp as a dead leaf. "This is the *men's* room."

"I'm in a lot of places I'm not supposed to be," she said, pulling him close to her. "Don't worry. Everything is going to be fine."

But it wasn't fine. Grandma Rose had lied to him. He'd forgiven her, though. The divorce wasn't her fault. It was his mom's fault. It was his dad's fault. Maybe it was his fault too. Grandma Rose had been living with them ever since that terrible day. She was tough, but Charlie knew she loved him more than anything in the world.

How could he think of leaving her?

"I know it doesn't seem right, but you have to get out of here," Grandma Rose said. "That man will kill you."

Charlie heard commotion upstairs. The gunman was trying to break the latch that held the attic door in place. It wouldn't take him more than another minute to break out. "I'm calling the police," he said, running over to the phone.

"There's not enough time," Grandma Rose said, her voice raised and ragged.

Charlie put the phone to his ear. "It's not working," he said, dropping the receiver to the floor.

Grandma Rose pressed against the ropes in vain. "Charlie, listen to me!" she screamed. Her tone scared him. "If you want to help me, then go to Miss Feldman's house. She'll know what to do."

"I'm not leaving you!" Charlie yelled back. Frightened out of his mind, he ran over to Grandma Rose and threw his arms around her. His tears begin to soak her shoulder.

There was a loud crash upstairs. The gunman was loose. Only seconds remained before he would storm down.

Charlie opened his misty eyes, seeing for the first time the man sprawled out on the dining room floor. "Who's that?" he asked, raising his head.

"His name is Ben," Grandma Rose said.

"Is he dead?" Charlie asked, walking over to the body.

She did not answer right away. "I think so."

The stomp of heavy boots could be heard at the top of the stairs. Their owner was muttering and swearing.

"Leave the body alone," Grandma Rose said.

"He might have a cell phone," Charlie said. Empowered by his own bravery, he knelt by Ben's still form. He pinched the edge of the man's jacket and peeled it back. Luck. He spotted a phone, tucked away in a small leather holster. "Found it!" he called to Grandma Rose.

Grandma Rose didn't hear him. She was in shock, eyes fixed on the lava-red face of the gunman, who cocked his gun.

Charlie was reaching for the cell phone when he stumbled upon something else: a second holster, this one harboring something entirely more powerful. He unbuckled the holster and pulled out the gun. *Heroes always help! No matter what!*

The intruder left Grandma Rose and headed for him.

Charlie stood up, quivering all over. He looked down at the dead body next to his feet. That would be him, if he couldn't pull it together. He took a deep breath, hoping his asthma wouldn't act up. He could already hear a slight wheeze in his throat. He lifted the gun.

The man stopped. "You don't want to do this," he warned.

The gun was heavier than Charlie thought it would be. It took both hands to hold it level with his enemy's chest. Was it loaded? Was it ready to fire? It probably didn't matter, he remembered, thinking back to an episode of *FuzzDroids* in which the heroes escaped after carving fake guns out of soap. "This gun is real," Charlie said, clarifying the matter for both the man and himself.

"I can see that. But it doesn't matter. You try and do anything and I'll kill your grandma. And if you don't put the gun down, you'll be next."

"Not if I kill you first," Charlie said, mimicking *RapidFire*. He hoped that his enemy couldn't hear his wheezing.

The man turned and pointed his pistol at Grandma Rose. She shrieked a split second before he pulled the trigger.

"No! No! No!" Charlie screamed, stopping only because his throat had snapped shut. He fell to the floor.

✠

Joe leaped forward and seized the gun from the brat's hands, throwing it aside. He leaned down and listened to see if the boy was breathing.

He wasn't.

In only a matter of minutes, he would be dead.

Joe fumbled for his phone. Xandria would know what to do.

⑦illuminated**seven**illuminated⑦

"Never leave your plans in the hands of an idiot," Xandria said, covering the mouthpiece of her phone. "Don't get me wrong, Joe is a completely capable guy. I just wouldn't put the life of my child in his hands."

The joke didn't get any laughs. August looked out the window of the plane and ignored her, imagining himself far away from the madness. He closed his eyes and focused on the drone of the engines.

Xandria snapped the phone shut. "Sounds like my associate may have done you a favor."

"Just tell me that my son is okay."

"He's fine," she said. "Your mother-in-law, however, may not make it through the night. Lucky you, huh?"

August turned to face her. "What have you done?" he whispered.

"I didn't do anything. Your little boy found a gun and accidentally shot her. She's alive, but she's going to need medical attention."

August leaned in closer. "I'm keeping a tally, and I swear, when all this is done, you'll pay in triplicate for every person you harm."

Xandria put a finger on his lips. "We don't have time for exchanging threats, as fun as it is. There's too much work to do." She opened the laptop and double-clicked on a set of three images, each one enlarging to fill the screen.

August had seen them a multitude of times while researching the history of the Gutenberg Bible. They were illuminations, beautifully strange images painted by hand around the borders of the printed text. The illuminations had intrigued August, and his research showed him that there was far more to their meaning than one might realize. "These illuminations are from the Morgan Library's copy of the Gutenberg."

"Correct! Glad to see I haven't gone to all this trouble for nothing," Xandria said. She passed the laptop to August, who set it on his tray.

"What am I supposed to do with this?" August asked, already fearing the answer.

"I'm going to give you the condensed version," she said. "During World War II, an Allied forces code-breaking center known as Station X intercepted a message from the Nazis. The Allies had acquired a five-hundred-year-old notebook that supposedly unraveled the Gutenberg mystery. It wasn't until after the war that Station X figured out what the notebook was: a journal kept by Gutenberg himself, which explained where to find particular images Gutenberg had commissioned for a select number of his Bibles. These images are like a riddle that he used to protect important information from people who wanted to destroy it."

"What was Station X? Sounds like something from a comic book."

"You know what they say about truth being stranger than fiction. Station X was the name given to the cipher-hacks working at the Bletchley Park mansion just outside London. Their efforts ended the war three years earlier than it would have without them."

"And you believe what they claimed about this journal? That Gutenberg was hiding something in the illuminations?"

"Of course I do," Xandria said. "And you would too if you read it."

"You've read the journal?"

Xandria laughed and rose from her seat. She unlocked the overhead compartment and reached into her bag, pulling out a small box. She tossed it to August. "Go ahead," she said. "See for yourself."

August slowly raised the lid. Inside was a worn, leather-bound notebook, tied shut with two thin cords. He didn't dare touch it, for fear that the oil from his fingers might damage its ancient pages.

"You book collectors are all the same," Xandria said, sitting down and snatching the journal out of the box. "Weak. Afraid. You forget that the value is the content of the books, not the books themselves." She released the journal's cords and let it fall open with such a flourish that August thought birds might spring from its pages.

"Tell that to the people I sell to," August said, infuriated that Xandria would be so cavalier with such a precious commodity. *What would it fetch at auction? One hundred thousand? Half a million? Less now, of course,* thought August as he watched Xandria flip through it.

Xandria turned to a passage near the middle. "The journal explains that there are three sets of images needed to complete Gutenberg's riddle."

"Three sets in three different Gutenberg Bibles?"

"Correct. But there are redundancies. Each set of images can be found in multiple copies of the Gutenberg. For instance, the set of images in your copy could also have been obtained from Gutenberg Bibles in France and Japan."

"Then why didn't you just steal those?"

"For one, your photographic memory will come in handy." How in the world did she know about that? "And for another, your copy provided a unique opportunity. *Leveraging*, you could call it."

"Leveraging? This isn't a business transaction. You're toying with people's lives."

"Whatever you want to call it, it's working," Xandria said. "After acquiring the three images from the Morgan Library edition, the only ones we need are the images in the Bible you have and the one your ex-wife is going to steal. And then, of course, there's the matter of the tenth image."

"What is that?"

"No need to worry about it now," Xandria said. "You've got nine other images to interpret first."

"What am I supposed to interpret?"

"Don't play coy with me," Xandria said, checking her watch. "You've got one hour to figure out the meaning of the first three images." She closed the journal and placed it back in the box, setting it on the seat beside her.

August resized the images and arranged them on the screen so he could see them all at the same time. "One hour. That's not enough time. This would take weeks, maybe even months for a team of researchers to figure out."

"One hour," Xandria said, stressing each word. "But tell you what. I'll make you a deal. Something to give you a little more incentive. Figure out these first three images in the next hour, and not only will I save the life of your son, but I'll put your mother-in-law out of her misery."

August shook his head. "I do this, and you make sure my mother-in-law gets medical help."

"Be reasonable," Xandria said. "I can't exactly call her an ambulance."

"I don't care how you do it," August said. "Just do it." He closed the lid of the laptop and locked eyes with her.

Xandria sat in silence for a moment. "We've established that you are in no position to negotiate," she said. "But I admire loyalty. You have a deal." Xandria peered at her watch. "Your hour begins now."

"Call for someone to help her."

"*After* you figure these out," Xandria said, raising the computer screen and pointing to the images.

August's mind raced. Where would he even begin? "I need some paper and a pen," he said.

"You've got a laptop right in front of you."

"No," August said. "I need to write it out. Feel it on the page. I need to see how the information works together. I can't do that on a computer."

Xandria considered the situation, then finally stood and opened the overhead compartment. She dug around in her bag and retrieved a small notepad and a disposable ballpoint pen. "Here," she said, handing over the items.

"Thanks." August grabbed the pen and began to scribble on the notepad. He split the page into three sections, labeling each of them:

> One—Two White Dogs Chasing Fox and Hare
> Two—King with Golden Globe
> Three—Split-Bearded Man with Sword

"Lie down with dogs, get up with fleas," August said, staring at the first strange image.

"Say again?"

"Nothing," August said. "I like to talk things through out loud. Kind of a habit." He turned his attention to the first image, a snapshot of a full page of a Gutenberg Bible. The majority of the page was composed of luminous Gothic text, appearing almost hand printed, with strokes of red denoting the beginning of each new sentence. The sentences were divided into two columns, each forty lines in length. August realized that this was an early print of the Gutenberg, as the standard column length of later Gutenberg Bibles was forty-two lines.

But the text was beside the point. The element on the page that August had to "interpret" was the illumination at the bottom, beneath the Latin script. The

image spilled forth from an embellished letter *S*, which sprouted forth a gnarled green vine curving and curling its way along the edge of the page in a curious collection of blue and red blossoms and gold-feathered flourishes. Four animals leaped in and out of the vine: two lean white dogs, one with a brown hare caught in its teeth, and one in close pursuit of a rust-red fox. The colors of the illumination were fresh and vibrant, giving an even more eerie appearance to the wild and somewhat vicious scene.

"I've seen this," August said. "But where?" He closed his eyes and rambled through the pages of a thousand books. He could almost feel the pages he needed in his hands. "Merlin," he said. "The image has some link to Merlin."

August launched the Internet browser and began a Google search for "Merlin Medieval Art." After what seemed like an eternity sifting through the results, he found a Web site that looked promising. He scrolled down the page to an image titled *Ambros [Young Merlin] Prophesies to Vortigern.* And there it was. "Wow," he said, amazed.

"What?"

"Look at this," August said.

"Two dragons fighting," Xandria said. "I don't see the connection."

"Look again. Look at the white dragon."

Xandria blinked at the screen. In the background of the image was a throng of people, many with their faces rubbed out. Their fingers, including Merlin's, pointed toward the bottom right corner of the image where two dragons—a white one and a red one—battled in a dirt pit resembling a boxing ring.

August used the cursor to position the first Gutenberg image next to the medieval piece. He traced his finger along the white dragon, and then along one of the white dogs in the Gutenberg illumination. "They match," he said. "Look at the dog's feet. They're claws, like a dragon's. And the dog's teeth! Look! They're biting the hare in the same way the white dragon is biting the red dragon. The curve of the neck . . . the angle of the body . . . Gutenberg must have used this painting as a model."

Xandria seemed cautiously impressed. "How did you know about this dragon image?"

Even now, he couldn't quite shake the feeling that his photographic memory was as much blessing as curse. "I probably saw it reproduced in a hundred books when I was an archaeobibliologist. It's a famous portrayal of the young sorcerer Merlin."

"But what does it mean?"

August enlarged the painting of the dragons. "Like most fables, there's far more than meets the eye. *Merlin the Sorcerer* is a symbolic peasant's tale. The true legend lies beneath the surface. For example, in the painting, the red dragon represents the people of England."

"And the white dragon?"

"The Saxons, but in a more symbolic sense, the forces of Germany." August scribbled something on the notepad. "The painter was using Merlin as a way to portray the confrontation between England and Germany. But in the Gutenberg illumination, the representations have changed. The white dog probably represents the Holy Roman Empire, which encompassed Germany in the Middle Ages. But the red dragon has been replaced by a hare."

"You mean a rabbit."

"No," August said, correcting her. "A rabbit and a hare are different." He pointed a finger at the illumination. "See the short ears and long hind legs? That's a hare, not a rabbit. It's a distinction that the illuminator would have wanted the viewer to understand."

"Why?"

"I think I may know the answer. A few years ago I sold a first edition of Jakob Grimm's *Deutsche Mythologie* to the prime minister of England, who wanted to give it to his daughter as a birthday present. I only got about forty thousand dollars for it because a couple of the pages were bent."

Xandria wagged a long finger and frowned. "Must have been a careless owner."

"I would suspect, yes," August answered drolly. "Anyway, Grimm was an enthusiastic fan of medieval literature; it was where most of his tales came from. One of his stories told of an old German festival called Ostara, which commemorated springtime or, more specifically, Easter and the story of Jesus' resurrection. Grimm explained that the name Ostara came from an even older story about a goddess who took the shape of . . ." August gestured toward the Gutenberg illumination.

"A hare?"

"Exactly," August said. "Meet the Easter bunny!"

"That's the reason we have an Easter bunny?"

"Yes. But that's not the mystery here," August said. "I think that Gutenberg is suggesting that the Holy Roman Empire possessed a dark religious secret." August stopped, feeling the impact of what he had just uttered. "I'm not quite sure what that means, but I'm certain that's the connotation."

"And what about the fox?" Xandria asked.

"The fox usually portrays dishonesty and trickery. The interesting thing is that in the illumination the second white dog has lost track of the fox, distracted by what appears to be an acorn made of gold coins."

"So maybe the powerful German, or a second powerful German, is letting treasure get in the way of the deception in front of him."

"Maybe," August said, jotting something onto the notepad.

His fingers danced on the keyboard and the second image—which was set inside the initial *M*—came into view: a king sitting on a throne, his garb a flowing, ruby-red tunic encrusted with jewels and topped with a royal-blue collar. The king held a golden globe in his right hand. His other hand extended up, with two fingers pointed toward the sky. The throne he sat on was simple and rustic, as was the crown set upon his head.

"Thirty minutes," Xandria said.

August ignored her, lost in the labyrinths of his mind. "The illumination begins the book of 2 Chronicles, which might be reason enough for the king holding up two fingers," August said, mulling the possibilities. "But the globe . . ."

Sensing that once again the illumination might be playing on a commonly known late-medieval painting, August trolled the Internet for images of fifteenth-century rulers in the Holy Roman Empire. He smiled, stumbling only a few minutes later upon another familiar image. "I think I found a connection," he said to Xandria.

Xandria looked at the laptop and saw an image labeled *The Holy Roman Emperor Sigismund.* She gasped, then shut her mouth quickly.

"You recognize this?"

"Yes," Xandria said. "What's the connection?"

August flicked the mouse pad, and the

Gutenberg illumination came side by side with the painting of Emperor Sigismund. "This is King Solomon," August said, pointing to the Gutenberg illumination. "Or, at least, it *should* be King Solomon, since he is the main focus of 2 Chronicles. But there's a problem with the representation."

Xandria studied the two images for clues. "The throne?"

"Close," August said. "Take a look at the crown." He lassoed the crown portion of the painting with the cursor and enlarged it. "This is not the crown Solomon would have worn. This is a *Saxon* crown."

"Just like the white dog."

"Correct," August said. "But you have to understand the history to see the implications. The first dukes of Saxony were simultaneously considered kings of the Holy Roman Empire. This continued well into the twelfth century, when Saxony was taken over by the Welfen dynasty."

"So what does the illumination mean?"

"I think it's suggesting that the power of the Holy Roman Empire sits on King Solomon's throne. Odd, to say the least."

"What's in his hand?"

"It's called a globus cruciger. In medieval paintings, it was common to show political leaders holding it. It means, literally, a globe with a cross on top. See, Sigismund is holding one. It shows that he holds the world in his hand, and the cross shows that he has been given the authority by holy rite."

Xandria compared the two images on the screen. "But the Gutenberg illumination shows the king holding a globus with no cross on top."

"Well, if both illuminations so far are about Sigismund, they could reasonably imply that his leadership of the Holy Roman

Empire was driven by an evil purpose. Jan Žižka—
the general of the Orphan army—battled against
Sigismund, claiming that he was driving the Holy
Roman Empire toward destruction."

"The Orphan army?"

"Followers of John Huss, the martyr who didn't
exactly see eye-to-eye with the Holy Roman Empire.
Some call them Hussites, then Orphans after Huss's
death. But I'm with those who think they didn't
acquire the name Orphans until after their leader,
Jan Žižka, perished in battle."

"Fascinating," Xandria said, tapping her watch as
if she were bored. "Only five minutes left."

August flew the cursor around the computer
screen and closed all the windows except for the
third Gutenberg illumination. This file, too, showed
an entire page of the Bible, this time from the book
of Romans. A flowering plant traveled along the
lower edge of the page, spiraling up into the initial
S. Above the initial stood a man wrapped in a flowing green tunic secured beneath his neck with a single gold clasp.
The man held two objects: in his left hand, a sheathed sword, and
in his right, a scarlet book, which appeared to be tied shut with two
black cords. His visage was bright and bold, lit from the light of
heaven that he seemed to be staring into. He seemed unaware of
the most unusual feature of the illumination: an ape, climbing a
thick green vine up the west margin of the page.

"Care to explain?"

"I'll start with the obvious," August said. "The ape."

"A monkey means mischief, right?"

"A monkey has a tail, something the *ape* in the illumination is clearly lacking," August said. "You really should go to a zoo sometime. You'd learn something."

"Maybe I will," Xandria said. She leaned in close enough for August to smell her cinnamon breath. "Maybe I'll take your kid with me. Show him the lions."

August tried to quell his anger. He needed to keep Xandria fixated on finding her answers. He highlighted the ape on the screen. "In the twelfth century, a man named Philippe de Thaon wrote a book called *Bestiaire*. It's a strange book of poetry, divided into three sections: beasts, birds, and stones."

"Stones?"

"Mostly diamonds and pearls, really," August said. "Philippe was trying to bridge early zoology with zodiacal study, and in doing so created an impressive work that was influential in medieval animal symbolism."

"And let me guess: you sold one of his books to the highest bidder."

"The buyer was from Norway. Owned a fishery or something. I don't remember his name. But I do remember his check for two hundred thousand dollars," August said, smiling. "I make a point of becoming educated about every book I sell. The edition I sold was Thaon's French translation. It made for a fascinating read, especially the chapters about evil beasts."

"Was the ape an evil beast?"

"The most evil of all," August said. "Philippe claimed that the ape was a symbol of the devil, trailing evildoers on the path to hell."

"But this ape is climbing up toward heaven."

August agreed. "So there might be a pattern here. The illuminator could be saying that someone or something evil is advancing in a holy quest. But take a look at this. Do you recognize the man in the illumination?"

Xandria looked again at the man in green. His beard forked into two points, making his wise expression take a turn toward one of cunning. "Who is he?"

"Make the phone call and I'll tell you," August said.

"Who is he?" Xandria asked again.

"Make the call," August said, dragging out the words, drawing a line in the sand.

Xandria pulled out the phone and dialed. "Joe? You can keep the kid alive for another hour. And stitch up the woman." She paused, listening. "I don't care how, just don't let her bleed to death. But if she gives you any trouble, shoot her. Got it?" She hung up. "No more fooling around. Who is the man in the illumination?"

August couldn't help but grin. He couldn't imagine the audacity it would have taken to have such an illumination created. It was the work of either genius or madness. Or both. "You know who it is. The man in the image is none other than Gutenberg himself. And this"—August carefully picked up the journal—"is the book he's holding!"

edilluminatedeightilluminatedill

The Thomas Jefferson Building—the central structure of the Library of Congress—stood in the distance like a white fortress surrounded by a moat of bustling boulevards: to the north, East Capitol Street; to the west, First Street; to the east, Second Street; and to the south, Independence Avenue. The gargantuan temple of the arts took laborers over eleven years to complete, and once finished, its interior was adorned with the work of over forty American painters and sculptors, their most magnificent production being the grand entrance, the Great Hall.

April sat nervously in the passenger seat of Norman's car, watching the sun sink, contemplating how she had come to the point of needing to steal the Great Hall's crown jewel.

"They were right," she said.

"Who was right?" Norman asked.

"The FBI guys were afraid I was going to take the Gutenberg, and now, here I am, trying to figure out how the two of us are going to sneak past Meng to do exactly that." She put her head in her hands. "How can this be happening?"

Norman put his hand on her shoulder. "The authorities will understand once you explain. I still think we should just call the police now and tell them what's going on."

"No. Any police involvement and they'll kill Charlie."

"But—"

"We can't," April said. "I'm sorry. But we just can't chance it."

Norman looked out the window of the car at Meng, who appeared to guard the entrance. "So how are we going to get in?"

April twirled the ends of her hair between her fingers, deep in thought. "I've got an idea," she finally said. She turned around and put her arms behind her back. "Cuff me again."

"What?"

"Meng probably doesn't know that I got away. And he certainly doesn't know that you had anything to do with it."

"What if one of your chaperones called him? That might be why he's standing there in the first place!"

"We've got to take that chance," she said. "C'mon. We're running out of time."

Norman reluctantly pulled out the handcuffs. "If he shoots us, I'm blaming you."

"Fair enough," she said. "Now, cuff me." She felt the cold metal slip around her wrists and click tight.

"So what's the plan?"

"We're going to have to improvise a little," she said, explaining the rest of her thin idea as they exited the vehicle.

Norman positioned April in front of him and began hustling her toward Agent Meng, who took immediate notice of their activity. "Sonofagun," Norman said. "He's going to put us down before we reach the end of the block."

"Just stay confident," April said, watching as Meng trained his pistol on them. "He's only going to let us in if he believes us."

They walked the remainder of the trip in silence, keeping a close eye on the gun.

"The library's closed," Meng said as they closed the gap to twenty yards. "FBI business. You two are going to need to get out of here."

"Agent Meng," Norman said. "It's Officer Briggs. We met earlier."

The gun lowered a little. "I remember. Hold on. Is that Ms. Adams with you?" The weapon rose back up.

"It is," Norman said. They were now at the bottom of the gargantuan steps leading up to the Library of Congress. "You didn't hear?"

"Didn't hear what?"

"Your boys had a little bit of an accident. Called me in to help."

"Why would they call you?"

Norman grunted in April's ear. "Because they knew I wanted to help."

"We don't need your help."

"Really? Because Ms. Adams would have gotten away if it wasn't for me. Seems she attempted a daring escape. Almost made it, too."

Meng stood flicking the safety on the gun on and off, on and off. "Come up here."

Norman pushed April up the stairs.

Meng pulled out his phone. "Stop right there." He dialed a number. He hung up and dialed another number. He put the phone away and swore under his breath. The door behind him opened, and a man in a dark-gray suit stepped out.

"Sir, we're having some trouble."

"I'm a little busy here," said Meng, stepping aside to reveal Norman and April.

"What are they doing here?"

"That's what I'm trying to figure out. You hear anything about an accident?"

"No."

Meng walked over to April. "Look at me."

She raised her head.

"You're in charge of the Gutenberg Bible, so you must know about the display-case security mechanisms, right?"

April remained silent. She knew more than mere curiosity drove his question. He'd already sent her away once to keep her from interfering. What would he do this time?

Meng put the tip of his gun under her chin. "Maybe it's a good thing you came back." He turned to the agent in the door. "Take them inside."

The agent took out his gun and waved Norman and April into the Library of Congress. Meng followed close behind. The Great Hall was bathed in an eerie red glow.

"What happened to the lights?" Norman asked.

"The FBI is running an unscheduled test on the grid tonight. The lights will come back on in a few hours. Long after we're gone." Meng grabbed April away. "Well, long after *we're* gone, anyway. You might still be hanging around."

The other agent pointed his gun at Norman. "Stand over by that wall," he said.

"Hey! I'm the one trying to help, remember?" he said.

Meng dragged April across the massive marble floor, which was inlaid with the signs of the zodiac. They passed over the sign of the ram. "April . . . April . . . let's see . . . are you an Aries?"

"Taurus."

"A bull? Really? I never would have pegged you for a bull. You just seem so . . . *un*bullish."

They walked through an archway into a room that was empty, save for two massive wooden display cases that stood to the left and to the right. The one to the right contained the Mainz Bible, which was of huge historic value but bore little interest at the moment. The one to the left held the Gutenberg, and as they peered through the glass, April felt her heartbeat quicken.

"Can you get the Gutenberg out?" Meng said.

April noticed that there were five other agents around the perimeter of the room, shrouded in the darkness. "I'm guessing you've already tried."

"There was a security measure we didn't expect. The Gutenberg Bible is lying on some type of trigger. Do you know how to turn it off?"

"You'll have to take off my handcuffs," April said.

"Get that security guard over here," Meng said to the agent outside the door on the other side of the Great Hall. The agent shuttled Norman over to the display case. "Unlock her cuffs," Meng told him.

"No problem," Norman said.

"Without opening your mouth," Meng said.

"Sure thing," Norman said, taking out a key and removing the handcuffs.

April rubbed at her wrists. "I need my gloves," she told Meng.

"Not tonight," Meng said, flicking his pistol's safety off.

April put her hand on the glass. It was cold, like touching a refrigerator door at the supermarket. She could see from a gauge positioned next to the Gutenberg that the temperature and humidity controls were still engaged, thanks to a backup power source. Obviously the antitheft controls were similarly wired. "I don't know anything about the security system."

"Try to remember," Meng said.

"You're just going to shoot me anyway."

"We're FBI, not CIA," Meng said. "You help us and you'll walk out of here alive. You don't want to leave your kid an orphan, do you?"

April met Meng's threatening glare. Was he conspiring with the woman who had August? "What do you know about my boy?"

"I've seen you with him here before. Cute kid. It'd really mess him up to lose his mother." Meng circled her. "Memory returning yet?"

"Take the panel off the back of the display case," April said.

"We've already done that," Meng said. "Next?"

"There's a keypad attached to the left side of the case. It's covered by a camouflage panel."

Meng waved his hand, and an agent ran to the back of the display case and shone a flashlight inside. "I think I found it," he said a minute later. "There's a bunch of strange pictures on the keypad."

"The signs of the zodiac," April said. "Just like the ones on the floor of the Great Hall."

"Interesting," Meng said. "Is there any connection?"

"You'd have to ask someone higher up than me."

"You seem to know everything we need to know," Meng said. "What's the code?"

"Taurus, Leo, Virgo, Scorpio."

"Taurus?" Meng said. "Are you part of the code?"

"It's just a coincidence."

Meng put his hand around her neck. "I don't believe in coincidences. Who do the other three signs belong to?"

April felt his fingers constrict her windpipe. Tears began to form at the corners of her eyes. "Please," she said, straining for air. "I'll tell you."

Meng released his grip.

"Dr. Winter, Thomas Jefferson, and Johannes Gutenberg." She gulped at the air. "Leo, Virgo, and Scorpio."

"Punch it in," Meng said.

They heard four short chirps from the back of the display case. "Seems good," said the agent. "I see a flashing green light."

"Push the light," April said.

"Do it," Meng confirmed.

"I'm pushing it now," the agent said. As soon as the words came out of his lips, a soft hiss of air could be heard escaping the glass lid of the display case.

"What just happened?" Meng asked.

"The case is acclimating its interior to the exterior temperature and humidity. Give it a few seconds."

"We don't have a few seconds," Meng said, placing his fingers under the lid and lifting. The glass rose skyward, its frame supported by a sturdy set of support hinges. The Gutenberg now lay exposed, the frailest of flowers on the verge of being tossed into a strong wind. "Lift it out so the trigger doesn't accidentally get activated. You're the only one here who's done it, so I trust you won't screw up."

April wiped her hands on her pants and reached forward into the display case. She put a hand under each side of the Gutenberg and—in a motion so prolonged that it resembled a slow-motion replay—closed the book so that it rested on its spine. Two spring triggers could be seen in the space where the front and back covers of the Gutenberg had been.

"The two sides had to be lifted simultaneously," Meng said, pointing the mechanism out to one of the other agents. "Or what?"

"I've never bothered to find out," April said.

"Now put it in the briefcase," Meng said, directing an agent. The agent opened a briefcase and set it on the floor at Meng's feet.

"That's really not a good traveling situation for—"

Meng cocked his gun.

April took the Gutenberg out of the display case and began inching toward the briefcase.

"You can move faster than that."

"This book is over five hundred years old," April said. "I can't begin to explain to you how delicate it is."

"Are you stalling?"

April leaned down and delicately placed the Gutenberg in the briefcase like she was laying a loved one in a casket. She straightened. "I guess I'm just not that anxious to die."

The briefcase lid snapped shut, the sound of metal grasping metal echoing in every corner of the room.

"You know I can't let you go," Meng said.

"Please," April said. "I swear I won't tell anyone."

Meng leveled his gun with her chest. "I wish I could believe you."

"Please!"

"Wait!" Norman said.

Meng turned his head. "Do you have a problem?"

Norman put out his hand. "No . . . I just think it might be a mistake to kill her."

"You're right. It is a mistake for *me* to kill her." Meng turned to one of the other agents. "Give him your gun," Meng instructed him. The agent handed his gun to Norman. "Better your prints on that than mine, and you can be the one to explain the gunshot residue on your hands." He lowered his own weapon.

"You might need her," Norman said. "If she's dead she's no good to you."

"Listen to him," April said, pleading her case. "There are things you don't know about the library. I can help—"

"Kill her," Meng said.

Norman took a deep breath and leveled the gun at April. "Five. Four. Three. Two—"

"Now!" Meng screamed.

April closed her eyes.

An alarm shattered the quiet of the Great Hall, followed by a burst of rain from the ceiling. Norman shot a bullet past April's right ear, placing it in the chest of the agent against the far wall. The agent crumpled. Meng lunged at Norman, but he was ready and struck Meng just below the chin with the butt of his gun. Meng fell, dazed.

"C'mon!" Norman yelled to April, the two of them running across the room to shield themselves behind the Mainz Bible display case. Pieces of the wall blew apart as gunfire whizzed by their heads and struck it. They ducked.

"I thought you were going to kill me," April shouted, wiping water away from her eyes.

Norman raised his voice over the din of the alarm. "You said *improvise.*" He checked the gun clip, then leaned around the display case and fired off a couple rounds. "They won't stick around for us. They've got the Gutenberg."

"They have one Gutenberg," April said. "I don't think it's the one they need."

"What do you mean, one? The library has another?"

"Not that the public knows about."

A few rounds ricocheted off the bulletproof glass of the Mainz Bible display case as the agents' feet splashed by. "They're not headed for the exit," Norman said. "Do you think they know where the other Gutenberg is located?"

"They must," April said. "Is it safe for us to move?"

Norman pulled a couple coins out of his pocket and threw them toward the far corner of the room. Bullets ripped the ground where the coins landed. Norman spun around the opposite side of the display case and fired a single shot at the exposed agent. The agent fell face-first into a pool of water, his head cracking on the floor. "Now it's safe," Norman said.

The two of them sloshed toward a flight of stairs that led to the wraparound balcony. As they reached the top step, the resounding alarm stopped, as did the torrent of water.

"How did you know about the alarm?" April asked, heading up another set of steps toward the Minerva mosaic that overlooked the Great Hall.

"Dr. Winter showed the display-case code to me: Taurus, Leo,

Aries, Aquarius. He also showed me the fire code set to a five-minute delay, the code you gave them."

"The delay was built in to allow someone to get the Gutenberg to a secure location before the water destroyed it," April said. "Who knew it would save my life?"

"Will we get to the second Gutenberg before they do?"

"I don't know," April answered. "And here's something else I don't know: if they planned to take the other copy, why didn't they want to keep me around to help get that one too?"

"Apparently they didn't think they needed you in the first place."

They exited a door that led into a long hallway on the second floor. They ran until April stopped before a set of ornate bronze doors. She pointed to a panel set in the upper left-hand corner. "The signs of Gutenberg are everywhere if you know where to look."

Norman squinted at the image set in the door. It looked like two shields—the kind medieval knights would have carried—hanging next to each other from a tree branch. The shield on the left featured an *X*, while the one on the right displayed an inverted *V*, set with three stars. "What is it?"

"It's a symbol taken from a colophon," April said. "Before there were title pages in books, printers used a colophon on the back page. It was basically just a few lines explaining who worked on the book. But it also included an image, a set of symbols unique to the printer."

"So that's Gutenberg's colophon?"

"No. The *X* is the Greek symbol *chi*, and the upside-down *V* is the Greek symbol *lambda*," she said, tracing the letters with her finger in the air. "The shield on the left represented a man named Johann

Fust. And the shield on the right stood for his business partner Peter Schöffer."

"And they were . . . ?"

"Gutenberg's associates," April whispered. She turned away from the door toward a gate on the opposite wall. She took out a key and unlocked it. "Come on," she said, opening the door behind the gate and entering the room beyond. She didn't bother turning on the lights; the layout of the room was etched on her brain. She grabbed Norman by the arm. "Follow me." She dragged him across thick carpet, past wooden tables topped with brass lamps.

Norman trailed behind April, now and then banging into the sides of benches. "The Rosenwald Room. This is your hideout, isn't it?"

"You could call it that," she replied.

They passed rows of bookshelves, moving toward the back wall. "Where are we going?" he asked.

April heard the door open behind them. She stopped and listened as two agents entered the room. April squeezed Norman's arm so hard he moved to pry her fingers off. She pulled him forward, farther into the enclave of rare books. They finally reached the back corner of the room, where the last bookshelf met the wall. The two sets of feet scuttled toward them. "They're getting closer," Norman said in April's ear.

She wasn't interested. She kept her back to him, her body pointed toward a small control box on the wall next to her, its wide, digitized panel glowing a soft orange. April put her hand against it, triggering a faint *click* from the bookcase.

A loud thud echoed behind them. April turned. The agents were an aisle away. She felt the ground quiver with every step they took. They were running. The lit panel next to April showed them exactly what to run toward.

"Stop!" one of the agents yelled.

"Go!" Norman said, tapping rapidly on April's shoulder. She grabbed him and fell into the bookcase. It gave way, not falling but spinning, toward the wall.

They crashed to the floor, and the case slammed shut behind them. April darted up while Norman was still dazed.

"We've got to hurry," she said, descending a narrow staircase on the other side of the room, though *room* was a broad term for this space. It was more like a tall, triangular closet with a hard concrete floor and three bare walls. The bookcase shook beside Norman. Apparently the agents didn't know how to get the bookcase to spin open, though they seemed determined to force the issue.

April was already twenty stairs in front of Norman when he started down. She stopped twenty steps later, where the descent diverged to the left and the right. Norman finally caught up to her. "Where are we?"

"Shhhh," she said.

"You are such a librarian," Norman said. He lowered his voice. "What is this place?"

"We're under the library. This is the way to the rare-book vault."

If Norman was shocked by the multitude of surprises—the bookcase doorways, the basement lairs, the secret vaults—he didn't let on. This was Washington DC, after all, a city known for its duplicitous underpinnings: gallant facades covering underground tunnels and covert antechambers. Secrets lurked everywhere. Their current situation was proof.

Seeing another question forming on Norman's lips, April put

her finger up again, this time not bothering with the sound effect. Instead, she balled up her face in the angriest display she could muster, which wasn't much, but more than enough to get the point across. *Quiet!*

Okay, okay, Norman mouthed. And then he turned toward a sound: there were voices coming from a doorway at the bottom of the left staircase. April began to creep toward the voices. Norman reached out a hand to stop her, but she evaded his grip.

April had almost reached the bottom of the stairs when she paused. There was something on the ground in front of her. A mouse, maybe, or a dead rat. But the proportions were all wrong. And then she realized what she was staring at: a human hand, severed at the wrist.

April caught Norman's attention and pointed to the hand, then to the wall. Next to the open doorway at the bottom of the stairs was a digital panel, an exact copy of the one she had placed her hand on above. The hand had been used to gain access to the door. No wonder they thought they didn't need her for this part of the job.

The growl of grinding metal filled the air. April motioned Norman closer. "They must be drilling into the vaults," she said. "But they're in the wrong place."

Norman followed her back up to the top of the steps. Instead of going back to the Rosenwald Room, she headed down the other staircase, which led to another vault, the only difference being that this one was sealed shut with a steel door.

April put her hand on the digital panel next to the door. It flashed red. "I don't have access to this room," she said.

"You've got access to the magical bookcase but not this?"

"Unlocking that access panel made this one impossible for me to open. Someone else with the proper clearance will have to open it. It's a check-and-balance system to make sure no one comes down here alone."

"Why does that matter?"

"It's so no one steals anything."

"Like the guys in the other vault?"

"Exactly. Only they couldn't have known they picked the wrong vault. Last week I personally moved the Gutenberg to this vault to compare it with some other illuminated books from the fifteenth century. But no one outside of our department would have known about the move."

Norman put his hand on the digital panel and watched it blink red. "Who else has access to this vault?"

"Just a few other people from my department."

"Was Dr. Winter one of them?"

"Yes, of course."

"Then I think he can help," Norman said, dashing back up the stairs.

"Where are you going?" April asked.

"To get a helping hand!"

nine

Xandria had given Joe two primary objectives: number one, keep the hostages alive, and number two, if drastic action became necessary, kill them. Joe had expected objective number two to be the difficult one. Objective number one should have been a given. Do nothing, and the kid stays alive.

Wrong. And it was worse than that.

To his left, Grandma was bleeding to death, and to his right, the kid was laid out on the floor, pale white. *Dead* white.

In a moment of clarity, Joe realized he could not tell Xandria about the boy. She needed him alive. Besides, if Xandria's next call was to kill them both, then his job would already be done. Why save them only to have to kill them again?

But Xandria might also call and say, "Let them go. We got what we needed." Or, even worse, "Put the kid on the line to talk with his dad." Their deaths could prove problematic. Why had he wanted to leave his desk job? Wasn't it enough just to be a part of the Orphans? Too bad he couldn't talk about it in his blog. It was certainly cooler than his stories about watching every season of *24* front to back for a third straight time.

"You've got to help Charlie," Grandma said, panting. "His inhaler is in the kitchen by the coffeemaker."

He stared at her, unmoving. What should he do? He pulled out his phone, wishing Xandria would call at any minute and say, "Kill the boy!" But the sight of the phone scared him. What if Xandria didn't come through? What if he let the boy die and then the police came and put him away for life? Objective one: Keep the kid alive. It was the *first* objective, the *most important* objective. Objective two would only come into play if the kid's parents failed to do their job. And they wouldn't, would they? Not with the life of their only son at stake.

"Please help him!" Grandma wailed.

Joe snapped out of his confusion. He ran over to the boy and leaned down. At first he heard nothing but a graveyard silence, but then he heard the faintest whistle from the collapse of Charlie's airways. "He's still alive," he said to Grandma. The comment didn't seem to lessen her anxiety.

He raced into the kitchen, knocking down a chair and a framed picture of Charlie along the way. He felt out of control. Where had Grandma said the inhaler was? Next to the refrigerator? The toaster? He raced around the room, peeling back flowerpots and napkin holders, looking for the little plastic gadget that could save the kid's life. Where was it?

He stuck his head out the kitchen doorway to ask. Grandma was hunched over in the chair—at least, as much as the ropes would allow—eyes closed and apparently unconscious. He yelled at her. She didn't respond. He turned back to the room and decided to take a sweeping approach, quite literally extending his arm and removing everything from the countertops. Pill bottles and coin jars and salt and pepper shakers and *everything* went crashing to the floor. Joe dropped to his knees and violently started sifting through the junk, hoping to stumble across the inhaler.

It was a broken coffee mug that finally reminded him where to look. He glanced around the fallen kitchenware. He needed to find the coffeemaker. Where was it? He looked up. It was on a small table across the room. Next to it, he saw a small white-and-orange device: the inhaler.

Rising, he glanced back at Charlie but could see only his feet. Was the kid still alive? He tried to remember how long a person could go without air. A minute? Two? Twelve? Hadn't that magician gone for the record in a barrel of water and failed? And how long did he go without air? Five minutes? Six? How long had he been searching? His head was dizzy.

The lights swirled as he swam over to the coffeemaker and grabbed at the inhaler. It slipped from his hand and broke apart on the floor. He picked up the two, no, three pieces and ran back across the kitchen toward Charlie, trying to put the inhaler back together.

He exited the kitchen and squatted by Charlie's side. The kid looked even worse, and this time there wasn't so much as a squeak from him. His airways were closed. Maybe for good.

"C'mon, kid," Joe said, sitting the boy up in his lap. "C'mon!" He pried open Charlie's pasty-dry mouth and shoved the inhaler inside. The side of the device was cracked, and the first depression of the cartridge only managed to make the inhaler fall apart again.

Joe swore. Maybe he should just give up.

He looked down at Charlie's face. A few freckles. A scratch on his chin, probably from slipping on his skateboard or something. A touch of chocolate on his upper lip, a sure sign the kid had finished off a full glass of Ovaltine or whatever kids drank these days for an after-school snack.

He couldn't let this kid die.

Joe reassembled the inhaler and curled his fingers around it to hold it together. He crammed the mouthpiece between Charlie's lips and squeezed down on the cartridge. *Pfffffffft!* Charlie didn't move. He hit the cartridge again. *Pfffffffft!* Again. *Pfffffffft!*

Nothing.

"Wake up!" Joe screamed. He slammed his fist down onto Charlie's chest and watched the child's eyes blink open. Joe sat in shock for a moment, before blasting a fourth and final shot from the cartridge. *Pfffffffft!*

Joe felt tears well up in his eyes as he watched Charlie suck in the bitter, lifesaving air. He sat fully upright, coughing and choking, but *breathing*. He was going to make it.

"Grandma," Charlie said weakly.

Joe looked over to the chair where Grandma Rose was fixed. A pool of blood had collected under the chair. Not good.

"You shot her," Charlie said.

"Your grandma would be fine right now if you hadn't been messing around with that stupid gun," Joe said, his relief vanishing. "This is *your* fault."

"Is she dead?"

Joe walked across the room and put a couple fingers against Grandma's neck. "No. She's still alive. But just barely." He took a closer look at the bullet wound in her leg, which was actually *two* wounds: entry and exit. He hoped the fact that it wasn't still in her leg was a good thing.

"What are you going to do?" Charlie asked.

Joe began to wonder if he had done the right thing by letting the kid live. "I don't know," he told Charlie.

"Call a doctor. Call 9-1-1." His pale skin had a little more pink in it now.

"No doctors. No police. Nothing like that," Joe said. "We have to figure this out ourselves." He began to untie the ropes holding Grandma. She wasn't exactly going to dash away in the condition she was in. He turned to Charlie. "Go into the kitchen and run the water in the sink until it's hot. Got it?"

Charlie nodded and sprinted to the kitchen. The sound of water running into the stainless-steel basin of the kitchen sink came only seconds later.

"And no funny stuff, okay?" Joe shouted. He listened for a response. "You hear me?"

"Yes," Charlie said, popping his head back into the room. "Now what?"

"Get a bowl and fill it up with the hot water. Grab some clean rags and bring everything in here as quick as you can."

"How do you know what to do? Are you a nurse or something?"

Nurse? What was the kid thinking? "Just get it!" Joe said.

Joe pulled Grandma Rose from the chair and laid her out on the floor. He propped the ankle of her bad leg up on the chair and tied a tourniquet around the top of her leg, tugging until he felt certain there was no possible way even a drop of blood could travel past the rope blockade.

Charlie entered the room a minute later, water sloshing out of a crystal punch bowl that Joe guessed had never been used. Probably a wedding gift. He helped Charlie set the bowl on the ground, then began sopping up the bloodied areas on Grandma's leg with the large rag Charlie had brought with him.

"What is this?" Joe asked, noticing the rag wasn't a rag at all. Hand-stitched flowers dotted the fabric, which was silky and smooth, definitely not the terry texture of cloth used to clean up spilled milk.

"It's my mom's best tablecloth."

Joe continued to clean Grandma's wounds, sponging up the blood and wringing it out in the crystal bowl. "Why did you grab your mom's best tablecloth?"

"It was the cleanest thing I could think of. Mom won't let a *crumb* drop on it whenever she uses it, which is only when really important guests come over."

Joe leaned back on his knees. "I don't think there's anything more we can do right now. But I think she's going to be okay. She's not losing any more blood."

"Thanks for helping her," Charlie said. "What's your name?"

"Joe."

"I'm Charlie. You'd make a good nurse, Joe."

"Doctor."

"Nurses don't have to be girls, you know."

Joe rolled his eyes, feeling silly explaining himself to a child. Of course he knew that. "I'm just saying that if I was going to go into the medical profession, I'd be a doctor, not a nurse. Like maybe a brain surgeon or something."

Charlie looked puzzled. "I don't think you could be a brain surgeon."

"Why not?" Joe asked, perturbed.

"Because I'm only eight, and I totally fooled you in the attic, which means you can't be that smart."

"You didn't fool me," Joe said. "I knew *exactly* where you were."

"Spell *lyceum.*"

"What?"

"If you're smarter than me, then spell *lyceum.* It's one of the winning words from the national spelling bee."

"How do you know that?" Joe asked. He tried to envision the word in his head. It was a little fuzzy. What was a lyceum anyway? A bug? Yes, he decided. Some kind of beetle.

"I know about *lyceum* because I met the winner who spelled it," Charlie said proudly. "Amanda Goad. She's from Richmond, Virginia, which isn't very far from here. My mom introduced me to her last year at the library." Charlie got a funny expression on his face, as if he was recalling the encounter with Amanda Goad, or maybe something humorous that had happened between them, or something odd she had said.

Joe was still turning the word over in his mind. "I'm not spelling nothing, kid," he finally said.

"I'm not spelling *anything,*" Charlie corrected.

"What?"

"Never mind."

There was a knock at the door. Joe and Charlie looked at each other.

"Expecting anyone?" Joe asked.

"Nope."

"Like a repair guy or something?"

"I don't know. Maybe."

"Well, yes or no?"

"I said I don't know. I'm eight."

"But you're a really *smart* eight-year-old," Joe said, hoping the flattery would help him remember. "So maybe you overheard your mom or grandma talking about someone coming over?"

"Maybe."

"Maybe yes? Or maybe no?"

"Maybe I don't remember."

Joe was about to shoot himself. The kid probably understood nuclear physics, but he couldn't remember anything actually useful.

Another knock.

"Don't move," Joe said to Charlie. Staying low, he maneuvered toward a window to the left of the door and peeked underneath the curtain. Although the light was dim, he could see a man in a dark blue jumpsuit standing on the front stoop. He was about six feet tall, Joe guessed, and wore round, gold-framed glasses. His curly brown hair and pudgy, pockmarked cheeks gave Joe the impression that he was pretty harmless. Plus, he was holding a weathered leather bag in one hand and a Jamba Juice cup in the other. Repairman for sure. But better to be safe than sorry.

"Charlie, I need you to open the door and tell this guy that your grandma is sick and he'll have to come back another time." Joe made sure that his tone left no room for disagreement.

"But what if he sees Grandma Rose?" Charlie asked.

"If you only open the door a crack, he won't see her," Joe said. "Just don't let him in, understand?"

"Okay."

"Really?"

"I won't let him in. I promise." Charlie walked over to the door.

There was another pound on the door. Loud. Impatient.

Charlie put his hand on the doorknob.

"Wait!" Joe barked. "Put the chain back first."

"Gotcha," Charlie said, reaching up and hooking the chain in place. And then, without another hesitation, he opened the door.

✠

Stanley Glass didn't ask questions. He sometimes wondered if it had something to do with his childhood—maybe with the Catholic school nuns swatting his hands with thick rulers when he failed to answer *their* questions, or maybe with his parents, who incessantly told him to be quiet, to stay in his room, to stay out of trouble, to stay out of sight. At other times he wondered if it had something to do with joining the military afterward, with the cruelty of his drill sergeant or the beating he endured after failing to answer a command.

Maybe.

It didn't really matter now. Now he was loved. Now he was feared. And all because he did exactly as he was told.

"Are you ready, sir?"

"Not quite," Stanley said, scanning the board on the wall. His phone buzzed. A text message. He ignored it. There were more important things at hand. Burner? Matcha? Performance? Which boost should he add? His phone buzzed again. He pulled it out of his pocket. "Sorry," he said to the register girl. He read the text:

no word from ben.

must B trouble.

go 2 house.

full clean.

Full clean. It had been months since he'd done a full clean. Luckily, all his gear was in the trunk of his Volvo station wagon. Gloves. Bags. Saws. He couldn't think of anything he was lacking.

"Sir? Please. We've got lots of people waiting."

Actually, there was *one* thing he lacked.

"Sir?"

Surely he had time to wait for a Jamba Juice. He'd been standing in line for twenty minutes already, not an uncommon occurrence for the busy location.

"Sir? I'm sorry, but the line is out the door, and I really need your order."

Stanley scowled and left his place in line. He was right in front of the register. So close. But he had to go to the job immediately. Time wasted meant a botched job, and that was something he couldn't chance.

He walked out the front door and saw a man taking the paper off the top of his straw. "'Scuse me," Stanley said. "What flavor did you get?"

"Razzmatazz," the man said, clearly pleased. He opened his mouth and aimed for the straw.

"And what boost did you get?" Stanley asked.

The man stopped an inch from the straw. "Um. Let's see . . . it's getting late, which means she wouldn't have put anything in that would keep me up all night. I'm a regular here, you see . . . they know exactly what I like."

"So like a Vita Boost or something?"

"Probably."

Stanley smiled. *Perfect.*

✠

He was just sucking down the last drops of the fresh, frothy concoction as he knocked on April Adams's door for a third time. The Vita Boost left a slight tingle in his mouth, and he wondered if it was going to put a tingle in his stomach as well. He had been having some stomach pain lately. He hoped his doctor wouldn't forbid his daily shot of Jamba Juice.

The door opened a crack.

"You can't come in," a boy said through the narrow opening. His eyes looked frazzled, like he'd been up all night drinking Coke and eating Sugar Pops.

"I'm here to fix the dishwasher. Your mom called me earlier this week," Stanley said, pulling a repair order from his jacket. He showed it to the kid. "The contact name I have is April Adams. Is that your mom?"

Charlie nodded. "But you still can't come in. My grandma is sick, and we can't have any visitors."

"Well, you're in luck, because I'm not a visitor," Stanley said, putting his fingers around the edge of the door. "I'm a repairman. I'm just here to do a job. That's it. Your grandma doesn't even have to know that I was here."

Charlie stood resolute. "Sorry," he said, starting to close the door.

Stanley locked his elbow to stop the door, then tensed his muscles for the push.

Charlie seemed perplexed by Stanley's inability to remove his hand. "I said I'm sorry, mister."

Stanley grinned. "Me too."

tedilluminatedtenilluminatedillu

T he airbus cut through the ink-black sky like a giant white whale. Most of its occupants slept peacefully, many enticed to their private dreamland through a mixture of melatonin and alcohol. A scattered few stayed awake to watch the movie, a B-grade, cable-network reject that didn't merit its captive audience. One couple argued quietly between themselves about the exact number of attendants that should stand in their wedding: the girl was up to seven, the guy was holding at three.

August was about to force them to agree to five when the cabin rumbled again.

None of the sleeping people woke. And none of the movie-watching people blinked. The cabin had been shaking the entire trip, and like voyagers set on the high seas and resigned to the ebb and flow of the waves, the patrons of the airbus had decided to set their worries aside and just ride out the whole ordeal.

August considered that the odds of the airbus crashing to the ground were relatively slim. He looked over at Xandria and wondered what his odds were, considering everything else.

"Call your wife again," she said.

"She said she would call when she had the Gutenberg and could send us the images," August said. "I can assure you that she won't forget."

Xandria held out the phone. "Call."

August cracked his knuckles, as well as his neck, before snatching the phone from her hands. Any behavior that showed he wasn't her pawn made him feel a little more in control.

He dialed. April's phone rang, but no one answered.

"She's probably right in the middle of getting it out of the library. It's a tricky job, you know," August said. "It's not like she can walk in and check out the Gutenberg like it's a copy of *Foucault's Pendulum*."

"Nice reference. Did you think I wouldn't know what that was?" Xandria said. "I've read *Foucault's Pendulum*. I thought it was boring."

"So did my ex," August said. "Of course, you're both wrong. It just went over your heads."

"Excuse me?" Xandria said. "You think because I'm a *woman* I couldn't possibly like an intellectual thriller. Is that it?"

"That's not what I meant at all."

"Right," Xandria said, the sarcasm dripping from her full lips. "Better stay focused on your own pendulum. It's getting lower by the minute."

The phone chirped twice.

"Text message," Xandria said, pulling the phone out of August's hands. She scanned the screen. "Trouble at the library. Your ex is asking for another hour."

A shiver rippled through August's body. Xandria didn't seem too fond of handing out favors. "One hour," August said. "You've got to give it to her. It's completely fair."

"Since when has any of this been *fair*?" Her sentence was punctuated by a loud rumble of the plane. Xandria gripped her seat, and August caught the faintest glimpse of fear in her eyes.

"What are you going to do? Kill my son? Do you really think I'm going to help you then?"

Xandria's face showed indifference, but she was listening.

"My cooperation is completely dependent on my family staying alive," August said, holding his ground. He knew Xandria wouldn't buy it, but it might keep her thinking rationally.

"One hour," Xandria said. "You can decipher the images in *your* copy of the Gutenberg while we're waiting on your ex."

Another shiver. This wasn't what August wanted to hear. "One problem," he said.

"What?"

"I don't have the Gutenberg with me," August said, almost chuckling as he said it, the words seeming so outrageous as they fell out of his mouth.

"You do," Xandria said. "I saw you walk on the plane with it. It's in that oversized metal briefcase right above our heads."

"I wish it were," August said. "That briefcase doesn't have anything in it besides some of my dirty laundry."

"So where is it?" Xandria asked.

August could tell by the tension in her voice that this was completely unexpected news, a loose thread that could unravel her entire plan. For a moment, he toyed with the idea of telling her it was back in Germany, that the Gutenberg wasn't on the plane at all. But the thought of her giving the command to execute Charlie quickly dispelled that notion. "It's with the checked baggage," he confessed.

"You checked it."

"Yes."

Her eyes held his. "I don't believe you'd do that. It's too risky."

It was risky, which was why August tended to favor the approach. What kind of book thief would expect him to plant homing devices in his rare books, shrink-wrap them, then slap a "Collector's Edition Reproduction" sticker on the outside?

"Well, it works. Obviously."

Xandria said nothing, which scared August. He couldn't tell if she was going to laugh or claw his eyes out. She did neither, instead turning forward in her seat and taking a few deep breaths. August felt lucky that Xandria had apparently visited a few psychotherapists over the years.

"Then I guess you'll have to go get it," she stated, in a voice so calm he almost didn't hear her.

"Go get it?" August said. "It's in the cargo hold! They don't exactly let people down there!"

"Excuses, excuses," Xandria said, reclining and crossing her ankles. "You and your ex-wife aren't very good at taking responsibility for your problems, are you?"

August contemplated the options. "There's no way I can do it."

"You're Superman, remember?" Xandria said with a smirk. She

slithered closer to August. "Charlie needs you to figure this out." Closer. "And I need you to figure this out too."

August could feel her body next to his. His heartbeat accelerated despite himself. He could smell her perfume swirling around him, both invigorating and toxic.

"Stay away from me," he said, rising from his seat. He clumsily climbed over her on his way into the aisle.

"Don't forget to get my book," she said sweetly. *"Foucault's Pendulum,* remember?"

August untangled his left foot from between her ankles. He tottered in the aisle, using the headrests for support as the cabin shook once again.

A flight attendant came bounding up to him from the front of the plane. "Sir, sir!" She scowled. "Maybe you didn't hear the announcement, but we need everyone in their seats. We've been experiencing some turbulence."

"Turbulence? Really?" August said, stalling while he thought about his next move. He looked a couple rows ahead and saw the kid next to the grandfather he had helped. August turned back to the flight attendant, his plans resolved. "I'm sorry . . . Janice," he said, reading the name on her badge. "I just wanted to check on my friend who got hit in the head earlier."

"Oh, right. You're the superhero guy. Time to retire your cape. Your friend is doing fine. We found a real doctor to check in on him from time to time."

"I'd really like to see him," August said, trying to plaster concern across his face. "I can see that there's an open seat right next to him. I'll buckle as soon as I sit down. I swear."

The flight attendant rolled her eyes. "You guys are all the same," she said. "Which means you'll bug me until you get your way." She backed up until August could enter the row with the old man and his grandson.

August quickly scooted in, careful not to bump into the old man, who was lying back in his seat with a cold compress against his head. August buckled his seat belt right away under Janice's watchful eye.

"And keep that kid in his seat too," the flight attendant called back, grabbing at seatbacks as she pulled her way to the front of the plane.

August waited until she was a safe distance away before speaking to the grandson. "Hi," he said. "Do you remember me?"

"Sure," the boy said. "You helped my grandpa."

August grinned. "How's he doing?"

"Okay, I guess. They gave him some medicine. He's been sleeping a long time, but that's better than being dead."

"Well put." He couldn't disagree with the kid's simple logic. He stuck out his hand. "My name is August. What's yours?"

"Clayton," he said, slapping a low high five.

"Clayton, I've got a question for you," August said, inspecting his ketchup-stained G. I. Joe T-shirt, beige camouflage pants, and black high tops. "What's your favorite thing in the whole world?"

Clayton didn't have to think twice. "Tiger sharks."

August was hoping for him to say something simpler, like maybe bubblegum. "Tiger sharks, huh? Well, that's pretty cool. I like tiger sharks too."

"They're not real tigers," Clayton said, lifting his eyebrows as if worried that he might be leading his new friend astray. "They're just a special kind of shark."

"Do they have big teeth?"

"Really big!" Clayton said, opening his own mouth wide.

August looked over to his right at the old man. August felt assured that he was fast asleep, even though the compress hid the eyes. August turned back to the boy. "What if I told you I could get you a tiger shark?"

The boy crossed his arms, skeptical. "Now?"

"Not *right* now. Tiger sharks don't like to fly, so we'd at least have to wait until we landed."

"You can really get me a tiger shark?" Clayton asked.

August paused momentarily. He wasn't going to lie to the kid. But if this horrible undertow turned into a favorable tide . . . "Yes," he finally said. "I most certainly can. But you're going to have to help me first."

Clayton didn't pause, didn't even question how on earth August planned on fetching such a creature for him. "Deal," he said, sticking out his hand like he'd made this transaction a million times: a big favor for a tiger shark.

August took his hand and shook it firmly. "I'm going to need you to listen to me very closely," he whispered.

☩

Janice was counting the carbonated versus noncarbonated beverages in the drink cart when the first scream rang out. "Did I just say thirty-two or thirty-three?" she asked Thad Hartman, who was in charge of peanuts.

"Did you hear something?"

"Thirty-two or thirty-three? Which was it? I don't want to have to count these all again."

Another scream.

"You better go check that out," Thad said, his arms full of small peanut bags.

Janice shot her worst glare at Thad and threw up her arms in disgust. "I'm completely lost. I'm going to have to start counting all over again!"

She flung open the curtain—which she had closed to have a moment of peace from the ever-needy passengers—and shuffled down the aisle toward the screaming. She could tell it was a young boy yelling. She slowed down. He was probably just freaking out after losing his Game Boy under his seat. Not exactly an emergency.

The scream blasted again, and a hundred tired eyes opened in response.

"Coming!" she said, hoping the boy would shut up and letting everyone know she had the situation under control. Were his parents deaf?

The scream turned into a frantic wail. People were getting up out of their seats, their confused and irritated faces pointed toward the commotion.

"Sit down, everyone. Sit down," Janice said, motioning for the people to return to their seats. She reached behind her to make sure the rubber band holding back her thick, brown hair in a ponytail was still in place. She'd once had a kid practically rip her roots out in a mad fit after spilling Coke on his pants, and she didn't want to chance another such encounter.

"I think he's having a heart attack!" someone said.

Janice sensed she might have misevaluated the situation. "Please, let me through!" she boomed, tearing down the aisle. The plane trembled, and she would have fallen if not for the kind arm of a businessman. "Could you get me a gin and tonic?" he asked, peeling back the edge of his noise-canceling headphones.

"Sir, we'll be taking drink orders later."

"I have to wait? I just want—"

"Sir. Please. Later. I have a non-drink-related emergency to attend to," Janice said, pulling away and plunging headlong through the gathering throng. "May I remind everyone that the seat belt sign is still lit? Sit down now, or you will be docked frequent-flier miles!"

Everybody sat down.

Janice finally reached the epicenter of the trauma, finding that the shrieking boy belonged to the old man with the head injury. "What's going on?" she asked.

"I think he might be dead," said the boy, tears pouring down his cheeks, his arms wrapped tightly around his grandfather.

Janice looked at the old man. He looked very pale, and his mouth was hanging open at an odd angle. If she had to guess, she'd say that the boy was right in his assessment. She stuck out her fingers to take a pulse, but the boy batted her away.

"Leave him alone!" he said. "You're not a doctor!"

"I'm just trying to help, you little brat!" she snapped, wishing she could reel the words back in immediately. "I'm just trying to help," she said again, using a gentler tone, looking around to make sure everyone observed her smoothing out the misunderstanding.

The other flight attendants came running toward Janice from both ends of the aisle. "What's going on?" Thad asked, coming up behind her.

"Where is the man who was just sitting here?"

"I think I saw him step into the restroom."

"Go get this guy's doctor," Janice instructed Thad. She ordered the gawkers back to their seats, then covered her ears against the boy's crying until the doctor finally showed up.

"Little boy," Janice said. "The doctor's here. We need you to sit down so we can take a look at your grandpa. Okay?"

"Okay," he said, suddenly releasing his grandfather. He sat down with a smile. The defiance that had creased his face only a moment earlier completely vanished.

Janice was stupefied.

The physician grabbed the old man's wrist to check for a pulse.

The whole plane held its collective breath, waiting for the announcement. Janice put a hand on her forehead. The old man was dead. She knew it. They'd have to ride the entire journey with a dead stranger propped up in one of the seats.

"He's alive," the doctor said, with as much surprise in her voice as was on the faces of the rubberneckers.

"Really?" Janice asked, her incredulousness more apparent than intended.

"Check him yourself," the doctor said, placing the old man's wrist in her hand and walking away.

The other flight attendants left as well, leaving Janice to soak in a bath of hot glares. No one had forgotten her pronouncement of the sweet boy as a little brat.

"He spit at me," she lied, shrinking behind the safety of the curtain.

☩

August reached the back of the plane just as Clayton's first scream ripped through the air. He stood outside the occupied restroom, feigning impatience, and waited until three flight attendants pushed past him on their way to the growing commotion. August didn't hesitate, entering the flight attendants' cubbyhole and throwing the curtain.

He listened to another siren blast from Clayton, which was followed by a long wail and then . . . was he crying? The kid was better than August expected.

He searched around the floor for the trapdoor that led to the storage compartment below. It wasn't hard to find. He lifted a thin utility mat and found the two latches he needed to open it. He was starting to twist the first latch when he heard the restroom door open. What if it was a flight attendant in the restroom? And what if the flight attendant was about to throw open the curtain and catch him in the middle of a federal offense?

He heard the restroom door snap shut. The prior occupant brushed against the curtain, and August flinched. His pulse doubled. He quickly tried to formulate an excuse in his mind: his dog was in the storage area and he needed to walk him? He would need to do better than that!

But he didn't need the excuse. The person walked away, and August realized he'd been holding his breath.

Not wasting another moment, August quickly twisted the latches of the trapdoor and pulled on the handles. It didn't budge. He pulled harder. Nothing.

Through the curtain he heard a muffled verbal battle going on between Clayton and a few other people. The kid wouldn't be able to stall for much longer. Once they figured out the old man was very much alive, the jig would be up.

August grabbed at the trapdoor once more and discovered the

explanation for his failure to open it: set in the bottom of each handle was a tiny keyhole. *But where was the key?*

The flight attendants!

August put his palms against his temples and rubbed hard.

Think. Think. Think!

He glanced around the small room for anywhere there might be a spare key. He started fumbling through the cabinets, the drawers, the drink cart; he was finding nothing. August was about to give up when he saw something sticking out of a small seat folded into the wall. He reached over and yanked the seat down, revealing a yellow purse.

Clayton hadn't cried out in over a minute, and at any moment the flight attendants would be returning. August unzipped the purse and rifled through it. Lipstick, lipstick, lipstick—how many colors did one person need?—a pink wallet, vanilla-mint breath spray, a New York subway pass, an old rabbit's foot keychain, *keys!*

August closed the purse back into the folded seat and dropped to the floor. There were at least ten keys on the chain, but only three or four looked small enough for the trapdoor locks.

He tried the first.

The second.

The third.

He heard voices from the other side of the curtain. Clayton must have run out of steam.

August slammed the fourth key into the slot and turned. *Click!* He opened the trapdoor and stared down into the storage compartment. It was completely dark. He looked up and saw a hand grab the edge of the curtain, but there was no stopping now.

He wondered if once he was down there he'd even be able to find his way around.

The curtain opened an inch. August could hear the flight attendants talking with a passenger about the crazy screaming kid and his undead grandfather. He dropped through the trapdoor and shut it over him, hearing the mat flop back into place. He was in. Seconds later he heard feet overhead. He couldn't hear the flight attendants' exact words, but he could tell by the rise and fall of their voices that they were questioning each other about something. He heard the folding seat open and shut, and a shrill voice followed.

August cringed, realizing he had left the key in the trapdoor. He heard the rug rolling back. The trapdoor rattled, then rose. August dived between two large piles of luggage, pulling in his legs just as a head popped into the light above.

"You see anything?" asked a voice.

"It's hard to see anything down here," the flight attendant said. He flicked on a flashlight.

August watched the beam float silently across the floor, then travel along the surface of the luggage and against the walls. Too late, he saw that his shoe was within view. He could almost feel the beam of light burning into his sole as it passed over.

"Are you sure you didn't leave the key in the lock?" the flashlight bearer asked. "I heard that you sneaked down here with Thad one time."

"What?" the voice overhead snarled.

"That's just what I heard!" The flight attendant disappeared and the trapdoor shut.

August thought he had avoided the worst. He uncurled his

body and stretched out in relief. Now he just had to find the Gutenberg.

"I'm a lucky guy," he said aloud, a vote of his own confidence. And then, like a heavenly response to his boasting, he listened to the unnerving scrape of the trapdoor lock turning.

illuminated eleven illuminated

Norman had taken the job at the library to avoid trouble. That was the idea. At least, that was his wife's idea. She'd had enough of nights lying awake and wondering if Norman, a cop then, was lying dead in a gutter somewhere. The library was safe, a haven for bookworms, not drug dealers. Books were the stuff of comfort, and even though Norman hated to admit it at the time, he was ready for a more comfortable life too.

Then what am I doing? Norman asked himself, creeping down the stairs to retrieve a severed hand. *This is crazy!*

The sound of the metal drill still purred from the open vault doorway below. Norman wondered how long it would be before the burglars realized they were in the wrong place.

Norman stopped two steps from the bottom and looked down at the object of his pursuit. The hand didn't even look real; it looked like a prop, something you might find on the floor of a horror-movie set or the back wall of a magician's shop. He had been in such a rush to fetch the grisly item that he hadn't considered how he might accomplish such a feat, which would put him in plain view of the drillers. His only chance would be if their backs were turned.

He peeked around the corner. For the moment, he was in luck. He saw two men, diligently probing one of the many steel doors that lined the walls. Strewn about their feet were the remains of the ten priceless books they had pulled from the vaults. Norman hated to think of the loss the mess represented.

The drilling stopped. Norman watched as one of the men placed the drill on the floor and pulled back the vault door. The other man hastily reached inside, pulling out a thick brown tome that must have weighed forty pounds. He threw it to the ground, obviously disgusted that it wasn't the book they were looking for.

The drill buzzed once again.

Norman slipped to his knees, reached out into the space lit by the doorway, and without another thought, grabbed Dr. Winter's absentee hand. During his stint as a marine, the grotesque artifact wouldn't have fazed him, but now, older and two careers removed from the action in the field, Norman felt a wave of nausea gnaw at his stomach.

The drilling stopped. "What do you think you're doing?" screamed one of the agents.

The voice replaced Norman's nausea with blinding fear. He jumped to his feet and sprinted up the stairs as fast as his arthritic knees would carry him. He could hear the shoes of the two vault-breaking agents slide on the concrete floor behind him. He felt shards of concrete hit his face as the blasts from their pistols struck the wall. Blinding fear transformed into survival instinct.

He crossed over the midpoint and headed down the stairway on the other side. "Catch!" Norman shouted down to April, tossing Dr. Winter's hand like a softball pitch.

April screamed and let the object bounce off her outstretched arms. "What are you doing?"

"Open the door!" Norman cried, slipping his way down the stairs. "They're coming!"

April gingerly picked up the hand and placed it against the glowing panel. The doorway slid open just as Norman hit the bottom of the staircase, and the two of them fell inside.

A hail of bullets ricocheted off the floor just outside the door. "Close it!" Norman yelled.

April had already pushed the button to close the doorway when Norman realized she'd made a terrible mistake: Dr. Winter's hand was still lying in the hallway.

"Just leave it!" April pleaded.

Norman dropped to the ground and snatched Dr. Winter's hand from outside the door just as it slammed shut.

Bullets smacked into the metal door. A string of obscenities hit the door seconds later.

"I'm not sure how long that will hold," April said. "We'd better hurry." She ran to the far wall, reached around her neck, and removed a thin chain with a key at the end of it, which she placed in the lock, turning clockwise until there was a faint click.

Fists banged on the door.

April smiled. "We might be in luck."

Norman shoved Dr. Winter's hand into his jacket pocket. "Severed hands, men with guns chasing us . . . I'd say luck is the one thing we *don't* have."

"No, you see, they must have only looked at the blueprints to the Jefferson portion of the Library of Congress." She reached inside the vault and pulled out a large wooden box. It was highly polished and smooth as a wet stone. April unraveled a thin leather cord holding the box together and lifted the lid, revealing the marvelous Gutenberg, lying just as it had been for nearly five hundred years.

"If they had looked at the blueprints to the Adams or Madison Buildings, they would have realized that the underground tunnels that connect them to the Jefferson Building could also be reached from this vault," April said, lifting the Gutenberg out of the velvet-lined box and setting it on one of the stainless-steel tables. She unbuttoned her blazer and took it off, wrapping it around the Gutenberg tightly and tying the sleeves around the top.

"Someone's been hitting the gym," Norman said, noticing April's strong physique, now outlined by her fitted T-shirt.

April blushed. "No, it's called being a mom," she said. "Sometimes I call my son my personal trainer." She looked at the Gutenberg package. Her blazer barely stretched around it. "I'm going to need your shirt too."

Norman took off his jacket, begrudgingly removed his button-down, and handed it to her.

"Looks like you've been working out too," April said, ripping his shirt in two and tying it at opposing angles around the Gutenberg.

"Please," Norman said, putting his jacket back on over his sleeveless T-shirt, which bore a long stripe of sweat down its center.

The pounding grew louder. They were using something bigger—a fire extinguisher, Norman guessed—to hammer their way through. The extinguisher must be looking pretty battered about now.

April picked up the wrapped Gutenberg like an awkward duffel bag and threw it over her shoulder. She pushed back the table, revealing a panel in the floor.

"Even the secret passageways have secret passageways!" Norman said.

"Before all the high-tech modern-day gadgetry, hidden corridors were a top line of defense," April said.

They lifted the large tile from its position in the floor and slid it aside. April entered the vertical tunnel first, grabbing the sides of the ladder inside and shimmying down as speedily as she could manage. Norman followed directly after her, yanking the floor panel back into place. He could still hear the men banging on the door. And then he heard a new noise: the drill.

"Hurry!" Norman said.

"I'm almost to the ground," April said.

"How deep is this thing? I can't see squat."

"Just keep going. You don't have much farther."

Norman was only a few yards from the bottom when light flooded the narrow shaft. At first he was happy to be able to see again, but when bullets began buzzing by his head, his mood soured. Seeing that he was only a few yards above the floor, he jumped, landing hard and rolling into the sidewall.

"Are you okay?" April asked, dragging him away from the raining gunfire.

Norman saw stars in the corner of his eyes. "I'm fine," he said, shaking his head. "Don't slow down because of me."

They sprinted down a long, curved passageway for several hundred yards before it dead-ended into a blank concrete wall.

"Are you sure you got your directions right?" Norman asked, pulling a flashlight out of his utility belt and examining the wall.

April walked up and knocked on it. "The tunnel should be on the other side," she said.

"*Should* be? You've never been down here?"

"Are you kidding? Do you see how creepy this place is?" She continued knocking on the wall until the sound under her knuckles changed. She pressed on the spot and slid back the stone facade, which revealed another glowing palm scanner. Norman took the cue and withdrew Dr. Winter's hand, placing it on the display. The scanner flashed, and an exit was produced in the wall as a portion of it dropped into the floor.

Norman heard the echo of boots coming from the passageway behind them. "Where does this go?" he asked, not really caring as long as it was away from the two guys trying to shoot him.

"I'm not sure," April said, poking her head into the darkness beyond. A thunderous rumble instantly answered the question. She pulled her head back just in time to watch the Metro Transit cars streak past.

"That's not what I call smart planning," Norman said.

"It was probably an empty tunnel a hundred years ago."

"But not now."

"No," April agreed. "Not now."

The footsteps behind them were getting louder. The two men would be upon them in seconds.

The last car roared away. April swung her legs out through the opening and dropped down to a slender ledge. The Gutenberg swung her off balance, and she began to fall toward the rail. Norman grabbed her.

"Careful, daredevil," he said. He pulled her back to the ledge, his other arm anchored to a fissure in the wall.

The almost surreal concrete web of the tunnel curved overhead, looking like something from an eighties sci-fi movie. In the distance she saw the tunnel stretch out into a larger section. A terminal. Maybe a city block away.

"Look," she said, pointing to the light ahead. "That has to be the Capitol South stop."

"Don't move!" a voice shouted from above their heads. Norman turned to see two angry faces staring back at them.

April grabbed Norman's hand and pulled him off the ledge, down to the track. Ignoring the pain that shot up from his ankle when he hit, Norman rose to his feet and ran with her, hunched over to prevent being punished by gunfire.

A deep rumble shook the ground.

"I thought we'd have more time," April said.

"I can't make it," Norman said from behind, limping.

April seized his arm and dragged him forward. "You'll never see your grandkids again!"

"They wear me out anyway," Norman whimpered, breaking April's grasp and lagging.

Behind them, Norman heard the two men drop down to the ledge. No shots. Maybe they couldn't balance quick enough to get any off.

The next train was screaming closer, and Norman watched himself gain distance on his own shadow as the headlights intensified.

He pushed his body to its limits, pure dread extinguishing any other thought than reaching the safety of the platform. A few businessmen spotted them and extended their hands to help April up from the track. He heard the screams of the idiot gunmen as they were overtaken by the speeding metro, and the screams of the witnesses, which lasted much longer, and then, finally, the screams of the brakes stopping for the terminal, applied too late for him.

✠

April strained her arm toward an open hand reaching from the platform. She wasn't going to make it.

"You can make it!" a shrill voice shouted from the gathering onlookers. Others were chanting, "Go! Go! Go!" In that split second, April felt as if she had somehow been transported into some gruesome futuristic sporting event.

She lunged and felt someone pick her up from the ground by her free arm. Her legs continued to spin as the metro rushed past her feet. After a dozen cars flew by, the train screeched to a halt and the harrowed passengers spilled out.

"Norman!" April yelled, searching the growing crowd for his face.

A Metro Transit Police officer broke the circle of people. "You're coming with me," he said to April. "It's against the law to be on those tracks. You could have been killed!"

"Where's Norman?" April asked, frantic.

"Who's Norman?" asked the officer.

"He was right behind me," April said. She turned to the crowd. "Did anyone help him?"

No one seemed to have an answer.

"I think I saw him fall under the train," one man said, stepping forward.

April's face went white. "No! He was right behind me." She started pacing, peering under the train. "Can you stop this train from leaving?" she asked the officer.

"Stop it? You don't think that—"

"Can you do it?"

The doors on the train started to close. April jumped in the way of the doors, and they reopened. A young man on the train yelled at her to get off. The loudspeaker blared a warning for all passengers to step away from the doors.

"Stop the train," April begged.

"Lady, you got to get out of the doorway."

"What if he's trapped under there, *alive*?"

"For all I know, you just escaped the insane asylum and are looking for something fun to do, " the officer said. He walked over and put his arm around her, pulling her away from the train. "Time to come with me before you cause any more trouble."

A few more people joined April, blocking the train doors from shutting.

A person stepped out from the crowd. "You have to check," he said. "What if she's right?"

The security guard was clearly agitated. "Get out of the way, people!"

They didn't move. "I saw him myself!" someone shouted.

A woman wearing a Metro Transit uniform came running to the scene. "Wait, wait," she said, out of breath. "I saw the whole thing. It was terrible. Two guys got hit. Then this old guy fell under the train." She pointed at April. "She was the only one who made it."

"Hold on," he said, taking out his walkie-talkie. He turned and spoke a few words into the receiver. He turned back to April after he was done. "Don't go *anywhere*. You understand?"

April nodded.

"I see him!" someone said a few cars down. "I see the guy!"

April rushed toward a group of people pointing between two of the railcars. She spotted Norman right away, lying flat on his back. "I can't believe you're alive!" she said.

"I am?" He coughed. "My wife's going to be disappointed. She has a good life insurance policy on me."

"Well, she'll have to wait a few more years to claim it," April said, crying and laughing at the same time.

Norman extended his arm between the railcars. "Take this," he said.

April leaned out as far as she could and took Dr. Winter's severed hand. "I can't leave you," she said.

"I'll be fine," he said. "You've got more things to worry about than an old man stuck under a train."

April heard the officer yell behind her. He wasn't happy. "I'll see you soon," she said.

Norman grinned. "Better believe it."

April secured the makeshift bag holding the Gutenberg over her shoulder and raced away from the escalating commotion.

twelve

Charlie fell backward as the front door smashed into his chest. The chain held, a remarkable feat, considering the force of the blow. An arm shot through the opening and grabbed Charlie by the collar. The repairman whose name badge said Stanley pulled Charlie hard against the crack in the door, nearly ripping him through it. Stanley leaned down to meet him eye-to-eye, moving his grip to Charlie's throat.

"I'm going to close the door just enough to let you unlock the chain. You got it?"

Charlie nodded, crying.

The door closed until it pressed against Stanley's wrist, caught neatly between the door and the jamb. Charlie reached up and began sliding the end of the chain to unlock it.

"Stop right there, kid," whispered Joe, who was still crouching by the windowsill at the hinged side of the door. He rose from his position, making sure he couldn't be seen through the window. "And don't look over here."

Charlie whimpered, the chain shaking in his hand.

"Open the door, now," Stanley said, pulling Charlie's collar tight around his throat.

Joe slammed his body into the door. The first impact cracked one of the bones in Stanley's wrist. The second one snapped it in two like a dry twig. Stanley screamed, yanking his crushed limb out the door.

Joe threw the door shut and ran over to Charlie, who had retreated to Grandma Rose's side. He pulled out his gun. "Is he a cop? Did you see a badge or anything?"

"He said he was a repairman," Charlie said, his voice strained. "His badge said *Stanley.*" He put the inhaler in his mouth and took a shot.

"Calm down," Joe said. He cocked his gun.

"What does he want?" Charlie said.

"Maybe the same thing as me. I dunno." Joe kept his eyes fixed on the front door. Why wasn't the guy trying to break it down? "Where's the back door?" he asked.

"In the kitchen," Charlie said, pointing.

"Stay right where you are," he said. Charlie nodded.

✠

Joe crept into the kitchen, staying low. He crawled forward slowly, keeping a wary eye on the glass panels in the back door. Maybe he was wrong. Maybe the guy had taken off. He had broken his wrist, after all. It was a pretty severe injury. Maybe the guy had given up.

The window next to the back door smashed inward, sending shards of glass flying everywhere. Joe spotted the culprit of the crash: a tiny silver canister. It bounced against the front of the refrigerator and spun to a stop in the middle of the floor.

"Oh, man," Joe said under his breath. He turned and dived out of the kitchen. There was an explosion of white smoke behind him. "Tear gas!" he shouted at Charlie. "Get up the stairs!"

"What about Grandma Rose?" Charlie asked as Joe pulled him up from the ground.

"I'll take care of it," Joe said. He leaned down and scooped her up, slinging her over his shoulder. She was a little heavier than he had expected, but his adrenaline was pumping hard, and he knew he'd have no trouble getting her up the stairs. "Go, go, go!" he said to Charlie, shooing him toward the staircase.

White smoke rippled toward them, and Joe's eyes felt the sting. Charlie hopped up the stairs two at a time, Joe following closely behind. They reached the landing and raced into Charlie's bedroom. Joe laid his passenger on Charlie's bed and ripped the blanket out from under her. He turned and shut the door, stuffing the blanket into the crevice between the door and the floor. "Do you have any tape?" he asked Charlie.

"I've got duct tape," Charlie responded. "I use it to build stuff."

"No time to show me your duct-tape robots, kid. Get me whatever you've got, and hurry," Joe said, snapping his fingers. He could see a few trickles of white fog sneaking through the cracks in the door.

Charlie fumbled through the drawers of his desk in search of the silver roll of tape. "I know it's here somewhere!" he said, dumping an entire drawerful on the floor. Marbles that looked like bloodshot eyes, rainbow-colored paper clips, dull-pointed pencils, batteries, gears, and a thousand other things went spilling everywhere. But no duct tape.

"Hurry!" shouted Joe.

"What's going on?" Grandma Rose asked, sitting up on the bed.

Joe and Charlie stared at her, frozen for an instant by the shock of Grandma Rose's awakening.

"I said hurry!"

"I'm trying!"

"Would someone please tell me what all the screaming is about?"

"Found it!" Charlie pronounced, standing with a scant roll of duct tape in his hands.

"Throw it here!"

Joe caught the tape and began plastering the gap around the door, sealing off the tear gas. The roll ran out as he got a quarter of the way down the right side. "I need more!"

Charlie dug around some more, finally coming up with a long broadsword made entirely out of duct tape. "This is all I've got," he said, obviously reluctant to give it up.

"I need it."

"Are you sure?"

Joe yanked it from his hands. He began ripping it to shreds.

"That took me a week to make. It's based on the exact dimensions of Excalibur."

"Kid, I'll buy you a real sword if we get through this alive!" Joe said, taking the strips of tape and pressing them over the gap.

"You promise?"

Joe didn't answer. He finished the job on the door and pulled out his cell phone. Dialed. Waited.

"What?"

"Xandria, it's Joe."

"I know that. Why do you keep calling?"

"Somebody's here."

It took Xandria a second longer than it should have to answer. "Who?"

"I don't know. But I'm pretty sure it's not the police."

"It must be the Order of the Dragon," Xandria said, the surprise in her voice showing a hint of admiration. "How many?"

"Just one," Joe said. "But he's not very nice. He blasted us with tear gas. We're hiding upstairs in the boy's bedroom."

"You idiot. Why didn't you leave the house?"

Joe knew the question was coming. "Because he'd pick us off running out the front door."

"Is everyone still alive?" Xandria asked.

"For now," Joe whispered. He looked over to Charlie, who was consoling his grandmother. He noticed for the first time how much the boy looked like his sister's youngest son. And who did the grandma remind him of? His aunt?

"Make sure they stay alive," Xandria said. "Especially the boy. His parents will do *anything* as long as he's okay."

"How are things going on the plane?"

"It's none of your concern," Xandria snapped. "Just do what you're paid to do, and everything will be fine." She hung up.

Joe put away his phone. "Shhhh!" he said to Charlie and Grandma Rose, who weren't even making any noise. He closed his eyes and listened. The house was still. He focused his ears on the depression of floorboards, the soft clomping of footsteps, the quiet click of a pistol being cocked. But there was nothing.

"Could someone tell me what's going on?" Grandma Rose demanded.

Joe walked over to the bed and sat down. "You think I'm the bad guy. But you're wrong. There's a guy outside that door who's way worse than me. And if he gets in here, he won't hesitate in killing us all."

"Why would someone want to do that?" Charlie asked, picking up his mangled Excalibur. "Did I do something wrong?"

"This isn't about you," Joe said. "This is about your parents."

"Is it because they got divorced?" Charlie asked.

Grandma Rose pulled Charlie back toward her. "No, dear," she said. "This is happening because your father owes some people a lot of money."

Joe shook his head. "No, it isn't! Why'd you tell him that?"

"Because that's the only thing that makes sense!" Grandma Rose said. "This couldn't have anything to do with my daughter! She works at a *library*, for crying out loud!"

"Maybe your daughter isn't as innocent as you think," Joe said.

"You don't know what you're talking about," Grandma Rose said. "You don't even deserve to be . . . well, just never mind." She put her hands over her grandson's ears. "Don't listen to him, Charlie."

"Believe what you want," Joe said. He heard a squeak outside the room, coming from the staircase.

"Is that him?" Charlie asked, quivering.

"Shhhhh!" Joe and Grandma Rose said in unison.

"What are we going to do?" Grandma Rose whispered.

"We're going to hide in the attic," Joe said. "Right, Charlie?"
Charlie smiled.

☩

Stanley's wrist pulsated under the makeshift splint he'd jerry-rigged
with wooden spoons and duct tape. That unforeseen incident would
make his job more difficult now, but maybe more entertaining. He
slipped the roll of tape over his good wrist and peered through the
lens of his gas mask at the door in front of him. It was covered in
hand-drawn pictures of dinosaurs, planets, moons, pirates, space-
ships—the typical icons of boyish youth. The only difference was
the detail: each picture was fully diagrammed with dozens of
arrows, each linked to a paragraph of explanation. For example,
four dinosaurs were linked to a sentence explaining they were
ornithischians and all shared the same hip bones, namely, the *ilium*,
the *ischium*, and the *pubis*. He was tempted to tear the pages off, just
to have something interesting to read the next morning with his
Jamba Juice.

One kick knocked the door down. The room was empty. Not a
surprise. But he knew they were up here somewhere. He'd watched
them hike up the stairs, scared as kittens caught on fire.

He swept the room with his gun, looking under the covers, then
under the bed. Behind the desk and in the closet. All the usual
spaces. Sometimes people were dumb enough to hide there. This
group was probably a little smarter. But not much.

The fact that there were three of them worried him very little.
Once he shot the big guy, the other two would make easy prey. A kid
and a grandma? C'mon. No problem, even with a shattered wrist.

Satisfied the room was empty, he slowly pulled up his gas mask, making sure the gas had fully dissipated, then walked out the opposite door into the adjoining playroom.

Some playroom. It was long and narrow, with bookcases lining the wall to his left. Each of the bookcases was completely filled, and as Stanley looked closer, he saw that the books were numbered. Starting from the top left, the spines were lined up in sequence: one, two, three, and so on. The books at the beginning of the order were simple picture books. But as the numbers grew, so did the difficulty. The entire Harry Potter series, the Lord of the Rings trilogy, the Chronicles of Narnia, and a slew of other fantasy titles comprised multiple shelves, and those were only halfway through the numbered sequence. The kid was definitely the son of a librarian.

A multicolored rug covered most of the hardwood floor. The pattern and numbers on it suggested it was used for games of some sort, though Stanley couldn't decipher what it was or how it worked. The place looked more and more like a surplus shop for Nerds 'R' Us. On the far wall were two large toy chests, and to their right, a set of ceiling-high cabinets. Stanley figured they were filled with test tubes and microscopes, but they also made perfect hiding places.

What interested Stanley most was the feature in the middle of the room, the one that extended down from the ceiling: a ladder, leading to the attic. Stanley was disappointed that his chase was already over. It was an obvious trap. A person would have to be dumber than bricks to fall for it.

Stanley advanced up the ladder backward. The groan of the stairs would draw them out eventually. They were probably counting the number of steps, waiting for him to enter the darkness of the attic. Stanley creaked the third step twice, just to mess with them. He might as well make it fun.

He got to the last step, right before the attic floor, and stopped. And waited. He turned his head and shouted into the attic. "Give it up! There's no other way out!" He almost laughed saying it.

A minute later he heard one of the toy chests squeak open, followed by the sound of two small feet hitting the floor. He couldn't see him, but he could hear the kid coming up, getting ready to spring the trap. Stanley felt a push on the ladder, but his weight held it in place. And then the kid, to his amazement, walked around to the front of the ladder. He grabbed the bottom and struggled to lift it before he noticed the imposing figure standing right above him.

"Hello," Stanley said politely. "I wish I didn't have to do this." He raised his gun and pointed it at Charlie. He caught the boy's eyes glancing at something over Stanley's right shoulder. The floor creaked.

Stanley swiveled, still holding the gun, and cut Joe off at the ankles with his good arm. The two of them tumbled down the ladder to the floor. Stanley pushed his legs against Joe and sent him flying into the bookshelves, their contents raining down upon him. Joe struggled toward his gun, which he'd lost during the fall. Stanley stepped on it. "Make one more move," he taunted.

The room stilled.

Stanley kept his own gun trained on Joe's head. "Where's Grandma?"

Joe slowly advanced to one of the toy chests and lifted the lid. Grandma Rose lay inside, curled in a fetal position.

Stanley tossed the roll of duct tape to Joe. "Wrap her up. Then the boy."

Joe didn't question the order. Soon there were two silver cocoons lying in the middle of the room.

"Now tape yourself up," Stanley said.

Joe's face twisted, puzzled. "I can't," he said.

"Then I guess I'll have to do it for you," Stanley said. He pulled back his arm, stepped forward, and unleashed a potent blow to the side of Joe's head.

Lights out.

Joe fell. Grandma Rose and Charlie cried out as his body hit the floor. Stanley winced at their shrieking. He peeled off two strips of tape and shut their traps. He spooled off a few more yards, making fast work of securing Joe. Then, one by one, he dragged all three of them downstairs.

He admired the bounty with pride, as he slipped on a fresh pair of thick plastic gloves and secured the splatter-shield over his face. He felt his heartbeat quicken as he envisioned the horribleness of what would happen next.

He smiled. It was time to earn his paycheck.

illuminated thirteen illuminated

One fact had eluded August concerning the cargo hold on airliners: they were cold. Really cold. Then again, he couldn't remember ever meeting anyone dumb enough to sneak into one during a flight.

They were dark, too. And the only thing that saved him from searching blind was the penlight from the first-aid kit, which August had unconsciously slipped into his breast pocket after assisting Clayton's grandfather.

Even so, August felt the flames of his hope begin to dwindle as he dug through the luggage. He willed himself to stay focused, to believe that he could somehow find the Gutenberg, decipher the illuminations, and escape from this cage before time ran out.

There were heaps of bags. Mountains of them. How would he find the Gutenberg? He tried to think of any distinguishing characteristics that might help him find the right bag. But he had put the Gutenberg in a decidedly indistinguishable bag, to meld in with the zillion other bags, to be completely lost in the general flow of bags, bags, bags. Attention, he had learned, was something to be avoided.

That instinct flowed from the Gutenberg itself. Most Gutenberg Bibles were kept in complete secrecy by their owners. The few lucky universities that held the rare book kept them under lock and key, usually unbeknownst to the most respected professors on their staff. The same was true for the handful of libraries that possessed copies. It was too dangerous to alert people to the fact that there was something of such excessive value within close proximity. It invited trouble.

Like the universities and libraries, August had gone to great lengths to dodge trouble. But it snagged him anyway. And now everyone he cared about was suffering the consequences.

He thought about that for a moment, catching a glimpse of his true feelings. Charlie. Now, that was obvious. Charlie was his son. His own flesh and blood. But April. He hadn't stopped to consider what she might still mean to him. Did she still mean something to him? *Plenty of time to think about that later.*

He toppled over another tower of bags. *Think! This is getting you nowhere! Think! There's got to be another way . . .*

He turned off the penlight.

Closed his eyes.

Yes.

That was it.

August began digging through the bags with his eyes shut. Although the fabric of the bag the Gutenberg was in looked like all the other bags, the truth was that it was unlike any other. Woven into its polyester fibers was a tear-resistant, nearly bulletproof, metal thread. The bag could endure some punishment, something August had to take into account when considering the rough handling it might receive from the baggage crew.

Not it.

Not it.

Not it.

He pushed through the bags, his hands out in all directions, scouring for the right texture, so distinct, like silk and steel at the same time.

Not it.

Not it.

Not . . . wait.

August opened his eyes. Verified with the penlight. He'd found it. He tugged at the handle and pulled it from under a stack of other bags. *They're going to think a monkey broke loose in here*, he said to himself, stacking a few suitcases to form a makeshift table.

Placing the Gutenberg bag on top, he unlatched the lid and pried it open. In the narrow beam of light, he gazed at the beautiful book that lay inside. He leaned down close to it and let the ancient perfume of its pages drift into his nose. *Musty* was the wrong word for it, though the implication of agedness was correct. It wasn't *stale*, either, for the book practically breathed. *Old.* The word he was searching for was simply *old.* But the kind of *old* that implied endurance and wisdom, the good things that outlasted the passage of years.

He removed the Gutenberg from its sturdy container, tore off the shrink-wrap, and wrapped the tome in a UCLA sweatshirt he stole from another bag. He was tempted to leave a note with his address and a promise to replace the purloined garment, but he thought better of making too many promises. He already owed someone a tiger shark, for goodness' sake.

Returning to the trapdoor, he inspected it once more for possible means of escape. There appeared to be none. Were there any other ways out? A quick glimpse around his surroundings revealed nothing, except for the hatch that led outside, the one the baggage crew used. But that wouldn't help. He couldn't exactly climb outside the airplane back to his seat. This wasn't a Jerry Bruckheimer movie, after all.

Still, he stared at the hatch.

A thought.

He scrabbled over bags, grabbed the release handle, and pulled it.

✠

Thad felt a tap on his shoulder. "Yes?"

"I need you to check out a problem in baggage." It was Janice. The concern on her face seemed genuine.

"What's going on?"

"Captain just alerted me that the door down there is open."

"The door . . . ?"

"The hatch."

"But how could that be open?"

Janice smiled, a smile that turned her concern to impatience. "That's why I need you to go down there," she said.

Thad walked toward the back of the plane, ignoring a number of passengers who asked for his assistance as he passed.

"What's going on?" one of the attendants inquired as Thad entered the safety zone behind the rear curtain.

"Janice thinks someone opened the hatch down below," Thad said, trying to make the story sound as absurd as possible.

"*Captain* says it's open," Janice said.

"Oh."

"Can you let me down there?" Thad asked.

"Sure," the other attendant said, chuckling. It was a fool's errand, an undesirable job for whoever happened to be at the bottom of the flight-attendant caste system.

The floor panel was removed, and the other attendants left to go pass out more pillows and drinks. "Just let us know when you're done in here," the last attendant said, slipping out the curtain.

Thad slid feetfirst into the hole, using his feet to find the ladder indentations in the wall of the cargo hold. He climbed down and removed a small flashlight from his pocket, shining the tiny beam around the entire area.

It was a mess. What had happened down here?

He pointed the beam toward the hatch, which appeared to be closed. Over the grumble of the engines he could hear a series of beeps, an indicator that the release handle had come unfastened. Maybe the turbulence had been severe enough to jar it loose.

There was a noise from behind him. Thad spun around. "Is anybody there?" he asked, hoping not to hear a response. None came. He adjusted the flashlight to project a wider beam, then waved it around, trying to illuminate as much of the compartment as he could.

The plane shook, and a pile of bags fell over. Thad's heartbeat tripled. He made his way over to the hatch and secured the release handle, fearing that somehow the door mechanisms would fail and the door would fly off into space. With the release handle in place, the hatch stopped beeping. The dullness of the engine roar took over until again he heard a noise—a scraping, scratching sound—coming from behind him.

"If there's someone down here, you need to come out right now!" he yelled, turning to face whatever monster was trapped in the cargo hold with him. He'd heard stories of animals getting loose: cats, dogs, snakes. Once an attendant even claimed a baby black bear escaped its cage and trashed every bag in sight.

Lies, Thad told himself. *Just lies.* He wondered why the flashlight beam was jumping to and fro until he noticed that his hands were shaking. *Lies! Nothing's down here!*

He tried to remember the lessons he'd learned at a "panic school" he'd attended five years ago to overcome his fear of flying. *Face your fears,* they had told him. *Face them head-on! Run toward your fears! Embrace them!* And so he did. The next day he filled out an application to become a flight attendant, and he'd stuck with it ever since.

Face your fears!

He could see the beet-red face of his panic-school instructor bellowing at him to conquer this moment. He gripped the flashlight with two hands and pressed deeper into the luggage catacombs. The sound was coming from right in front of him. Thad got closer, squinting. He reached out and grabbed the handle of the suitcase, the only barrier between him and the creature on the other side.

He yanked the suitcase away, shrieked like a girl, and fainted.

✠

Xandria tried to concentrate on the book in her hands. But she couldn't shake the fear that gripped every thought as she waited for August to return. What would she do if he didn't return? She put the possibility out of her mind. It wasn't an option.

Her phone rang. It was Cornelius. She looked down the aisle for the fifth time in five minutes. Where was August? She should not pick up the phone without knowing precisely what her situation was. She held the phone like she was wringing the life from it. Finally, it died.

Cornelius would just have to wait. He wouldn't be happy, but she could handle him. She could handle any *man*. After all, none of them could be worse than her father used to be.

Used to be.

She was glad he was dead. It was a horrible thing to think about anyone, much less a parent, but the world was an improved place in his absence. Cornelius was a saint compared to her father. She often wondered what could have created a monster like him. Escaping the clutches of his household had been the most freeing moment of her life. She often replayed in her mind the formative events of her childhood.

Meals were quiet, her father seated at the head of the table, with her sister and herself fixed at the sides. They would watch him drain a flask of whiskey between bites of cube steak, his nightly indulgence. "What are you looking at?" he would begin calling out as the liquor took hold. The interrogation always devolved into a completely unwarranted explosion of anger. The house was dirty. The food was awful. The money was disappearing. Everything was their fault. And so they paid for it.

Xandria tried for years not to blame him. Not directly, anyway.

He was suffering. Their mother had died—a victim of cancer—and he was left in the wake, trying to take care of two small girls who missed their mother. How could he make up for the loss? He couldn't. He tried his best, but he couldn't. Xandria and her sister pulled away from him as a result. Fearing loneliness, her father began putting restrictions on them. They were not allowed out of the house for days at a time. He pulled them out of school. They soon found themselves scared and friendless.

And that's when the real pain began.

Religion had always been a part of her father's life. But somehow, combined with alcohol, it turned into something ugly. Something evil. He would rant about how God had created women to serve men. Unless his two daughters learned how to serve him, they would never make it to the holy hereafter. But there was nothing holy about his brand of servitude.

Late one night, Xandria heard screaming coming from her sister's room. She hid under her covers and stuffed her pillow in her ears. It wasn't enough to muzzle the sound of her sister calling out to her for help. But what could she do? Their father was too strong, even drunk, for Xandria to stop him. Her sister continued to call out. Xandria rose from her bed and opened her bedroom door. Her sister's door was directly across from hers. It was cracked open. The sounds coming from inside nauseated her. "Help me," pleaded her sister. "Please . . ."

She looked down at the scars on her arms, her legs, her chest. They felt like they were burning. Then she heard her sister's voice again, more frail this time.

"Xandria . . ."

She walked back into her bedroom and shut the door. She fell to the ground, her back against the door, and cried. A few minutes later she heard the heavy footsteps of her father staggering down the hallway toward the kitchen, surely to find something more to drown his misery in. Xandria waited to make sure he wasn't returning and opened her door, quickly slipping across the hallway and into her sister's room. She closed her door and turned on a small lamp. What she found haunted her for the rest of her life.

✠

"Excuse me, is that seat taken?" Xandria hadn't even looked up when August approached with his big bundle, which was just fine with him. Better that she wasn't watching the clock.

Xandria startled, and it took her several seconds to formulate a reply. "You did it."

"Don't seem so amazed," August said. He climbed over her and dropped into his seat. "Did you know they keep pets down there? I found a black cat the size of a horse."

"You've only got thirty minutes left."

Okay. So he was still on the clock. August unwrapped the sweatshirt, revealing the Gutenberg. "What are we looking for?" he asked, pulling the notepad he had scribbled notes on earlier from the seat pocket in front of him.

Xandria opened the red journal. "Judges, John, and Daniel."

"Forgive me," August said to the book, gingerly flipping the pages. "I've never touched the Gutenberg without gloves," he explained.

"Be gentle."

"Believe me, I am," August said. He turned back a few pages,

realizing he'd flipped too far. "Here it is. Judges. Any clues from Mr. Gutenberg?"

"That's what you're here to figure out, remember?" She returned to her book.

August placed his hands over his ears to block out the noise and focused on the image in front of him. It was a strange one indeed.

The illumination was based around the general framework of the initial *A*. The background of the figure was in gold, while the initial itself was in blue. The circle of the Gothic initial housed a pattern of burgundy and rose, appearing like a school of fish biting each other's tails. Stemming from the left side of the initial was a series of vines, also in blue, but sprouting flowery blossoms in green and red and gold.

But it was the characters that comprised the lines of the initial that fascinated August the most. The vertical line held a man, entirely blue, save for the scant white lines that drew his shaggy beard and windswept hair, and his beady, pointed eyes. Even more bizarre to behold was the ghostly blue face staring out from between his legs. And to complete the spectacle, an angry blue swan curled around the top of the initial, held between the two hands of the blue man.

The image posited a million questions that needed to point to one unifying answer. What was the key? August put the pen to the notebook:

Four—Blue Man and Swan

"There's something wrong about this swan," August said, fixing his attention on it. "The feathers, the neck, even the top of the head are right. But look at the mouth."

Xandria took a closer look. "It has *teeth*."

"Exactly," August said. "So what is this illumination trying to say?"

Xandria closed her book. "Did the *Bestiaire* explain imagery involving swans?"

"Most definitely. Birds were a favorite device of painters, and especially illuminators, because they usually depicted the inner wars of the church. The swan was used as a symbol of the martyr. First the swan sings, then it dies."

"Swan song."

"Right."

"But what about the teeth?"

August looked more closely at the swan. "The teeth are suspiciously like that of the dog we saw before. Maybe the reference is related as well."

Xandria got out her laptop and dug up the image of the two fighting dragons. "It looks like you might be right. Are you saying that this new illumination has the same meaning as the last one?"

"No," August said. "Only that the reference of the dragon is the same. But there's something new here. Something we didn't have before."

He took the laptop and launched the Internet browser.

"What are you doing?"

"I'm searching for medieval factions of the church that used the dragon as their primary symbol," August explained. He clicked through a few Web sites until he landed on one that displayed a picture of a dragon curled in a circle, its tail curved and wrapped around its own neck. A pair of scaly wings was folded on its back, creased in half by what August remembered to be the Red Cross of Saint George. He enlarged the image on the screen and positioned it next to the illumination. "Eerily similar," he said. "And who does this symbol belong to?"

"The Order of the Dragon," Xandria whispered.

August scrolled down the screen and confirmed Xandria's proclamation. "How did you know that?"

"They were assassins, a covert arm of the Holy Roman Empire," she said. "They almost entirely destroyed the Orphans during the 1400s."

"Is the Order of the Dragon still around today?"

"Yes and no," Xandria said. "There are some people who claim to be part of it, but for the most part, they're just Dracula enthusiasts."

"Dracula?"

"Vlad II Dracul was one of the first members of the Order. His son was Vlad III the Impaler, the historical Dracula."

"But is there still a true Order of the Dragon?"

Xandria nodded, examining a piece of lint on her skirt. "I've been told that there are members of their society within most of the Western governments."

"Sounds a bit far-fetched."

She placed her hand over his. "Says the man holding the ancient book, searching for mysterious clues."

"Touché," August said, sliding his hand out from under hers. He returned his attention to the illumination. "Here's something I didn't see before," he said. He pointed to the open mouth of the swan-dragon. "It's attacking the blue man. Eating him alive. Perhaps suggesting that the Order of the Dragon is retaliating, or gaining some revenge."

"But why is the dragon combined with the image of the swan? The Order was full of evil princes and kings, not holy saints."

"Maybe someone in the ranks of the Orphans was a traitor, working secretly for the Order of the Dragon," August ventured. "It could make sense: the swan flows out from the arm of the blue man and then turns *back* to bite him! Also, the notion that the Order is evil would be in the eyes of the beholder. I bet *they* would consider themselves saints."

"And the ghost between the blue man's legs?"

"An emerging force, perhaps? Something born from the war between the Orphans and the Order of the Dragon?" August said, jotting the ideas in the notebook.

Their conversation was cut short by a female flight attendant. "Would you care for a—wow! What kind of book is that? It looks old!"

Xandria drilled August with her ice-blue eyes. "People always think that," August said, looking up, smiling. "But it's just a copy. A real one of these babies would be worth millions."

"I'm guessing you still wouldn't want to spill Diet Coke on it," the flight attendant said.

"Probably not," August agreed. "Maybe next time."

"And what about you, ma'am?"

"No thanks."

"Pillow?"

"Nope."

"Blanket?"

"Thanks anyway."

The flight attendant left.

August began flipping pages to find the next illumination.

"Matthew, Mark, Luke, and finally, *John*," he pronounced, producing the desired page. He peered at the image that sat perched on its side, an image much simpler than the last one. Or at least it appeared that way.

The letter *N* provided the frame for this image, rendered in shades of red. Splashes of gold and green once again outlined the initial, surrounding the regal figure held captive inside: a brown eagle, its stoic visage directed toward the sky. A golden halo circled its head, and a simple white banner hung from its beak, grasped at the bottom by its left claw.

"Gutenberg is giving us the bird again," August said.

"Not funny."

"I'm not kidding," August said. "Just like the swan, the eagle was a classic symbol used in religious imagery." He took out his notebook, writing:

Five—Eagle with Banner

"Have you ever heard of Spenser's *The Faerie Queene*?" August asked, continuing to make notes.

"Did you used to quiz your wife like this?"

"No, she used to quiz *me* like this."

"That must have been awful."

"It was kind of a game we played," August said, replaying in his mind some of their more lively discussions. "We both loved books, so it was like a contest to see who loved them more."

"Sounds exciting," Xandria droned. "Now tell me about this *Faerie Queene*."

"Spenser served with the English forces in Ireland in the mid-1500s. He wrote *The Faerie Queene* in an effort to secure his place in the royal court. But he angered the queen's secretary, Lord Burghley, and as a result, was paid practically nothing for his epic work. To rectify the situation, the queen ordered a payment of one hundred pounds—an incredible sum at the time—to be given to Spenser. When Lord Burghley heard about the payment, he was quoted as saying: *What, all this for a song!*"

The corners of Xandria's mouth lifted a fraction of an inch. "My aunt used to say that every time she opened a present. I had no idea where it came from," Xandria said. "But what about the eagle?"

"Spenser's *Faerie Queene* contained a legendary tale about the rebirth of the eagle, which is similar to stories of the ancient phoenix. The story went something like this: When the eagle gets old, it flies toward the sun until its wings are burned. It then dives toward the sea, and after emerging from the water three times, is born new again."

"So the eagle is a Christ figure," Xandria said.

"Yes, not unlike the symbol of the hare," August said. "But the banner the eagle holds puts a twist on the meaning."

August took out his notebook and wrote down the two words printed on the banner: REX ROMANORUM. "Latin was never my strong suit, but this one is pretty easy. It means *King of the Romans*."

"Another reference to the Holy Roman Empire?"

"One and the same," August said. "You remember the illumination of Emperor Sigismund?"

"Yes."

"There's something I didn't think to show you about the painting,"

August said. "It didn't seem to matter at the time, but you only saw half of the original image." August called up the painting of Sigismund on the computer screen, then grabbed the margin of the window with the cursor and dragged it out, revealing an entirely new figure.

"This is Charlemagne," August said, pointing to the majestic character opposite Sigismund. Charlemagne was easily a foot taller and appeared elevated and regal in comparison with the hunched figure of Sigismund. To add further to his dominance, Charlemagne held an impressive sword, while Sigismund gripped a dainty scepter.

"I thought Sigismund looked impressive earlier," Xandria said. "But now he just looks pathetic."

"It was probably important to the painter to represent Sigismund as the lesser of the two men," August said. "Charlemagne deserved a more favorable portrayal as the very first *Rex Romanorum*. Which brings us back to the eagle. As you can see, the Holy Roman Empire used the eagle as their symbol."

Shields emblazoned with the eagle's image hung over both Charlemagne's and Sigismund's heads. It was the same as the eagle in the illumination.

"So it appears that Gutenberg is trying to connect everything," August said. "The illuminations point to the kings, the Holy Roman Empire . . . as well as the Orphans and the Order of the Dragon."

"But you still haven't figured out *what* connects them," Xandria said.

"Maybe the next illumination will shed some light," August said.

"Ten minutes left."

"It's not enough time."

"It never is, is it?"

August carefully peeled through the Bible, stopping at the book of Daniel, the final stop of the hour. Only ten minutes left. Probably nine now. At least the image was fairly straightforward.

Six—The Lions' Den

A single initial—the letter *A*—fitted with a memorable scene: a man, presumably Daniel, fixed between two snarling lions.

"It's pretty self-explanatory," August said. "I don't see anything out of the ordinary yet."

He rolled the story of Daniel in the lions' den around in his mind, looking for a clue. From what he could remember, God shut the mouths of the lions to protect Daniel. He inspected the illumination. Yes, it appeared that the lions' mouths were closed.

So why was Daniel afraid? The Daniel in the illumination was clearly frightened, covering his mouth and looking worrisomely at the lions surrounding him. This was a faithless Daniel. Interesting, but certainly not the crucial piece of information he was searching for.

"Five minutes."

"I know, I know . . . ," August muttered. And then he saw it, like a light emerging from a mist. "Amazing. Again, the key is with the animals."

Xandria glanced at the illu-mination, keeping her watch up and in clear view. "The lions? Yeah, I saw those."

"No. Something else. Let your mind drift away from the obvious."

She looked again at the

image on the page. The illustration of Daniel and the lions was set within the bottom arch of the initial *A*, which was yellow-green and branched into a series of vines and bulbous flowers, flowing out in shades of purple and blue. August pointed to a spot of gold in the *A* and, following it, to a new set of characters that emerged from the field of green: an old man, holding a small creature with a flat nose and tiny pointed ears.

"What is it?"

"A hedgehog, another medieval sign of wickedness. Legend said that the hedgehog shook grapes from the vine and carried them away on his spines. People believed that the devil did the same thing with men's souls."

"And the man holding the hedgehog?"

"The man is wearing a robe and a beard, suggesting he is wise, or powerful. The peculiar thing is that he isn't *holding* the hedgehog; he's *releasing* it. That's why Daniel is afraid. He's not scared by the lions; he's scared by the evil about to be released into the world."

"A good analysis. Too bad you were a minute over your time," Xandria said, tapping her watch.

"You can't kill someone just because I'm a minute late."

"Rules are rules," Xandria said. "Without them, we'd still be living in huts and trading wheat for bearskins. It doesn't matter if it's a minute or an hour, late is late."

"Please. I'll do anything."

"Oh, don't worry about the lives of your precious ex-family," Xandria teased. "I've got something far worse in mind."

She reached over and ripped the illuminated page out of the Gutenberg Bible.

illuminatedfourteenilluminated

April watched the time slip away like dirty bathwater down a drain. "Can you go any faster?" she asked the cabdriver as they crawled under the streetlights. She had hoped to reach Dr. Winter's house by now.

"Lady, have you ever been to DC? Traffic is murder here." He paused. "Actually, *murder* is murder here."

"What?"

"You know, the crime rate is so high . . . it's an old Washington joke," the cabbie said.

Murder. April looked at Dr. Winter's hand, which she'd stashed in a Styrofoam cup filled with ice, purchased from a vendor outside the metro. Dr. Winter wouldn't be at his house.

"How far are we from the hospital?"

"Six—seven blocks."

April held up her watch to catch the beam that passed through her window and checked the time again. "We've got to go faster. If I give you an extra twenty, will you honk your horn to move these cars?"

The cabbie honked once. "That do it for you?"

April rolled down the window and strained to look down the street. "Might be construction on the bridge."

"Maybe."

"This is taking too long," she said. "Just let me out here." She shoved a wad of bills through the window divider.

"Do I still get my extra twenty?"

"Yes," April said, climbing out. "But only because I saw the picture of your wife and kids on the dashboard."

"Actually, that's my—yes, thank you! They will be so happy!"

April slammed the door and dashed to the sidewalk, then started running as best she could with the hand and the bulky old book.

Several minutes later she entered the emergency entrance, becoming hyperaware of her dirty clothes, matted hair, and smeared makeup in the bright neon lights of the lobby. She was about to apologize to the woman behind the check-in counter when the woman spoke, completely unfazed by April's battered state.

"It's about a thirty-minute wait," she said, handing April a clipboard.

"I'm here to see a friend," April said, handing the clipboard back to her. "Dr. Winter?"

April got his room number and dashed toward the elevators. She stepped inside, finding herself between two rather handsome doctors.

"Did someone help you already?" one of them asked as the doors closed.

"Yes," April said. "I'm fine."

"Are you hurt?" the other doctor asked, pointing to the blood-spattered cup in her hands.

"It's . . . um . . . a cherry Slurpee," she said. "I spilled a little."

The doors opened and she raced out, leaving the confused doctors behind. It only took her a few moments to find Dr. Winter's door. She pushed it open and was relieved to see that he was lying behind a curtain, giving her an opportunity to place the Gutenberg under a chair by the door.

"Dr. Winter?" she called out.

"Yes?" a voice said.

An electric shiver ran up April's spine. There was no mistaking the rich baritone of Dr. Winter's voice, however weakened it was. She wanted to turn and run out the door, but Charlie's life was at stake. Maybe her mother's too.

"Are you okay?" April asked. It was a stupid question, thoughtless. Of course he wasn't okay. He was missing a hand.

"April, is that you?"

"Yes," she answered, tiptoeing forward. She walked around the edge of the curtain, not quite knowing what she would find. She gasped. Dr. Winter was sitting up in bed, bathed in bandages, which covered his right arm, his midsection, and his eyes.

"I'm glad you're here," Dr. Winter said. "I thought that maybe they got you too."

"Who?"

"The Order of the Dragon."

"I thought you were one of them," she said.

Dr. Winter laughed, then winced, grabbing at his ribs. "No," he said. "I would never enter the ranks of such vileness."

"Then are you an Orphan?"

"How do you know about the Orphans?"

"I was kidnapped by some men who thought I was one."

"I'm sorry about that," Dr. Winter said. "They didn't take your hand too, did they?"

"No."

"Well, that's good."

"The pain must be unbearable."

"It was. But the good doctors have kept me very happy," he said, motioning to the IV beside him. "Can you do something for me?"

"Sure."

"Take the bandages off my face."

April reached toward the bandages, stopping just before her fingers took hold. "Did they take your eyes too?" She hated to ask, but some of the security measures at the library required an eye scan.

"They were kind to me in that regard," he said.

She removed the bandages and gasped again.

"They only took one," Dr. Winter said. He closed his left eyelid over his empty socket. He glanced down and saw that April was holding a large Styrofoam cup. "What's that?"

"Your hand," she said, backing away. "I put it on some ice. You could still have it reattached."

Dr. Winter smiled crookedly. "Could you call in a doctor for me?"

"After you answer a few questions," April said quietly.

Dr. Winter continued to smile. "Let's see what the questions are first."

"You know, you probably don't need this anyway," April said, shaking the cup. "I hear that prosthetic hands have come a long way."

"Enough," Dr. Winter said. He winced. "What do you want to know?"

"Are you a member of the Orphans?"

"Yes."

April's eyes filled with tears. "Then did you know my son was going to be used as ransom to get the Gutenberg Bibles?"

Dr. Winter closed his only eye. "I gave the order."

"You couldn't."

"It had to be done!" Dr. Winter proclaimed. "But I swear, your son was never going to be hurt."

"I don't understand. You had full access to the Gutenberg. You could have just walked into the vault and taken it yourself!"

"It's not that simple. The Gutenberg Bibles will be destroyed. My job would have also been destroyed in the process. Someone else needed to take the blame for taking the Gutenberg. Someone besides me," Dr. Winter said. "I'm sorry it had to be you."

"Me too."

"It might be hard to understand, but I act as a guardian for the Library of Congress. There are *hundreds* of books there that hold age-old secrets. Who knows what other treasures could be found? The library is important to the welfare of the Orphans!"

"It's also important to the Order of the Dragon. Their men took the Gutenberg from the Great Hall."

"No!"

"And they stole the one from the vault too," April said, hoping Dr. Winter believed her. She wasn't a very good liar, but she took the chance in case she needed the Gutenberg as a bargaining chip later.

"I can't believe it," Dr. Winter said. "Maybe if I'd asked you to join the Orphans in the first place, this never would have happened."

"I would never join any organization that puts people's lives in jeopardy," April said.

"That's because you're only taking a narrow view of the situation," Dr. Winter said. "Come now, April. You understand history. My life, your life, your son's life . . . they all mean *nothing* in the context of history."

"They mean everything to me," April said. She shoved the Styrofoam cup in Dr. Winter's face. "Stop playing games, and tell me exactly what I need to do to save my son."

"Very well," Dr. Winter said, sighing. "I presume you understand who the Orphans are?"

"I know that they were warrior monks back in the 1400s."

"Warrior monks? That's certainly a colorful title," Dr. Winter said. "I suppose you're somewhat right. The Orphans were a feuding clan back then, with their armored wagons and swords and such. But they were more than that. They were the defenders of a great secret, a secret they didn't even own."

"What secret?"

"It wouldn't be a secret if I told you, now, would it?"

April shook the cup with the hand. "Did I mention it was your *right* hand? You're right-handed."

"I'll tell you as much as I know," Dr. Winter said, grimacing again. "The secret had to do with the Order of the Dragon. They were said to possess something so powerful that the Holy Roman Empire was completely at their command."

"What was it?"

"Only Gutenberg knows. At an early age, he had a fateful meeting with John Huss—the father of the Orphans. Huss was being led through the streets to the middle of town, where he was to be burned at the stake. He handed the young Gutenberg a token— an ancient coin—that would change the course of his life. From that point on, Gutenberg swore his allegiance to the Orphans." He paused.

"What did he do for them?" April asked.

"Gutenberg's work developing the printing press became central to the Orphans' plans. They knew that putting the Bible in the hands of commoners would create radical social change. And it did, ushering in not only the Reformation, but the Renaissance too."

"Get to the point," April said, irritated. "How does the Order of the Dragon come into play?"

"The Order was first known as the Dragon of Saint George, formed to fight the onslaught of the Ottoman army. Each of the twelve members bore a sculpted dragon on their helmets. They were regarded as the fiercest soldiers in the land, but even so, each of them fell until only one remained: the Serbian prince Stefan Lazarević. The organization disappeared, until the German emperor Sigismund revived them under a new banner in 1408."

"The Order of the Dragon," April whispered, hardly sensing the words had drifted from her mouth.

"Exactly. The newly arranged *Societas Draconistrarum*, which is where the term *draconist* comes from—"

"*Draconist?* That's a word?"

"It's what the members of the Order call themselves. You won't find it in a dictionary, but my ghastly state attests to its reality. The term was first used by Emperor Sigismund. He chose the popular Prince Lazarević as the Order's first member, allowing him to convince a number of other powerful individuals to join their ranks, including Vlad II, Dracul of Wallachia."

"Dracula?"

"Dracula's *father*. He swore his allegiance to the Order as a way to continue his battle against the Ottoman Empire."

"I'm confused. It seems like the Order was simply trying to defend the power of the Holy Roman Empire. But from the way you talk about them, there must have been something far more sinister going on. I guess what I'm trying to ask is: was the Order of the Dragon good or bad?"

"What kind of a question is that?" Dr. Winter asked. "I believe it was Napoleon who said: 'History is the version of past events that people have decided to agree upon.' Whether the Order of the Dragon is good or bad will be determined by this night, by whether the Order succeeds or fails."

"Succeeds or fails at what?"

"At claiming the secret!" Dr. Winter pronounced. "The Gutenberg Bible is what they want. You see, Gutenberg acted as a spy among the kings and princes of his day. He walked in their courts. He heard their conversations, their plans, all because he was creating works of art for them: Bibles."

"The illuminations!"

"Yes. As you know, commoners could never have afforded the workmanship of an illuminator. The very inks cost a fortune, and the work took months, even years, to produce. Gutenberg realized this gave him the opportunity to expand his knowledge of the secret the Order was holding, as well as a method for hiding the evidence once he was gone: he hid it in the illuminations, in the very Bibles the Order commissioned. It also offered safety, for a Bible in the hands of a commoner could have been destroyed, but the Bibles commissioned by the members of the Order were treated like the fine works of art that they are."

"Gutenberg recorded their secret and preserved it under their own noses! Brilliant."

"It was brilliant, save for one problem: the Orphans were destroyed, and with them, the knowledge of what Gutenberg had hidden in the illuminations."

"The Orphans were destroyed? I thought you said that *you* were part of the Orphans."

"Newly formed, I should have added. The Orphans came into existence again during the World Wars, when the Order of the Dragon came into power once again."

"Hitler was a Dragon?"

"Have you heard of the Thule Society?" Dr. Winter asked.

"Sounds familiar."

"They were later known as the Nazi Party, after Hitler took command. The Thule Society was full of occultists, but was mostly based on the same principles as the Order of the Dragon. The name changed, but the philosophy remained the same."

April fiddled with the plastic lid of the Styrofoam cup, drumming on it with her fingers. "So let me see if I have this straight: the Orphans have been trying for hundreds of years to get their hands on Gutenberg's secret knowledge of the Order, and somehow, my innocent family and I are now mixed up in the mess."

"Calling it a *mess* seems so provincial, considering the enormity of the situation, but the simple answer is yes. Only something went dreadfully wrong. The Order of the Dragon shouldn't have had any idea what the Orphans were up to."

"I'm only telling you this because I want to save my son," April said cautiously. "The men at the library were FBI agents. Is that possible?"

"Entirely," Dr. Winter said. "The Order of the Dragon has always existed right under the authority of unaware governing bodies. Emperor Sigismund instituted his Order inside the Holy Roman Empire. Hitler formed his Order at the core of the Nazi Party. So it doesn't surprise me that the FBI would be a perfect hiding place for the Order today. They've always emerged where the power is. Think of the things they can get away with."

"Like breaking into the Library of Congress?"

"Precisely."

"So what about my son?" April asked. "And my mother? And what about August? Can't we help them now that the Orphans' plans have failed?"

"There might still be time to save the Gutenberg secret from the hands of the Order," Dr. Winter said.

"The only thing I care about now is saving my *family*," April said. "If the Order knew about the plan involving me, then they probably know everything else. My family could be in terrible danger." She set the Styrofoam cup down and took out her cell phone. "I want you to call it off."

"I can't."

"You can and you will," April said.

"No, you see, the Orphans exist worldwide. I was the primary contact, but there are others who can step in, others who have probably already taken my place to make sure the plan is carried out."

"But it's too late. I told you, the Order took the Gutenberg Bibles from the library!"

"It's not my decision anymore."

April held the cell phone limply in her hand. "I don't care," she said. "I want to talk to the man holding my son hostage."

Dr. Winter gave her Joe Radford's number. April dialed. A man answered, and she put the cell on speakerphone, holding it out in front of Dr. Winter.

"Hello?"

"Joe, it's Dr. Winter. Our plans have been disrupted," Dr. Winter said. "The mission is off."

"Sir?"

"You heard what I said. The mission is off." Dr. Winter looked at April and shook his head. *This won't work.*

"I'll leave right away."

April hung up the phone. "Sounds like you have more power than you're letting on," she said.

"No!" Dr. Winter said, his face twisted in dismay. "Something is wrong. He never should have just blindly accepted an order like that!"

"Right. Now talk to the woman on the plane."

"Xandria," Dr. Winter said. He muttered something over and over under his breath as April punched in the digits from her last call to August, making sure to first enter a code to block her caller ID. Three rings later a woman's voice answered.

"Who is this?" Xandria asked, her voice tinny on the cell's small speakerphone.

April held out the phone to Dr. Winter, who struggled to come back to his senses. "It's me," he finally said. "I had to use another phone. My apologies."

"What happened to your phone?"

Dr. Winter looked over to April, not knowing what to say. April made a face like an animal dying, sticking out her tongue and leaning her head over.

"It died on me," Dr. Winter said. "Bad batteries, perhaps."

Xandria didn't dwell on the topic. "We've just deciphered the second set of images. We're waiting for the third set to arrive."

"There's been a change of plans," Dr. Winter said. "I'm afraid I'm going to need to call off the mission."

"Why?"

"You won't be getting the third set of images. They've been taken out of our control."

"April didn't come through?"

"The Order got to her first," Dr. Winter said.

The phone crackled. "That's terrible news," Xandria finally said. "So what am I supposed to do now?"

"When the plane lands, walk away. Say good-bye. I don't care how you do it, but the plan is off."

"We were so close," Xandria whispered. She hung up.

April put the cell phone in her pocket. "Why do you look so upset? You just put an end to all this madness."

"I'm afraid this is only the beginning," Dr. Winter said. "Something else is at work here. I only agreed to terminate the mission because I knew my order would be dismissed. But they said yes. They agreed and they quit. Which could only mean one thing."

"What?"

Dr. Winter opened both eyelids wide, revealing his dueling features in their horrible fullness: a crimson abyss and a blinding fear. "You're in the hands of the Order now."

illuminatedfifteenilluminated

Stanley threw Joe's phone aside, unzipped the bag, and examined the contents: bone saw, mortise chisel, three-inch nails, a hand drill with a diamond-point bit, other assorted toys, and rags—lots of extremely absorbent rags.

He peered down at his three playmates, supine on the dining room rug, wondering which one would go first. Joe, Charlie, and Grandma Rose were wound tightly in their silver cocoons, wrapped from shoulder to toe in duct tape.

He always liked to save—when time permitted—an eyetooth from each of his victims. He had a necklace full of them. The skin around his neck had become raw from where it wore on him, but he didn't mind. It seemed like penance, his personal style of self-flagellation, so the necklace remained, despite the constant pain.

"Which one of you shot Ben?" Stanley asked, ripping the tape away from each of their mouths. He bent down over Grandma Rose. "Was it you? You seem like the feisty type."

"Get away from me," she said.

Stanley *click-click-click*ed a pair of pliers before her eyes. "Ben was nice, unlike me. He probably would have let you live. But I suppose that's why he failed. He was *too* nice, and in a dog-eat-dog world, only the wicked survive."

"I thought the Order of the Dragon was supposed to be a *holy* order," Joe said.

"We are!" Stanley said, moving over to Joe. "Haven't you heard of the teachings of Rasputin?"

"Rasputin was the antichrist," Joe said.

"No, Rasputin was a Russian starets, a healer and a prophet," Stanley said. "He understood that our depravity was our greatest connection with God, and that if we embraced it, we could have communion with him. The greater the crime, the greater the connection."

"You're out of your mind," Joe said. "And so was your friend Ben. I'm glad I sent him to hell."

"I'm tired of listening to you," Stanley said. He pried open Joe's mouth and stuck in the pliers. He wriggled the tool as Joe growled, then finally yanked free the tooth he desired. "You'll be first!" Stanley said, holding his tooth up in the air like a jewel.

"The Orphans have always made good martyrs," Joe said, spitting blood. "Bring on your worst."

Stanley took a long, curved hook out of his bag and stuck it in the duct tape between Joe's feet. With two hands, he dragged him across the slick wooden floor, stopping by Ben's lifeless form. "I'm going to make it my worst for his sake," Stanley said. "Brothers of the Order look out for one another, even after death." He pulled Joe into the kitchen.

✝

Grandma Rose felt like she was stuck in a downward-spiraling nightmare. And the worst part was, her grandson was along for the ride.

"What's going to happen to Joe?" They were the first words Charlie had spoken since he'd been bound.

"I don't know, Charlie," she answered, a half lie.

"I like him."

"He shot me in the leg, I'll remind you."

"He told me he only did it to make me drop the gun. It was my fault."

Grandma Rose took a deep breath. "It wasn't your fault."

"It's *all* my fault! Why do you keep telling me it's not? Joe could have stopped him if it wasn't for me."

The sound of a saw or a drill—some kind of mechanical terror—came from the kitchen. The barely audible sound of someone trying *not* to scream vibrated beneath the noise.

"Charlie, tell me about school. Or the last book you read. Anything."

"My mom and dad's divorce?"

"I wasn't going to suggest that, but if that's what you want to talk about, that's fine." How were they going to get out of here? Could they roll? Where would they roll? They couldn't exactly open the front door.

"It hasn't been good."

"Well, sometimes, Charlie, two people just aren't meant to—"

"To be together? That's what the counselor said too. But then I asked her if that meant that I wasn't supposed to be born."

"Charlie, of course you were supposed to be born!" She scanned the room for some obvious means of freeing themselves.

"But not if Mom and Dad were never supposed to be together!"

Grandma Rose suddenly understood that Charlie never bought any of the pat answers, any of the easy outs provided by the counselor, by his mom and his dad. Or by her.

"You know what I was thinking about earlier, Grandma Rose?"

"What, dear?" she said, looking at him as if seeing him as his own person for the first time.

"The time you took me out for ice cream."

Grandma Rose had to think for a minute. She'd taken him out for ice cream a million times. "Oh," she said, following his train of thought. "You mean when I first came to live here?"

"Yeah."

"That was a hard day for all of us, Charlie. I wish you could remember all the other times we've gone out for ice cream. The fun times, I mean."

"I've forgiven you, you know."

"Forgiven me? For what?"

"For lying to me. You said that everything was going to be fine. But it hasn't been fine. I've seen Mom crying sometimes. And Dad seems lonely too. He doesn't have any friends."

"Your father has plenty of friends," Grandma Rose said, resuming her search of the room. Her eyes landed on the sewing basket by her chair in the living room. "He has all those fancy parties."

"He told me that those parties are just to get more people to buy his books. Really rich people come to his parties. They aren't his friends, though."

"Well, he certainly doesn't seem to have a problem spending more time with them than his family," Grandma Rose said. She shut her mouth, wishing she'd kept quiet. "Sorry. That probably wasn't very fair to your father."

"Why do you call him that? He's my *dad*. You don't have to hate him so much. He doesn't hate you."

Grandma Rose gave a fake laugh. "*Hate* is a very strong word, Charlie. I don't *hate* your father."

"Dad."

"*Dad*," she forced out. "I don't hate your dad. I just don't agree with some of the decisions he's made." She tried to roll toward the sewing basket but couldn't even turn over. A blaze of pain shot up her leg. "Why did you say he doesn't hate me?"

"Well . . ." Charlie said, as if needing to buy himself an extra few seconds. "Sometimes I complain about you to him, and he tells me that you only want the best for me and there's no way Mom could get along without you."

This was news. "What do you complain about?" Grandma Rose asked. She couldn't help asking.

"Nothing. Stupid stuff," he confessed. "You made me eat spinach once after my mom said I didn't have to eat it."

"Spinach is good for you. You can't live on ice cream, you know." She discovered that she could move the fingers of her right hand and started wiggling them, probing for a weakness—a seam, maybe— in the tape. Joe hadn't bound her impossibly tight.

"Has anyone tried?"

"Tried what?"

"To live on ice cream. I mean, people are always saying you can't live on ice cream or cookies or candy bars or whatever, but do they really know that?"

"I think it's a pretty good guess to say that you can't live on ice cream."

"There are Eskimos who live on nothing but fish! I bet they used to say, 'You can't live on fish!' But they were wrong. Eskimos do."

"Tell you what, Charlie. If you ever ask me to cook you only fish, I'll be more than happy to do it," Grandma Rose said.

Charlie laughed. Grandma Rose laughed too.

A sickening sawing sound echoed from the kitchen. Charlie's laugh turned to a whimper.

"Listen to me, Charlie," Grandma Rose said. "You have to concentrate on my voice. You can't hear anything else, okay?"

"Okay," the boy murmured.

"Can you move at all?"

"No."

"Can you roll?"

"I'll try." Charlie wiggled in his cocoon, then began rocking until he built up enough momentum to turn over. "I did it!"

"Good!" Grandma Rose said.

"What should I do?"

The awful sawing grew louder. Grandma Rose tried not to dwell on the pain Joe was enduring. He was probably dead already. She wanted to say good riddance, but she couldn't blot out the thought that—despite the fact he'd put a bullet in her leg—he was actually a good man beneath it all. Misguided, but good.

"Grandma?"

"Charlie, I want you to roll over to my chair. Beside it, in the basket, are my sewing tools. There's some scissors in there."

"But we can't even use our hands!"

"One thing at a time," she said, keeping her voice steady. "Go get
the scissors."

"Okay," Charlie said. He didn't waste any time, rocking to build
up momentum. He gathered up enough force to turn over, then
kept on rolling, right up to the side of Grandma Rose's chair. He
was able to move his feet just enough to scoot himself up to the side
of the wicker basket beside the chair, which he pulled over with his
teeth. Everything inside spilled out—needles and pins and thread,
and finally . . . the scissors!

"Hurry," Grandma Rose said. The noise from the kitchen had
masked the noise of the basket toppling, but there was no telling
how long they had before Stanley returned.

"I'm trying," Charlie said through a muffled mouth. With the
scissors secure between his teeth, he rocked until he had enough
momentum to roll back over to Grandma Rose. He dropped the
scissors next to her. "Now what?"

Grandma Rose's hand slowly began to emerge through the silver
bindings. "Now we try to get out of here," she said.

✠

Stanley was neat. He'd always been neat. As a kid, he used to arrange
his socks by color, and then by day. His sports trophies were lined in
a row by date, and then by height. He used to come home during the
school lunch hour just to make sure nothing was out of place, that his
mother or younger brother hadn't disturbed the order of his life.

Stanley came to understand that not only was he neat; he was a neat *freak*. So it was no surprise to him that his compulsive neatness would play a vital role in his work as a professional cleaner.

It was difficult in the beginning: hacking people into pieces was a dirty business. But with an intense desire to find a solution, and a voracious appetite for serial killers' biographies, he made progress.

First came the floors. A thick tarp usually did the trick, though he had been surprised at how many were easily compromised by a sopping of blood. Towels or rags followed, lining the edges of the tarp. This prevented any excess from spilling out onto the floor.

Next came the procedure itself. The victim had to be calm. A rapid heartbeat meant a quick flow of blood, and that in turn meant that splattering was likely, a definite problem. How to calm a victim had become the problem to overcome for the last eleven months. He'd tried poetry as a possible method, but that just seemed silly now. Most of the time it only made the victim more anxious, more ill at ease with the surreal goings-on. He'd most recently settled on a mild tranquilizer, stolen from a veterinarian he dated for a short time, though it bothered him to use anything so counterfeit. Killing was *natural*, and the drug so artificial. Using it seemed like cheating. But it worked.

And, finally, there was the cleanup, the very essence of the professional cleaner's services: to leave no evidence. None at all. The appearance was to be that the victim—or victims, as was often the case—simply vanished. Disappeared. It didn't matter why. What mattered was that not a trace of them could be found. Stanley often amused himself watching *C.S.I.* reruns. The show was science-fiction. True investigators were usually far less scrupulous in their examination and far more interested in figuring out what brand of beer they would order at the bar that night.

Joe had been difficult. He was large. He was fatty. His bones were thick. Unusually thick, actually. Stanley wore out three blades just cutting apart the legs. And the tranquilizer had not worked very well. Not that it mattered. Joe seemed determined not to make a squeak. Stanley had found the whole thing a little disconcerting. One of the things he enjoyed most about the process was how human it felt. Joe's absence of fear, his lack of screaming and writhing, seemed so alien. In fact, Stanley noted that the expression on his face toward the end was almost angelic.

Martyr, indeed.

Stanley poured acid into a bowl and began to contemplate who his next victim would be. The kid? The grandmother? They would make equally boring work. Little struggle. Little resistance. They would yell at first, but they would quickly allow their minds to leave the unpleasantness of the present. They would still be alive, barely of course, but they certainly wouldn't be present. Their brains wouldn't allow it. Stanley had seen it time and time again, the sudden shift from shock to horror to nothing.

The grandmother. She seemed like an appealing choice for a date on the tarp. He'd start with her toes. Then fingers. Then . . . well, he'd just let the spirit lead. Maybe he'd let the kid watch. Or maybe . . .

The kid. A less-obvious choice, but putting him next in line would certainly drive the old woman up the wall. It was surely the more evil choice, something that would amplify the intensity of the religious experience. He'd have to do it slowly, take his time, give the kid small enough doses of the tranquilizer to keep him aware of exactly what was going on. And then he'd repent afterward, and bathe in the glory of God's mercy.

It was beautiful, really.

"I'm almost done in here," Stanley called out. "Joe was excellent, just excellent. A true model of decency for each of you."

He lined up his tools on the kitchen counter, as he'd done before: smaller utensils first—picks, scrapers, scalpels, and such — that eventually led to the larger devices, the drill and the saw. He stopped for a minute, noting that one of the saw teeth appeared to be chipped. He contemplated changing the blade, but finally agreed with his better judgment to move on due to the constraints of time.

In a final step of preparedness, he placed a new paper mask over his mouth, a new plastic cap over his head, and new plastic gloves over his hands. He examined the gloves for any imperfections, holes, and tears, things that might allow the victim to enter his personal space, or the opposite, for a flake of his skin or a fiber of his hair to exit and incriminate him. Everything looked good. Solid.

☩

"As soon as you can, run!" Grandma Rose said, hacking away at the remaining tape around Charlie's ankles.

"Are you ready?" Stanley called out, exiting the kitchen. He stopped, surprised. Charlie kicked at the bonds, only making it harder for Grandma Rose to finish.

"I don't think so," Stanley said. He strode forward.

"Stay back!" Grandma Rose said, holding the scissors up like a dagger aimed at Stanley's neck.

Stanley held his arms out wide. "You're only making this harder on yourself."

Grandma Rose didn't know whether it was the sheer rage inside her or the powers of heaven that allowed her to do what happened next. She pulled back her arm and propelled the scissors forward like a dart, lodging the razor-sharp points squarely in the middle of Stanley's throat.

Stanley fell to the floor and grabbed at the scissors, wrenching them from their tender position. Blood spilled through his fingers as he held his neck, clawing his way toward them with his other hand. "I'll kill you!" he gurgled, red foam forming at the corners of his lips. "I'll kill you all!"

‖illuminated‖sixteen‖illuminated‖

Xandria wasn't worried that August had stormed off. Tearing out the illuminated page had sent him into silent shock. And then tearing out the two other illuminations sent him shouting over the edge. He needed a minute to collect his thoughts. And she needed his head to be clear in order to decode the rest of the clues. Besides, what was he going to do? Explain his dilemma to one of the flight attendants? They wouldn't believe him. As long as they were on the plane, his world was in her hands.

She heard the phone buzz. She answered immediately, expecting the call. "You got my message?"

"Yes," Meng said.

"Winter just called. He said that the Order took both Gutenberg Bibles from the library."

"We got the one from the Great Hall, but it had redundant information. The one we needed got away. The girl took it."

"April? She's alive?" Xandria was shocked to hear the news. Winter had lied to her in more ways than one. "What about her son?"

"We haven't received confirmation from Stanley yet, but I think it's safe to say that he won't fail."

"I never thought you would fail either."

"We were only supposed to frame her, not babysit her. But one of our agents just spotted Ms. Adams leaving the hospital where Dr. Winter was taken. We're following her now."

"Does she have the Gutenberg?"

"Yes."

"Where is she headed?"

"We're not sure. But Gomez is on her."

"Call me when you have the book." Xandria hung up. The situation was getting more complicated by the minute. If she was going to pull this off, she needed to have every angle of the mission under her control.

Control. That's what she was all about, what she needed to survive. She'd learned that lesson the night her sister was beaten to death by her father.

Control. Her father's power over her kept her from telling the truth to the police. They'd questioned her for hours, but she never wavered from the story he had given them: that a kid from down the street had broken in, stolen some money, and then raped and killed her sister. The kid was from a poor family. He had a criminal record, something her father knew would bolster his case. The police took the kid in the next day. He didn't have an alibi, at least not one that was willing to talk to a cop, so he was put behind bars. Months later, Xandria read that he was beaten to death in a gang riot. She left the paper out for her father, folded with the story on the front. He picked it up and threw it in the fireplace.

Control. Years later, on the anniversary of her sister's death, Xandria found it for herself. Her father let her out of the house only to attend public school. Xandria did well there, making friends and impressing teachers. In her senior year, she secretly began applying to universities with the aid of the school's guidance counselor, a bohemian, recent divorcé named Russ.

Russ promised that once the right schools came knocking, her father would see that the wisest decision was to let her move away to pursue a career. Xandria was amazed at Russ's tenacity. He would often show her a stack of applications he'd spent all night preparing on her behalf. He spent lengthy amounts of time with her in counseling, discussing everything that troubled her. No story seemed too long for him. No problem seemed too discouraging. Russ was always positive. He was always kind. Which was probably why Xandria didn't see it coming when, one late afternoon in February, he locked the door after she came into his office.

He told her that he needed something in return for all his efforts. He'd fallen in love with her, he said. She didn't know what to think. She certainly was appreciative for everything he had done, but there wasn't anything more to it. Not love anyway. It could turn into love, he said. But it could start as something simpler.

Control. Russ used it over her that day. She rushed home in tears, not sure what to do. Her father was home early, something she hadn't anticipated. He asked her what had happened. She tried not to tell him, but he was drunk and shook her until she spilled the horrible events. He tore out of the house like a mad hornet, murder on his mind. She thought she saw him put a gun into the pocket of his coat.

Later that night, she got the news that her father had found Russ at a local bar and shot him, but not without getting shot himself by the barkeep. Both of them died within minutes of each other.

Xandria tried to find remorse in her heart for their lost lives but couldn't. They were gone, and she couldn't be happier. Their absence brought even greater rewards. Her father had stashed away a large amount of money he received when her mother passed away. He had probably hoped to keep it for himself after she was gone, but now it was hers. And Russ's efforts to find a university weren't in vain. By year's end, she was enrolled at one of the finest institutions in the world.

Control. She found it. And she understood the price to keep it.

✠

August knew it was time to return. He was only playing into Xandria's control of the situation by staying away. She wanted to infuriate him, confuse him, keep him guessing. But he needed to remain focused if he wanted to save his family.

He glanced out a window on the short trip back to his seat. He could see moonbeams shimmering off the silvery slivers of clouds, then shooting down to the shadowy waters of the Atlantic Ocean. Everything was so quiet, so calm. Everything seemed to be in order. But it wasn't. Everything was falling apart.

It wouldn't be long before they landed. He still didn't know what would happen once they stepped off the plane. But that was something he couldn't control. And this was.

"Mind if I take my seat?"

"I was just about to come find you," Xandria said, not moving and so forcing him to brush against her legs on the way by. "There's been a development."

August picked up the ancient Bible from the center seat and ran his fingers along the jagged edge where the illuminated page used to be. "No development can be worse than this."

"It is. April has the Gutenberg we need. But the Order of the Dragon is going to kill her to get it first."

August looked up. "How would you know that?"

"Because I just talked to them," Xandria said.

As frightened as August had been before, his fear doubled. The Orphans were one thing. The Order of the Dragon was another. The Orphans were misguided; the Order, however, was cruel and merciless. If Xandria had aligned herself with them, then April and Charlie would both die. "You're one of them," he said.

She put a finger to her temple for a moment before saying, "I understand that it might look that way. But let me explain the truth: two years ago, I met a man named Dr. Winter at a convention in Berlin."

"The head of the library's archaeobibliology department?"

Xandria nodded. "We talked many times over the course of the weekend, and eventually the subject of the Orphans came up. On the last day of the convention, he explained to me that he was part of a new formation of the Orphans, which he wanted me to join."

"And you said yes."

"Not right away. I had a long list of reservations. But Dr. Winter—

as you probably have heard from April—can be quite persuasive. After a month of e-mails back and forth, I joined. Over the course of the next year I devoted all my time to the Orphans, hunting for clues about the secret that had died with Gutenberg. I found nothing. And then, one day, through a short string of miracles I can't begin to explain, I came into possession of Gutenberg's journal."

"The one that Station X found."

"The very same," Xandria said. "Not long after, I was contacted by a man named Cornelius Hood. He had somehow heard that I had the journal and was willing to pay any price to have it. I told him it wasn't for sale. He said that there were other ways to convince me to give it to him. I hung up the phone. The next day I woke to find him standing at the foot of my bed. He pointed a gun at my head and told me that the journal was not mine to own, that it belonged to an ancient German society, a powerful organization that had nearly vanished after the World Wars."

"The Order of the Dragon."

"I wasn't eager to die, so I told him about my involvement with the Orphans, thinking he might spare my life to get information. That ended up being a wise decision, because more than that, he asked me to join the Order."

"As a spy."

"Yes. But secretly I was doing the opposite."

"So you're a double agent?"

"This isn't *Mission: Impossible*."

"But you know every move the Order is going to make."

"Not exactly. They don't trust me. But they take their chances because of my position with the Orphans."

"So that's how you found out that they're after April."

"Yes. But there's still time to help her. The only thing that both the Order and the Orphans want is the Gutenberg Bible she's carrying. If she puts the Gutenberg down, then the Order's field operative will let her go."

"And you'll still get the last three illuminations, because the Order will give them to you."

"See? Everyone wins. But only if she gives up the book," Xandria said. She got out the phone and handed it to August. "Call her. Make her leave the Gutenberg behind. It may not be that easy, because right now she probably thinks it's the only bargaining chip she has. But if she doesn't, they'll kill her. And you see how things will fall apart after that."

August wasn't sure what to believe, but Xandria's story seemed to make sense. In any case, April would be safer without the Gutenberg. He dialed her number.

"Hello?"

"It's me."

"August!"

"There's no time to talk. Right now, all I need you to do is put the Gutenberg down and get away."

"What do you mean?"

August could tell she was on foot. She was slightly out of breath, and he could hear the traffic rushing by in the background. "I wish I could explain," he said. "Listen, is there a man following you?"

"Give me a second." There was a pause. Some traffic. A few other passing voices. "Yes. There's a guy with a long scar on his chin."

"A long scar on his chin?" August repeated.

"That's Gomez," Xandria said. "He's the one who needs to pick up the book."

"Okay, April?"

"I'm still here."

"The man following you is named Gomez. I want you to leave the book at the next available spot, and then run. Don't look back."

"August, there's no way I'm letting this go. I have to get to Charlie."

"There's no time. Just put the book down and get out of there."

"But what if keeping it is the only way to get Charlie back?"

August felt the tension rise. "That's not how this works. If you keep the book, they'll kill you and Charlie."

"Are you sure?"

"April. You have to trust me."

"It's been a long time since I've been able to do that," she said.

The phone went dead. August slowly brought it down from his ear.

"Is she going to do it?" Xandria inquired.

"I'm not sure," August said.

illuminated**seventeen**illuminated

April kept her pace steady, fighting the impulse to sprint away from the man behind her. She could practically feel his breath on her neck. She needed to stay in control. But she also needed to make a decision. Fast.

Leave the book or keep it?

If she kept it, she might have something to trade for Charlie's life. But what if August was right? What if the only reason they were holding any of them hostage was to get the Gutenberg? Holding on to it would only make the situation worse.

How close was he?

April held up her watch, acting like she was reading the time. The reflection showed he was not far behind. And getting closer.

She held the book tightly in her arms. Letting it go seemed like letting Charlie go, like releasing the only power she had to keep him alive. But that probably wasn't the truth. The truth seemed closer to what August had said. But what if he'd been misled?

It was a horrible decision.

Making the wrong choice could mean death for Charlie.

And Grandma Rose.

Not to mention herself.

April held up her watch again to take a peek at her pursuer. Was he closer? Yes. He was most definitely closer. Was he just following her? Or was he waiting for the right moment to pull her into a side alley and slit her throat?

April saw an alleyway ahead. She would have to cross it. There was no other path but directly across the alleyway.

But before it! Her savior! A bench! A perfect place to set the book and run away! It was a sign.

April kissed the book and placed it on the bench. And ran. She ran harder than she'd ever run in her life, which wasn't much of an accomplishment. She'd barely ever stepped foot in a gym. Her slender appearance was the result of lucky DNA, not hard work. "Where do you work out?" people would ask. She'd usually tell them the Y, or someplace she remembered reading about in the paper. It was bad, lying to people, but it felt better than telling them the truth: that she did nothing. So while they tried their hardest and still got bigger around the middle, she ate ice-cream sandwiches and napped on her couch and woke up every morning feeling slim.

But now she regretted her laziness. She panicked a little. She was already running out of breath. There was that other part about the gym, wasn't there? The keeping-in-shape part. She'd forgotten about that. She sucked in more air, but it didn't seem to help. She ran harder. Her side was killing her. Was this what it was like to be a runner? To endure this kind of pain? She could never do it.

She tried to raise her arm, to peer into the dark reflection of her watch to get a view behind her. But it was jiggling too much. There was no way to know whether he was back there or not.

She tried to listen for footsteps behind her. But all she could hear was the *thump, thump, thump* of her own feet, and her heart pounding in her ears.

She had to stop.

She had to.

Stop.

April collapsed at the side of the road and waited for a cold blade to slice her throat. She waited, her lungs heaving so hard she thought they might pop like balloons at the end of a birthday party.

She waited.

✠

April opened her eyes. She couldn't see anything. She was light-headed, and her ears were ringing. She blinked. She saw something, a stoplight, some traffic. But no man, and no life-stealing blade.

Was she safe? April rose to her knees. There was no one chasing her. Had it worked? Had Xandria told August the truth?

Her breathing began to return to normal, and with it, her rational thought. *Charlie.* She needed to get to Charlie.

She stood and waved down a taxi, got into the car, and gave the driver the address. He hit the accelerator, asking if she was okay. She answered no. He shrugged as if it really didn't make any difference.

It was a long drive. Probably not if it had been a normal situation, if she was simply running across town to pick up a book that had just been released or to get some tea with an old college friend. But now the trek seemed like an eternity. She asked the driver if he could speed up. He shrugged, the same way he had before. He didn't understand. Or maybe he just wanted to act like he didn't.

"Stop here," April said. They were two blocks from her house. She could see that the lights were on. But the shades were drawn, and there was no way to see anything inside. She gave the man his money. She didn't tip. It could be considered a mean thing to do, but she felt like he had deliberately taken his time, racked up a couple extra bucks on the meter. He was keeping her from seeing her son. A son who could be hurt, or dead. He couldn't know that. But April kept her change anyway. She shrugged at him as he sped away, shrugging being the only language he seemed able to interpret.

April began walking toward her house, keeping out of the urine-yellow luminescence of the streetlights. She couldn't be too careful. She'd learned that, if nothing else.

She was only two houses away. If Xandria was right, then no one but Charlie and Grandma Rose would be in the house. Whoever had been there before should have been told to leave, now that they had their precious Bible.

April reached the left side of the house. She considered walking up to the front door, knocking, her mind filling with the sweet image of Charlie and Grandma Rose embracing her, thanking her for saving them. But she knew that kind of Pollyanna thinking would have to be saved for another day.

She chose to go around to the back. She could look in through the kitchen window and get a feel for the situation. If everything was okay, if Grandma Rose and Charlie were sitting there making cookies, then she'd simply walk back around to the front, or let herself in through the rear door and offer a good reason for doing so. They wouldn't care. They would be safe and happy.

April walked around the back of her house, scowling and rejoicing at the fact that the security light over the stoop was still unfixed. The cover of darkness kept her well hidden as she tiptoed toward the kitchen window.

She peered inside, just one eyeful.

It was enough.

What she saw could fill a thousand nightmares. She fought the urge to vomit and forced herself to look again. She had to know who the victim was. Please, not Charlie. Please, God.

It wasn't Charlie. It wasn't Grandma Rose, either. It was, in fact, someone she didn't recognize at all, not that she could have recognized anyone, the body being in the state that it was in. But the parts were too big to belong to either Charlie or Grandma Rose. She was sure of that.

April heard an unfamiliar sound. Or rather, a familiar sound in an unfamiliar setting. Her father had been a carpenter. Not by profession, but by hobby. He built all kinds of trinkets and toys, desks and chairs. The sound of his saw had become married in April's mind to the wonderful things he produced. But this sawing was different. This sawing spewed death.

The sawing ended. April was grateful at first the terrible noise had retired, but she realized there would be another victim. A smaller one perhaps. And soon.

What was she supposed to do? The police would take too long

and might only endanger her son and mother, considering they were still in a hostage situation. There would be no survivors.

She forced herself to look back into the kitchen. She pulled away. Had he seen her? She waited for the back door to open, for the man in the surgical mask and cap and gloves to come out and grab her by the neck. But the door stayed shut. He hadn't seen her. But she'd seen him, seen that he was . . . cleaning up? Almost like one might clean up after feeding a large group of dinner guests. Clean up? What kind of killer was this? It was like the kind she'd read about in magazines, trashy rags, the ones she always made fun of but read when she couldn't help herself. Yes, serial killers did this type of thing. So what was he doing inside her house?

April dashed around to the front of the house. One of the windows' curtains was pulled back a crack, just enough to peek through. She caught her breath. Tears streamed down her cheeks, and she brushed them away. *Stay in control. Stay in control!* Her little Charlie and her poor mother were tied up on the floor, squirming. Probably trying to get away, knowing the butcher was only a heartbeat away.

She could run to a neighbor, explain, get their help. Maybe someone had a gun. This was DC, for goodness' sake. People here had guns, needed guns, just to stay safe. Not that she'd ever had one. Not with Charlie in the house. Who was she fooling? Keeping a gun scared her to death. But her creepy neighbor next door might have one, right? What was his name? She couldn't remember. She'd never asked him. She'd seen him staring at her through his window one time, the creep. No. Even if he had a gun, he could be more trouble instead of help.

April tried the front door. Locked. Of course. Keys. Keys. Where were her keys? On her desk back at the library. She was wasting too much time. How could this be so hard? She would have to bust out the front window. She looked around for something to do the job, getting on her hands and knees, digging behind the shrubs. She found a plastic action figure. A penny. An old newspaper. Dirt. Nothing like she needed. Where were the baseball bats? Where were the tire irons?

She heard a voice cry out from inside, a deep moan growing into an unspeakable siren scream. Time had run out. She was too late. The tears began to swell in her vision. *No! No! NO!*

She looked up through her tears and caught the reflection of the streetlight off the birdbath. She ran to it, dumping the top over, soaking her feet and nearly crushing her toes. It was heavy. But her adrenaline was pumping. She'd heard of mothers doing incredible things in dire circumstances. Lifting cars. Telephone poles. A concrete birdbath was nothing. She picked it up and carried it to the front window, heaving it forward, through the glass.

The window gave way and the curtain came down. The birdbath rolled forward and struck the butcher in the leg. He fell. He appeared to be bleeding from the neck. There was blood everywhere.

April stumbled through the window. Charlie and Grandma Rose were nearly free of their bindings, but they seemed immobilized. Then April saw why: the butcher was rising to his feet. He was still very much alive, despite his damaged state. April got between the two opposing parties. "Leave my family alone," she said.

The butcher laughed. A trickle of blood escaped his lips, mixing with the blood drenching his shirt at the neck. He staggered a bit.

April reached down and picked up Grandma Rose's pink-handled scissors, the ones she never let Charlie cut construction paper with. They were stained crimson and stuck to her hand. They were expensive: heavy and deathly sharp. April swung them back and forth, feeling almost stupid, like a character from *West Side Story*. But she could see a hint of fear in the butcher's eyes. He knew she meant business.

He lunged, a little off-kilter. Still, it was enough to knock April to the ground. He was on top of her, his face right in hers. He grabbed her by the neck and squeezed. April tried to swing the scissors at him, but he held her arms down. She couldn't move.

He squeezed tighter. April swung her arms wildly. It was no use. Even weakened, he was too strong. Her vision tunneled.

And then.

The butcher rolled off.

April's lungs seized, sucking oxygen back into her body. She sat up and rubbed her neck, still feeling the phantom hands of the butcher locked there. She saw him lying in front of her.

Dead.

April looked past the body. Grandma Rose lay slumped on the floor, a gun in her hands. The smell of gunpowder was still in the air.

"Joe gave it to me," she said.

Who's Joe? April wondered.

She felt Charlie's arms wrap around her from behind. She turned to hold him. They both were crying. "Shh, shh," April told him. "It's all over."

"But what about Dad?" Charlie asked between sobs.

April didn't say anything. She didn't have an answer yet.

She took out her cell phone and dialed 9-1-1. Grandma Rose needed help, even though she said she was fine. A gunshot wound and she says she's fine. Typical.

"What about Dad?"

April listened to Charlie ask the question again. The child had been traumatized beyond reason, and still he was thinking about someone other than himself. What a gem. What an amazing kid.

"You have to help Dad."

April heard the words and didn't quite know how to process them. She was still shaking. She looked at the dead body—no, *two* dead bodies—lying in the room. Their home had become a morgue.

She heard a siren in the distance. In moments the place would be swarming with police and EMTs.

"You have to go, Mom. Dad needs you."

April knew what she wanted to say. She wanted to explain that August didn't need her. That he never had and never would. That there was no way she could help him anyway. He was unhelpable. She opened her mouth and struggled for the words to say. She found nothing.

Flashing lights and sirens flooded the room.

"Go."

April stared at Charlie. He was a child. He couldn't possibly understand that she simply couldn't go.

"Go."

It was Grandma Rose.

"We'll be fine. Go."

April went.

She dashed through the kitchen, careful not to touch anything, not to even look at the horribleness there. She opened the back door and ran. She didn't even know where she was going at first.

She needed a car.

She ran through her own backyard and then through the backyard of the neighbor behind their house, out to the next street. She saw police cars and emergency vehicles streaming toward her house. Charlie and Grandma Rose would be well looked after.

She raced down the street, down one, two, three, four blocks to a small gas station. She stopped near the pay phone near the road and pretended to use it. A man driving a small black Honda pulled in. He got out and filled up, then went into the convenience store. Maybe he needed a coffee. Or a Snickers bar. April didn't see that he took his keys with him.

She hung up the phone and strolled over to the car. No one was watching. She looked in the driver's-side window and saw the keys lying on the seat. It was almost too easy. She opened the door, and the car alarm went off. She jumped into the car and started the engine. Who on earth would turn on their car alarm and then leave the keys in the car? It was entrapment! For a moment April felt a twinge of sympathy for the legions of car thieves who roamed the DC streets.

She gunned the car, watching in the rearview mirror as the owner came running out the door of the convenience mart. He was shaking his fists. And running. April pulled out of the parking lot, just about ramming the vehicle into a truck. It was almost a very short-lived chase.

But she made it, barely clearing the front bumper of the truck and spinning into the next lane. She pressed the accelerator to the floor, watching as the fist-shaking man became a pinprick in the distance.

She slowed down driving through town. How long would she have before the police would notice her? She felt the impact of what she had just done. She was a criminal. She could go to jail. Her hands began to shake on the wheel.

What was she going to do once she reached New York anyway?

August could walk off the plane, and she could be standing there, looking like a fool.

"What are you doing here?"

"Oh, just thought I'd steal a car and drive up here and make sure you're okay."

"Why?"

"Because Charlie asked me to."

April wished she'd had time to think about the situation. How had she acted so impulsively? Stealing a car? Driving to New York? The last time she'd done anything so rash was when she bought a pint of Häagen-Dazs at the grocery store, something she felt guilty about for weeks.

She almost hit the brakes. She couldn't *drive* to New York! What was she thinking?

The airport. She could fly.

She aimed the car at Dulles International Airport. She could ditch the car in short-term parking and make the 9:35 flight if she hurried.

It was barely a plan, but it was all she had.

D etective Jensen showed up late. He liked it that way, because instead of being one of the mindless drones digging through the senseless rubble of a crime scene, he walked in with a fresh per-spective and a clear vantage point.

"What do you got?" he asked the first investigator he spotted.

"Looks bad," the investigator said. The badge around his neck read *Wallace*. "Two dead bodies in the front, and one really dead body in the kitchen."

"*Really* dead? What do you mean by that?"

Wallace looked a little pale. "Go see for yourself."

Jensen walked over to the kitchen door and surveyed the scene.

Two investigators were carefully picking through the evidence, taking photographs, scribbling on their notepads. Jensen looked around the room again. He still hadn't stepped foot inside. "Where's the body?" he asked.

One of the investigators looked up from his notepad. "Here, here, here, here, and here," he said, pointing at various locations with his pen.

"Oh, man," Jensen said. "Any idea who it was?"

"Not yet," the investigator said. "It's going to take a while to put this back together. Most of the body has been melted."

"Melted?"

"Gone. Acidized. Killer knew what he was doing. Half an hour from now there wouldn't have been anything left," the investigator said.

"Is the killer still at large?"

"We don't think so," the investigator said. "If what the kid said is right, then the killer got shot by the grandma."

"Kid? Grandma?"

"You haven't talked to them yet?" the investigator asked.

"No. I just got here. Where are they?"

"Last I knew they were loading Grandma up in the ambulance. Shot in the leg and refused medical treatment. They finally convinced her to go, but on the condition that the kid went with her."

"I'll see if I can catch them," Jensen said. It was always better to get info at the crime scene than after witnesses had time to think about things. "Get me a full report right away."

"Will do," the investigator said, picking up a severed toe.

Jensen made his way to the door. "Found something interesting," Wallace said.

"Can it wait? I've got to catch the ambulance before it takes off."

"I'll walk with you."

"Fine," Jensen said. Wallace was obviously anxious to impress one of his superiors. They exited the house. There were flashing lights and a gathering of reporters. It was a mess. Half the neighborhood was standing outside the yellow police tape.

"Both of the bodies—the intact ones, I should say—had medallions around their necks," he said, scurrying along at Jensen's side.

"Medallions?"

"Yes. Really strange-looking ones. Here, I took a Polaroid of one." He stuck out the picture.

Jensen took it and held it at an angle to catch some of the streetlight. A large gold dragon, curled upon itself, held a double-armed crucifix in its sharp claws. The cross bore several words. Latin, from the looks of it. "Any idea what it means?"

"I'm glad you asked," Wallace said. "I looked it up. You see, my phone has an Internet connection, and I just had to—"

"What does it mean?"

"Um. Sorry. The words on the right side—oh, it's Latin, but the way—"

"I knew it was Latin."

"It means 'Oh, how merciful is God.' And the words on the left mean 'Just and Faithful.'"

Ahead of him, Jensen could see a woman being loaded into the ambulance. She seemed to be arguing with one of the EMTs. A boy—her grandson, he guessed—stood resolutely beside her. "So do you have any idea what the medallions mean?"

"Maybe."

"Maybe? Well, what is it?"

"It's just that . . . it seems a little weird."

"Weird? Weird is a body being split into a billion little pieces. We're way beyond weird, so tell me what you know."

"This is only the first thing I found. I could only do a quick, limited search with my—"

"Wallace!"

"Okay. Sorry. The medallions were worn hundreds of years ago by an organization called the Order of the Dragon."

"Sounds like a cult."

"It might be. But this is the weird part," Wallace said. He looked around and lowered his voice. "I'm pretty sure I've seen it before. On a couple of our men in the locker room. One of the guys tried to cover it up, but I'm certain that it was the same medallion. You don't see many guys wearing medallions these days, you know?"

"You've obviously never worked in New York," Jensen said. He put a hand on Wallace's shoulder. "Good job. Now put everything together in a nice, neat report, and hand it in to me by tomorrow morning. You hear me?"

"Yes."

"Good," Jensen said. They reached the ambulance. "Now let me do my job."

Wallace scampered away.

Jensen grabbed one of the EMTs and pulled him aside. "What's the deal with Grandma?"

"We finally got her to lie down. She was pretty wound up," the EMT said. "Not that I blame her, after what she's just been through."

"Heard she got shot."

"Yeah. The bullet went right through. Whoever pulled the trigger must have been a bad shot, missed anything vital."

"Is she on any sedatives?"

"No. Refused them."

"Maybe you should put her on something," Jensen said. "I've got to interrogate the kid, and I don't need her interfering."

"You're interrogating the kid now? Where? In the ambulance?"

"It's as good as anywhere. Speed is the key. We still don't know all the facts," Jensen said. "For all we know, there could still be a killer on the loose."

"I thought that—"

"Yeah, exactly. We *think* we know what's going on. Maybe we're wrong. The kid might give me new information. So can you juice the old lady?"

"Normally I'd say no," the EMT said. "But she needs it. She's been through a lot." He climbed inside the ambulance and began adjusting the IV attached to Grandma Rose. She started to complain but quickly settled down.

Jensen climbed in and sat down next to Charlie, who was wrapped in a blanket. He reached out and took Grandma Rose's hand. "Hello. I'm Detective Jensen. I'm here to find out more about what happened tonight."

Grandma Rose just blinked. She said something softly under her oxygen mask, but Jensen couldn't make it out.

"Is she okay?" Charlie asked.

"She's going to be just fine," Jensen said. He let go of Grandma and shook Charlie's hand. "I'm Detective Jensen."

"I'm Charlie," the boy said. "Are you a *real* detective?"

"Real as could be," Jensen responded. He pulled out his badge and handed it to Charlie.

The boy took the impressively heavy item in his hands and rubbed his fingers over it. "Awesome," he said.

"Can I ask you a couple questions?" Jensen asked.

"I'm not sure."

Another EMT jumped in and shut the back doors of the ambulance as the vehicle pulled away from the curb.

"I'm sure your grandma would say it was fine," Jensen said. He looked over to Grandma Rose, now sleeping. "But let's not bother her now. She needs to rest."

"It's been a hard night," Charlie said, sounding like he was parroting something he'd overheard.

"Yes. It looks like it has been," Jensen said. "Think you can talk about it?"

"I don't know."

"It would really help us in our investigation," Jensen said, placing special emphasis on the last word.

"You need my help?"

"Your help would be the best of all," Jensen said. "The biggest help would be to know if there is anyone else involved who wasn't at the house."

"You mean who wasn't dead?"

Jensen chuckled to hear Charlie put it so matter-of-factly. "I suppose, yes. I guess I mean did anyone leave before the police arrived?"

"I don't know."

"You don't know? I really could use a sharp mind to help me figure this mess out. Detective work takes remembering a lot of details. Things other people would miss," Jensen said. "For instance, I noticed that there were some footprints in the kitchen that were too small to be a man's. But the shoe type was different from the kind your grandma wears." He pointed to Grandma Rose's smooth-soled loafers.

"So whose foot was it?"

"I don't know," Jensen said. "But I bet you do."

"Huh," Charlie said, thinking. "I think I might remember."

"Really? You would make an excellent detective."

Charlie beamed. "I didn't want to say it before, but my mom was there for just a few minutes."

Jensen didn't know what he was expecting to hear, but this certainly wasn't it. "What was she doing there?" he asked.

"She helped us get away from Stanley," Charlie said.

"Who is Stanley?"

"The guy with the big cut in his neck. My grandma threw her scissors at him."

"Ouch," Jensen said. "Was Stanley trying to hurt you?"

"He was trying to kill us. He took Joe first. Then he came back to get us."

"Who's Joe?"

"He's the guy who tied us up. I tried to shoot him, but he shot Grandma Rose first. And then I had an asthma attack."

"Let's get back to the part about your mom," Jensen said, trying to make sense of everything. "Was she there the whole time?"

"No. Just at the end," Charlie said.

"So then where did she go?"

"Is she going to be in trouble?"

Jensen made sure his face oozed concern. "Only if you don't tell me where she went."

The ambulance rumbled down the road. The attention of the EMT crew was focused on Grandma Rose, whose vital signs were steady and stable. The driver said they were only a few minutes away from the hospital.

"I can only help you if you help me," Jensen said. "Where's your mom?"

Charlie sighed. "She went to go find my dad."

"Where is your dad?"

"On a plane."

"So she's going to the airport?"

"I guess."

"What's your dad's name?"

"August Adams."

Jensen nodded to indicate admiration. "I know that name," Jensen said. "I've seen him in a magazine, right?"

"He's kind of famous, I guess," Charlie said, shrugging.

Jensen got down from the seat and faced Charlie eye-to-eye. "I need to know the truth," he said in earnest. "Is your dad in some kind of trouble?"

"Can you help him?"

"I think we both can," Jensen said.

The ambulance stopped at the emergency entrance to George Washington University Medical Center. The doors opened, and two men carried Grandma Rose out the back, rolling her inside the hospital. "The boy is supposed to stay with her," one of the EMTs said.

"Change of plans," Jensen said. "I'm taking the boy."

"You sure that's okay?" the EMT asked.

Jensen shot him a look.

The EMT gave a thumbs-up and got back in the ambulance, which took off to aid another victim of the DC nightlife.

A black car pulled up into the ER driveway. Jensen approached it and opened the door, waving a hand to Charlie to step inside. "I've got a special treat," he said.

"What is it?"

"You ever meet a real FBI agent?" Jensen asked.

Charlie smiled and stepped in.

☩

Agent Meng got the call just before getting on the jet. They were bringing the boy to him to take to New York. "Wasn't Stanley supposed to get rid of him?" he asked Jensen.

"Stanley is dead."

"You're kidding," Meng said, truly surprised. "I have to be honest, I'm not exactly sad to hear the news. That guy was serial-killer material, if you ask me."

"He took his work seriously, that's all."

"So why don't you finish the job and get rid of the kid?"

"Because April got away too. She's headed for New York."

"So the boy is bait in case something goes wrong."

"I don't know. I'm only passing on what I've been told," Jensen said. "If you've got a problem, take it up with Cornelius."

Meng, in fact, did not want to do any such thing. Others who had made the mistake of crossing the Dragon Master tended to "disappear" not long after. "How long before you're here?"

"I can see you right now," Jensen said.

A minute later Meng watched a black car pull up beside the jet. Jensen hopped out and brought Charlie over to meet him.

"This is Agent Meng," Jensen said. "He's with the FBI."

"Cool," Charlie said, taking in the airplane. "You're going to take me to my dad?"

"I sure am," Meng said. "Have you ever been on a private jet?"

"Nope."

"Neither has Detective Jensen," Meng jabbed. Jensen shot him a frown. "C'mon, my man." Meng gave Charlie a hand up the steps.

"Have a good flight," Jensen said.

"What are you going to be up to while we're gone?" Meng asked after Charlie ducked inside.

"I have to keep an eye on the grandma," Jensen said. "I might have to pull the plug on her later."

"Grandma duty. Nice," Meng said, ascending the stairs. "You get all the good jobs." He chuckled.

"Hey, you're the one doing the babysitting."

Meng didn't bother responding. He had more important things to do than play verbal volleyball with wannabes like Jensen. He closed the door to the jet and walked over to Charlie, who was sitting in a leather recliner. On the table in front of the boy was the Gutenberg Bible Gomez had retrieved, which seemed almost to hum with energy.

"I know what that is," Charlie said. "My mom showed me one at the library."

"She did? You're quite a lucky kid, then. Most people go their whole lives without seeing anything like this," Meng said, sitting in the chair opposite the boy. He thumbed through the pages until he reached one of the illuminations that had been sent to Xandria.

"It's like a comic book!" Charlie said.

"Oh, it's much better than a comic book," Meng said, turning the book to face Charlie.

"You've obviously never read *Watchmen*," Charlie said.

"You've read *Watchmen*?"

"No," Charlie confessed. "But my dad gave me first editions of the original set that I can read when I'm sixteen, but only if I'm really, really careful and don't bend the corners of the pages."

"Does your dad force you to be so careful with all your books?"

"Pretty much. My mom too. She's an archaeobibliologist."

"A what?"

"Arch-ae-o-bib-liologist," he pronounced.

"That's a big word for a little kid."

"I know how to spell *lyceum* too," Charlie said. "L-Y-C-E-U-M."

"Great," Meng said, thinking he might have preferred grandma duty.

The jet engines fired up, and they shot down the runway. Within seconds they were airborne.

"So when you saw this book before, did your mom let you look in it?" Meng asked.

"No. I had to sit on a chair across the room. I couldn't even *breathe* on it."

Meng promptly picked up the book and set it on Charlie's lap. "Go ahead," he said. "Look at it all you want."

"Really?"

"No lie," Meng said. "And . . . oh, never mind. That might be too hard for you."

"What?"

"It's an FBI job. I don't think a kid could do it."

Charlie lit up like a firecracker. "I know I could do it! Please, please, please!"

"Okay. But I told you. It's a hard job."

"I can do it," Charlie said, his face marked with determination.

"Do you know what an illumination is?" Meng asked.

"Yeah. That's the picture part."

"So, if I told you three illuminations, three pictures, do you think you could find them?"

"No problem," Charlie said. "That's all?"

"And then, could you rip those pages out for me?"

Charlie opened his mouth wide, like he'd just been told that Santa Claus was real after all. "What? Are you crazy?"

Meng put his hands on the great book and began to lift it from Charlie's lap. "It's for a classified FBI project. I knew it would be too hard for a kid."

Charlie kept his hands on the book. "It's not too hard," he said. "But my parents would kill me."

"Your parents don't have to know," Meng said, letting the book fall back into Charlie's grip. He described the three illuminations and explained where they could be found.

"Are you sure this is okay?" Charlie said, finding the first illumination after a brief search.

Meng held his right hand up in an odd formation, a blend of Scout's honor and Vulcan salute. "Dragon's Oath," he said, taking the ripped page from Charlie's outstretched hand.

"What's that?" asked Charlie.

"I'll let Cornelius tell you," Meng said. He placed his hand on Charlie's head and tousled his hair like a coach might one of his star player's.

So much to learn.

He wondered if the kid would live long enough to fully understand.

illuminatednineteenilluminatedl

The passengers aboard Flight 1213 began to stir. People who had sat next to each other for hours in silence began to talk for the first time, knowing that the end of their flight would come inevitably soon, a safety net to save them from a verbose neighbor. August wished he'd never said a word to his traveling companion, as if that somehow could have prevented the avalanche from crashing upon him.

Xandria passed the laptop to August. "We land in an hour," she said.

The final images had arrived. "I'll have less than forty minutes before they shut me down," he said. He quickly jotted down the illumination labels on his notepad:

Seven—Knight in Green
   Cape with Sword
Eight—Ox with Banner
Nine—Creation

"Freaky knight, you're first up to bat," August said, taking full view of the seventh illumination from the book of Maccabees. "You won't see this one in today's Bibles," he murmured. The image started with a red initial *E* at its center. As with most of the others, the initial was curved, encircling the figure trapped inside: a knight, dressed in thick blue armor and draped in a green cape. The knight held a long sword in his right hand. His left hand rose, palm open, to heaven.

"Doesn't look like a nice fellow," Xandria said.

"No, he's not," August said, recognizing the face in the illumination, with its flowing brown hair and penetrating eyes. "Take away the beard, leave the mustache, and I think you'll know who this is: the father of Dracula. This is most definitely Vlad II Dracul."

"But the cape is wrong," Xandria said. "It should be black and red, right?"

"You watch too many movies," August said. "Vlad III really confused the history of his father. *Dracula* literally means 'son of Dracul,' which has been wrongly translated as 'son of the devil.' *Dracul*, the title Vlad II was given, means 'dragon' in the Romanian language, not 'devil.' The name was given to him when he joined Emperor Sigismund's nobility."

"And the cape?"

"The color of the draconist's cloak was in fact green, as is depicted in the illumination, not black as most people have come to believe," August said. "But black looks much more sinister on the movie screen, I must admit."

"Let me guess why you know so much about this," Xandria said.

"I sold an Archibald Constable and Company mustard-yellow-with-red-lettering 1897 first edition of Bram Stoker's *Dracula* for twenty-five thousand dollars. My dad bought it back in the fifties for less than five hundred. What a bargain! He couldn't have known that only a few decades later a Dracula-boom would occur. But lucky for me, it did," August said. "The fascinating thing was the history behind the story, which in many ways is far more horrific than the fairy-tale version."

Xandria smiled almost imperceptibly. "How so?"

"For one, though the real Dracula is best known for the torture and amputations he inflicted on others, he was a tortured person himself. When he was only eleven years old, he was taken hostage by a sultan and held captive in Turkey. His gruesome stay ended only after his father was killed. By the time he returned to his home-land, he had become—to put it lightly—a world-class sadist."

"That's when the impaling started?"

"Correct. His first act after taking back his father's throne was to gain some revenge against his captors. On Easter Sunday, he invited his father's assailants to a great feast. They thought he was trying to mend fences. They were wrong."

"What happened?"

"He had the older ones impaled immediately."

"Naturally."

"But they were lucky. The rest were forced on a fifty-mile hike to the capital city of Poenari. Many didn't survive. Those who did were ordered to build Dracula an incredible fortress, known today as Castle Dracula."

"Sounds evil."

"Spooky, evil, all of the above," August said. "This illumination might indicate that we're dealing with something equally wicked."

Xandria's attention shifted back to the image of the green-caped knight. "So we've got Dracula's father in his ceremonious Order of the Dragon attire. And is he saluting?"

"Definitely not," August said. "For two reasons: First, he has his left hand raised. He should be saluting with his right hand, which was called the *weapon hand*. Second, even if it were a rare left-hand salute, the sword should be lowered. This sword stands high and ready for battle."

"What does it mean?"

"His left hand is in a position that suggests he's offering something. Combined with the sword, it could mean that he's offering something for battle. Or in exchange for a battle," August said, thinking aloud. "Say the Order of the Dragon has something—a secret, or a treasure—something they hold in exchange for war? It's like Vlad Dracul is saying, 'Choose one, the sword or the secret.'"

"I'll take the secret."

"Me too. And hopefully the next two images will tell us the rest of the story."

He shuffled the images on the screen, bringing into view the next illumination. The ox was set in the lower outpost of the initial *L*, which was rendered mostly in ruby- and rose-reds and blossomed with emerald- and sapphire-colored vines. The ox itself was portrayed in a warm chocolate, decorated with two ivory horns atop its head. Most curious was the banner emblazoned with a Latin word, *lumen,* which the ox pinned down with its left hoof.

"The ox was the symbol for Saint Luke," August said.

"The four evangelists had symbols?"

"Yes," August said. "Saint Matthew was represented by a man, because his book starts with Jesus' genealogy and, therefore, his place in human history. Saint Mark was represented by a lion, which corresponded with Jesus' kingship. Saint John was represented by an eagle, which we saw earlier, signifying the lofty nature of his poetic story of Jesus. And Saint Luke, which we see here, was represented by the ox, a symbol—almost universally—for sacrifice," August said.

"It sounds like there's nothing too odd about the ox, if it's in keeping with the usual symbolism for Saint Luke."

August tapped his finger on the screen. "No," he said. "There's one thing that's off here."

"What?"

"The reason the gospel writers were represented by a man, a lion, an eagle, and an ox was because of a passage from the book of Revelation," August said. "Let me read you something from the Gutenberg."

Xandria retrieved the great book and handed it to him.

August flew through the pages to the last book, the Apocalypse of Saint John. He turned to chapter 4 and read the words to his audience of one. "*Et in conspectu sedis tamquam mare vitreum simile cristallo et in medio sedis et in circuitu sedis quattuor animalia plena oculis ante et retro. Et animal primum simile leoni et secundum animal simile vitulo et tertium animal habens faciem quasi hominis et quartum animal simile aquilae volanti.*"

Xandria tapped a foot. "You have about twenty minutes left."

"I'm actually surprised at how easily this is coming to me," August said. "My dad forced me to take Latin as a kid. He called it 'resurrection class,' because . . . you know . . ."

"Nineteen minutes."

"It means, roughly, 'And in the sight of the throne was a sea of glass. And around the throne were four living creatures, full of eyes. And the first living creature was like a lion, and the second living creature like an ox, and the third living creature had the face of a man, and the fourth living creature was like an eagle.'"

"Fascinating. And we are right back to where we started."

"Right. But here's the important part, in the next verse. 'And each of the four living creatures had six wings, and they were full of eyes.'"

"Lots of eyes, these creatures."

"Plenty. But it's not the eyes I'm concerned with. Look at the ox in the Gutenberg."

Xandria looked. "No wings. Imagine that."

"No wings," August echoed. "Without the wings, you just have a regular old ox."

"Meaning?"

"That perhaps this isn't a symbol for Saint Luke," August said. "Thaon's *Bestiaire* said that the ox was a predictor of weather. Combine that with the Latin word on the banner . . ."

"*Lumen*," Xandria read.

". . . meaning 'light.' This could mean that the ox sees light ahead. The answer to the riddle, maybe?"

"You don't think the symbolism of the saint means anything?"

August shrugged. "Maybe it suggests that the answer won't be achieved without sacrifice."

Xandria let her head drop back against the headrest. "We've all sacrificed," she said.

"Some more than others," August responded.

"You're still alive," Xandria said.

"For now," August said. "We'll see how Leo Kahn feels about that." He shifted the images on the computer screen to display the ninth illumination, a portrayal of the creation story from Genesis. It was by far the most unusual and elaborate illumination he had ever seen.

"Sir?" It was Janice.

"Yes?"

"We need you to turn off all electronic equipment."

"Give me one minute."

"Sir, I'm sorry, but I really need you to—"

"Please," August said. "Just give me a minute. Make your rounds, and by the next time you walk by I'll have it off. I swear."

"I'll be back *soon*," she said.

"Not a problem."

"I don't need a problem."

"And I won't be one," August said.

Janice kept on walking.

August stared at the illumination, committing it fully to memory in case Janice made a quick return and shut him down. The image was composed of three main parts: higher vines and birds, lower vines and birds, and a giant letter *I*. The vines seemed ornamental, as did the birds, except for a large one in the lower right-hand corner, a peacock. "This," he said, pointing to the vibrant bird, "was a symbol for immortality."

"Not pride?"

"That came later," August said. "The peacock is an ancient bird, as are the myths that have followed it. Long ago, it was thought that every time the peacock awoke, it cried out in fear, because it dreamed that it had lost its beauty."

"Sounds like pride to me." Xandria picked up August's pad and began to review his notes.

August studied the initial *I*, which stood like a colossal pillar on the electronic image of the Gutenberg page. Inside the pillar of the *I* were four distinct sections: on the bottom, the Garden of Eden with its antediluvian occupants, Adam and Eve; next, an ocean, brimming with life; growing from that, a forest full of four-legged creatures, big and small; and finally, a wise, old man, his face beaming with its own inner light.

"There's so much," August said to himself, trying to figure out where to start. He chose Adam and Eve. The image was typical: they were naked and unashamed, a pre-Fall representation. The two wildlife settings didn't provide much more. The fish were in a classic motif. The wildlife frolicking in the forest gave August some hope, but nothing seemed to jump out at him. "Why am I not seeing it?"

"Maybe you're looking too hard," Xandria offered, setting down the notepad.

August put his hands up by the sides of his head, creating a set of blinders. He focused. He focused hard. Nothing.

"I was serious," Xandria said. "Let your subconscious do the leap, not your mind. You'll never find it if you keep looking directly at it."

"Please don't distract me. I'm trying to—"

The world evaporated. August lost himself in the illumination. He was in the forest with the animals, mucking about in the damp soil,

wet with weeds and moss. He stood
next to the deer, next to the
leader, the buck. But what did
they call it back then? A hart.
This was a hart. The hart of
the story. He counted the
points on the hart's antlers.
There were seven, an important symbolic number. It meant
perfection. This was a perfect hart.

August looked deeper, stretched further. The hart was concerned. Why? August followed the hart's eyes to its cavorting young
only a short distance away. But the distance was significant, because
something was between them. A wolf.

"*Physiologus*," August said.

"Excuse me?"

"There was a book called the *Physiologus*, similar to the *Bestiaire*.
Back when I was an archaeobibliologist, we used it like a reference
book. The *Physiologus* was the ancient church's symbology standard.
It made repeated mention of the hart."

"Heart?"

"H-A-R-T. Hart. A deer. Or a stag, really. In the image second
from the top, you'll see the hart, anxious about this wolf that sepa-
rates him from his children."

"Nature isn't pretty, is it?"

"The *Physiologus* mentioned an enemy of the hart. In fact, both
animals were enemies of each other. When the hart saw its enemy,
it retreated to the stream. And when the enemy saw the hart, it
turned to its hiding place high above in the rocks."

"You mean the wolf?"

August smiled. The connection was right there. And he'd almost missed it. "No," he said. "The enemy of the hart was the dragon."

Xandria shivered. "But what about the wolf?"

"The wolf is not the true enemy," August said. "I think the wolf represents the idea that evil will lurk in the craftiest of ways. The wolf was sly, an enemy to both the hart and the dragon."

Janice came back. She was frowning.

"Done!" August said, shutting the laptop off. He shot his best grin and waited for Janice to huff and move on.

"Time's up," Xandria said. She handed August the Gutenberg Bible. "You did an amazing job. No one has been able to dig underneath the illuminations like that."

"Glad to hear you say it, because now you can call your goons off my family," August said.

"As soon as we land."

"Call now."

"No electronic devices while landing," Xandria said. "You'll just have to wait."

August knew she was right. He shuffled back through his notes, reading through the nine images:

> One—Two White Dogs Chasing Fox and Hare
>
> Two—King with Golden Globe
>
> Three—Split-Bearded Man with Sword
>
> Four—Blue Man and Swan
>
> Five—Eagle with Banner
>
> Six—The Lions' Den
>
> Seven—Knight in Green Cape with Sword

Eight—Ox with Banner

Nine—Creation

He shook his head. "It still doesn't add up to me."

"It's like I said before," Xandria said. "You think too hard. You don't understand what to do with what you've seen."

August struggled to understand. "You said there was a tenth image, and I'm guessing that's the string that ties everything together. So what is it?"

Over the loudspeaker, the pilot announced they would be landing in just a few moments. He apologized again for the weather, making some joke about his control over it, or lack thereof. No one seemed very amused.

"The tenth image?" August inquired again.

"After we land," Xandria said. The lights flickered overhead as the cabin trembled. "That is, if we don't crash first."

◊illuminated**twenty**illuminated◊

April pleaded her case once more to the woman behind the ticket counter. *Brandy,* her tag said. She could tell the smile Brandy wore was beginning to wear thin.

"Ma'am, that flight leaves in thirty minutes. You won't even make it through security."

"You don't understand," April said. "This is a matter of life and death. Literally life and death."

"Overreacting isn't going to make me help you," Brandy said, scolding with a teacher's tone.

"I'm not overreacting," April said, her fuse an inch from detonating emotional dynamite.

Brandy punched some keys, stared at her screen, then repeated the process in silence.

"What are you doing? Are you looking for a seat?"

Brandy looked up. Her face said, *Do you mind?*

"I'm sorry," April said. "I'm just . . . it's really important."

"There's nothing," Brandy said, shaking her head at the computer screen. "Not. A. Thing."

"I could fly standby, right?"

"Yes, but it's the end of the day, and I've already got about ten people waiting before you to get on the next flight to New York."

"Ten?"

"There were some delays earlier," Brandy explained. "But I will put you on standby if that will get you to move out of my area. There are lots of other customers with extremely important life-or-death trips."

April nodded an emphatic yes. She was groveling at the feet of the aviation queen, and no amount of slighting was going to prevent her from getting on that plane to New York. She took her ticket and rounded the corner. Stopped. The security line was incredibly long. How could that be? Hadn't most people already made their flights? How could there be this many people still needing to fly?

"It's a bear," a tiny grandma at the back of the line said to April. "I swear, sometimes I'm not sure it's worth it. But then I see those grandkids. I've got four of them. Joshie is five, and he's the most adorable—"

"I'm so sorry," April said. She felt horrible for cutting off this sweet old woman. "My mind is spinning a little. Is this really the end of the line?"

"I'm afraid it is."

"I've got a flight in"—she checked her watch—"oh, I'm never going to make it."

The grandma scooted over. "Why don't you get in front of me? Would that help?"

There were about a hundred people in front of her. It was a generous offer, but it wouldn't make any difference. "That's okay," April said. She stood, paralyzed.

"Why don't you just walk up to the front?" the grandma suggested. "I'm sure once they hear the reason you're in such a hurry, they'll understand."

"I don't think so," April said. She'd heard horror stories about people butting in line.

The woman lifted her heels off the ground and leaned in to meet April's eyes. "It's for your family, isn't it? I can tell."

April felt moisture develop under her eyelids. "Yes."

"Then just do it! You'll never see any of these people for the rest of your life! So who cares if you offend them? You go around this world trying not to offend people, and you'll never get anything done."

April's heart sped up. She felt her hands get a bit sweaty, the same way they did every time she gave a lecture at the Library of Congress. But she always went through with it. Somehow, she never backed down. "Thank you," April said, leaning down and giving her a quick peck on the cheek.

"Go get 'em," the grandma whispered, giving a swinging punch in the air.

In some strange way, the outburst was exactly what she needed. She strode confidently past the line of people, whose faces, if April had stopped to look at them, all bore the same curious expression. *She wouldn't dare, would she?*

April did dare. She reached the front of the line, where a guy in his forties—gray suit, all business, talking loudly on his cell phone—was putting on a sideshow for everyone.

"Yeah, yeah, yeah," he said. "Well, you can tell Jack that if he comes in with anything short of *three million dollars*, then he can forget it!"

"Excuse me."

"What?! Jack said that?! Well he's just an idiot, now, isn't he?"

"Sorry, sir, excuse me."

"Hang on, I've got someone bothering me," the dealmaker grumbled. "What?" he asked April, hand over the mouthpiece of his cell phone.

"I know this seems a bit unorthodox, but I wondered—"

"Can I see your badge?" the dealmaker asked.

"Badge? I don't have a badge."

"Then you can get back in line," he said, returning to his call.

April began to hear the jeers, which she had managed to block out until the dealmaker ruptured her bubble of confidence.

Get back in line!

The nerve!

We all have to wait, lady!

You better be the president of an airline!

A hundred pairs of bothered eyes bored into April. She could feel herself shrinking, wanting to become invisible. She'd made a huge mistake.

And then there was the tiny little grandma, an ant from April's vantage point, a speck of a dot, swinging her arm like a prizefighter. *Don't give up now!*

April grabbed the arm of the dealmaker.

"What do you think you're doing?" he said, trying to wrench his arm away.

April wrapped her hand around his tie and pulled his face down to meet hers. "Listen, buddy, I've had a really bad night. A really bad night! Worse than you could ever know. So unless you want to tick me off—and let me tell you, you don't—then let me get in line!"

The dealmaker smiled, delicately slipping his silk tie out of April's fingers. He placed his palm on her shoulder and pushed her away. "Go back home, Mommy," he said with a chuckle.

Something in April's mind snapped. She yanked the cell phone out of his hand and flung it down the hallway, watching it skip like a flat rock across the shiny floor.

"Unbelievable!" the dealmaker said, throwing his arms in the air and racing after his beloved appendage. "Would someone call the cops on this lady?!"

"Do it yourself," said the woman standing behind him in line. She wore soft curls in her hair and barely a shadow of makeup. She turned to April. "Hard day, dear?"

"The hardest," April said, stepping in line and slipping off her shoes. She tossed them into a bucket with her messenger bag. No one objected.

"That guy was a jerk," said the woman in curls. "Am I right?" she asked the other people in line.

Yes, they all agreed. *Certifiable jerk.*

"Thank you, thank you, thank you," April said to everyone.

"Just keep it moving," said a security guard, his hand held out to accept her identification and boarding pass.

April handed the information to him, then grabbed her shoes

and bag off the belt as soon as they were within her reach. She sprinted toward the gate in her socks and checked the departure board. The flight she needed was listed as *on time: boarding.* There was still hope. But not much.

Arriving at the gate, she could see that most of the people had already boarded the aircraft. She raced up to the empty counter, where a pleasant young woman was stationed.

"Can I help you?" she asked.

"I need to get on that plane," April said.

"I don't think there's going to be enough space for you," came the sad reply. "But we can try!"

April propped her elbow on the counter and leaned her forehead against her fingers. "That means I'm not getting on."

"Probably not," the woman said. She pointed to a group of people standing a few yards away. "They're all waiting to get on too. A few of them have been here since early this morning."

"Thanks," April said to her. She turned and walked over to join the group. They all looked tired, and a bit desperate. April knew what they were feeling—she'd once spent two long days trapped in Chicago's O'Hare airport during a blizzard.

"Four of us aren't getting on," a pudgy member of the group said. He wore a Hawaiian shirt and looked a little sun-fried. "I counted everyone that walked onto the plane. There are eleven of us—counting you—and only seven spaces."

"So why are the rest of you waiting?"

"I guess, just in case a miracle happens," a woman in the group said. She held a picture of her kids in her hands. There were dark circles under her eyes. She'd had enough. She wanted to be home. "You never want to give up hope."

"I know what you mean," April said, watching as the last few stragglers spilled from the gate into the Jetway.

A voice began calling names over a loudspeaker, and one by one the group diminished. Hope felt like sand running through April's fingers. "Wait," she said. "I have to get on that plane."

"Your story can't be any worse than the rest of ours," a man said. He left quickly, hearing his name called.

"No! You don't understand!"

The woman holding the picture put a hand on April's shoulder. "I have a son with leukemia. I've been here all day, and I mean, *all day*. My family needs me, and I need them," she said. "Is your situation worse?"

April tried to weigh the words in her mind. But how could she? Of course this woman needed to go home! April shook her head.

The last name was called. The happy recipient of the invitation skipped—literally skipped—to the gate, waving as he departed.

"Sorry," the woman at the counter said, leaving her post.

April was stunned. "I didn't make it," she said to the woman with the picture.

"It'll all work out," the woman said, biting her lip.

April watched as she walked away. She waited for a minute, waited for a miracle. And then she began the slow journey to the exit. She cringed, thinking about seeing the people she'd passed in line. They would laugh, say something about karma or universal justice. They'd be glad to see that she had failed.

She was almost halfway down the airport corridor when she heard a voice call out behind her. She spun around. Was someone calling her name?

"April Adams?"

"Yes?"

It was the woman from the gate. "Can't believe I found you! I thought you'd probably already be gone!"

"What's going on?"

"Something happened," the woman said, a little out of breath. "Follow me. I'll explain at the gate."

☩

April boarded the plane, beaming. She really didn't know why. She had no reason to be happy. She was flying directly into a maelstrom, but just getting on the plane felt like the accomplishment of a lifetime.

Everyone from the standby list was aboard the aircraft, including the woman with the photograph, who was especially ecstatic. "I guess we got that miracle," April said to her, stopping for a brief second on the way to the back row.

"Who knew the Boy Scouts would come to the rescue?" she said.

April laughed, having just heard the story of how their seats were vacated. The leader of a Boy Scout troop discovered that they were one member short. "Where's Henry McManus?" he asked his boys. No one knew. And then Travis Wilmore—an Eagle Scout—raised his hand. "He might have gone to get something from McDonald's to take on the plane." The Scout leader was livid. "What? That line was a mile long!" he said. He reported the missing member to a flight attendant, but even after several announcements over the airport intercom system, Mr. McManus could not be found.

"C'mon, boys!" said the leader. "A troop never leaves a member behind!"

"This one does!" said Eagle Scout Wilmore. The Scout leader promptly tore a merit badge from the astonished boy's shirt. He then proceeded to march out of the plane, his entire troop behind him, including the emasculated Eagle Scout.

"I wonder if they give merit badges for snarfing french fries," the man in the Hawaiian shirt said as April sat down across from him.

April smiled. But her mind had wandered. She took out her cell phone, seeing that she still had a couple minutes before she'd be forced to put it away. She dialed information.

A woman at the hospital answered. April inquired whether her mother had been admitted as a patient there and was transferred to a nurse. Yes, came the reply. The nurse described how difficult Rose had already made life for the nurses on her floor. *That would be my mother,* thought April. Do you need to speak with her? No need, April said. She just wanted to make sure Rose was okay.

Feeling secure that her mother and therefore Charlie were in the safe haven of the medical establishment, April dialed information again, this time getting the number for Dr. Winter's hospital. She punched in the number.

"Hi. I'm trying to reach a patient. Last name Winter?"

The operator connected her, and a nurse answered his room extension.

"We're prepping Dr. Winter for surgery. You'll have to call back."

"Oh, please. This is his . . . um . . . *sister* . . . and I really need to speak with him."

"Sister? What's your name?"

April had a brief loss of functionality before coming up with a name. "Wanda," she said. "Wanda Winter." She slapped her forehead. She sounded like a character from a Roald Dahl book.

"Wanda Winter, huh?" The nurse covered the receiver and said something to her patient. After a pause, April heard Dr. Winter's voice.

"So good to hear from my dear beloved sister! I thought you were dead!"

April felt even more stupid. "I'm so sorry."

"Don't be. I never talked much about my family at the library. Not like you, anyway."

"How are you doing?" April asked, redirecting the conversation.

"I won't be playing tennis anytime soon," Dr. Winter said. "But the doctors seem to think I'll be all right. Where are you?"

"I'm at the airport," she said. "I'm going to help August."

"Oh, my dear girl," Dr. Winter said without endearment, like something he'd say after hitting a dog with his car. "What are you planning on doing?"

"I don't have a plan."

"Sounds like you have everything under control."

"This isn't about control," April said. "This is about doing the right thing. But you wouldn't know much about that, would you?"

"Is this why you've called?" Dr. Winter asked. "Because I needed another beating?"

"No," April said. "I think you're severely screwed up in the head, but I also believe you hate the Order of the Dragon as much as I do. So I need your help."

"With what?"

"With . . . I don't know . . . *anything*! I feel like I'm deliberately walking into a furnace!" April said. "I guess I just want some fireproofing."

"Tolkien wrote, 'It does not do to leave a live dragon out of your calculations.' You need to know what you're getting into, April."

"What am I getting into?"

"Did you ever read *The Hobbit?*"

"Yes. Charlie and I read it together a few years ago."

"Do you remember the part when Bilbo sneaks into the dragon's lair? Do you remember how frightened he was?"

"Sort of."

"Why was he frightened?"

"I guess because he knew that the dragon could crush him with one blow. Or sneeze and roast him to death."

"Exactly. Bilbo understood the power of the dragon," Dr. Winter said. "Do you understand the power of *your* dragon?"

April thought through the question. It was classic Winter. Non-direct. Specifically nonspecific. "I know the Order is extremely dangerous," she said.

Dr. Winter laughed. "I'm not talking about the Order," he said.

"I don't understand," April said. "What else could you be talking about?"

"Your pretending not to know tells me that your dragon is still very much alive," Dr. Winter said. "Use the time you have to search your soul. Because just like Bilbo, your dragon will have to be slain before the treasure can be reclaimed."

"Dr. Winter, I—"

"I'm sorry, but I'm going to have to let you go. The nurse has just walked in with a healthy dose of Percocet, and I'm not going to say no to another round!" He hung up.

April wished she hadn't called him. Talking to Dr. Winter was the verbal equivalent of being a cat who chased a beam of light on a wall: all flashes of brilliance, but no tangible substance.

She put away her cell phone and closed her eyes, listening as the engines roared and they sailed down the runway and up into the stars. She drifted off for a moment, sensing the need for some rest before she reached the mayhem that surely awaited.

But in the darkness of her restless slumber she saw two yellow eyes staring at her. They began as pinpricks but steadily grew until they engulfed the full range of her inner vision.

This was the dragon Dr. Winter had spoken of, not a dragon of flesh and blood, but the breed that had quietly crept into the catacombs of her heart.

She felt the fire of the dragon's tongue, smelled the malice of his breath. And then, quite unexpectedly, she understood the beast's true nature. She knew the dragon's name.

Fear.

twenty-one

Charlie bounded down the steps from the plane. "I've never been in a limo before," he said, eyes widening as he watched a black stretch pull up, its side door opening to greet him.

"Today's your lucky day," Meng said, following close behind. Charlie climbed in and immediately began poking around every square inch of the vehicle. "Is there a TV in here?" he asked.

"Afraid not," Meng said. "But don't worry, I've got plenty of things we need to talk about."

"FBI things?"

"Something like that," Meng said.

Charlie answered what seemed to him like an endless barrage

of questions from the agent. *This is very helpful to my investigation,* Meng reminded him. Charlie smiled. He felt like a real superspy, not just the kind he pretended to be at home.

It wasn't long before they drove into a featureless warehouse district. "Where are we?"

"In a secret FBI location," Meng said.

"Cool!" The limo pulled in front of one of the warehouses, and they jumped out. Two agents met them at the warehouse door. Meng flashed them a look, and they entered.

"Follow me," Meng said. Charlie didn't question the order, trailing behind Meng to a boxlike room set up in the middle of the cavernous storehouse. Meng opened the door to the room and pointed to a chair. "Take a seat," he said.

Charlie sat. "What do we do now?" he asked.

Meng pulled up a chair next to him. "We wait for Cornelius," he said. Charlie didn't bother asking who Cornelius was. Just the way Meng said his name let him know that he was someone important.

✠

Charlie watched as the man walked in. Slender but solid. Strong cheekbones. Charlie knew that was good. He'd heard his mom say it once. He wore a suit. Black. Black shirt. Black tie. Charlie figured he was older than his dad. His hair was silver, but he didn't look too old. Maybe a premature graying. He'd heard Grandma Rose talk about that.

"Charlie . . . or should I call you *Chuck* or *Charles*?" the man asked. "I don't want to assume."

"Charlie is fine."

"Charlie, my name is Cornelius. It's nice to meet you." He turned to Meng. "Would you mind leaving us for a while?"

Meng let himself out without a word.

"I trust that Agent Meng treated you well?"

Charlie nodded. "He was nice."

"That's a good way to put it," Cornelius said. "Agent Meng is what we draconists call a salamander—a slimy, disgusting waste of God's good dirt that only is good for the smallest of errands, the tiniest of tasks."

"Did you say *dragonist?*"

"*Draconist,*" Cornelius corrected. "A member of the Order of the Dragon."

"I thought you were with the FBI."

"Agent Meng is with the FBI. And there are many departments of the government—both here and abroad—that contain people from our membership. I, however, have no time for such petty organizations. You're so young, you have no idea how hard it is to get anything done in this world."

Charlie sank in his chair.

"I'm sorry," Cornelius said. "Does it frighten you to hear that I'm a draconist?"

Charlie nodded.

"I heard that one of our men visited you at your house. It sounds like he made quite a mess. Please accept my sincerest apology. I can tell you that he acted against my direct orders," Cornelius said. "He was sent to *save* you, not hurt you."

Charlie stared into his eyes. He still hadn't seen Cornelius blink. "Really?"

"Cross my heart," Cornelius said, doing so with his long forefinger.

"But let's move on. You can't change the past, but you *can* change the future," he said, drumming the words out to a full march.

Charlie perked up. "That's true."

"I'm so glad you agree. So. The future." Cornelius stood and flipped a switch on the wall. The table in the middle of the room lit up, the entire top becoming a pool of white light. He left the room, a second later returning with the three pages Charlie had ripped out of the Gutenberg. He placed them side by side on the table in front of Charlie. "I was told you tore these out."

"I did," Charlie said with caution, not sure if he was accepting blame or praise.

"Excellent job," Cornelius said.

Charlie breathed a sigh of relief.

"Agent Meng probably would have made a mess of these pages. But not you. You respect the book."

"My mom won't think so," Charlie said. "She's going to kill me."

"Your mother will do no such thing. I can assure you of that," Cornelius said. "How could she be mad at you for something she's done herself?"

Charlie cocked his head to the side, puzzled. "My mom would never ever rip pages out of the Gutenberg. She'd rather be eaten by wolves."

Cornelius straightened the pile on the table, aligning it just so. "Wolves? How about dragons?" he asked. He leaned down and whispered in Charlie's ear. "Listen to the truth: before this night is over, your mother will rip three pages out of the Gutenberg. And she'll do it because the life of someone she loves dearly will be in danger."

Charlie said nothing, sitting still. Suddenly he leaped toward the door. His chair clattered to the floor, tripping Cornelius, who clawed at the air. "Come back here!" he said.

Charlie threw open the door and ran out into a wide warehouse. Five men in black suits were there, waiting. Charlie skidded to a stop. The men stood like an impenetrable wall.

"Going somewhere?" Cornelius wrapped his icy hands around Charlie's neck.

"Please don't hurt me."

"Hurt you? I would never hurt you," Cornelius said, dragging the boy back into the room and forcing him into his chair. "In fact, I have a *gift* for you." He pulled something from his jacket pocket. A syringe. Without warning, he plunged it into Charlie's neck.

Charlie screamed.

The needle slid out. Charlie touched his neck, and his finger came away with a small circle of blood on it. "You've been injected with a digital sensor. If you try to escape this room, the only thing left of this warehouse will be a smoking hole in the earth."

✙

Cornelius strode across the warehouse floor, the other men leaving a visible distance between themselves and the Dragon Master. The legends of Cornelius's cruelty were well known in each division of the Order: in Russia, for disemboweling a Mafia boss; in Australia, for having a priest devoured by pigs; in Brazil, for setting a mother on fire in front of her daughter. All in the name of a holy crusade. Some members of the Order questioned the purpose of the crusade, whether the treasure they sought really existed at all. These doubting Thomases were extinguished without question. Other members held fast to the Doctrine of the Dragon, as Cornelius called it. These believers moved up quickly through the ranks.

Agent Meng was such a believer, and although Cornelius despised the agent's hands-off approach—Meng always delegated any lethal tasks to his underlings—the Dragon Master couldn't deny his loyalty.

"I need you to do something for me," Cornelius said, exiting the warehouse. Meng was waiting dutifully right outside the door.

"I have Garcia ready if you need to dispatch the kid."

"No," Cornelius said, Meng's sleight of hand all too obvious. "I need you to go to the airport."

"I thought Xandria was bringing August."

"She is. I want you to bring me April."

"She made it here? I can't believe it."

"She's proving to be a difficult assignment for you," Cornelius said. "Consider this your opportunity to redeem your position."

Meng walked over to the waiting limo. "I won't fail you, sir."

"Good," Cornelius said. "And please stop calling me *sir*. *Master* will suffice."

☩

Meng flashed his badge, bypassing security, and walked down the concourse toward the gate where April would be arriving. He checked his watch. Twenty minutes.

Coffee. Coffee would be good. Coffee would be amazing. He was already beat, and this long day wasn't over yet. He needed something to wake him up, keep him sharp. He got in the line at Starbucks. It was a few people deeper than he was hoping. He wanted to be at the gate fifteen minutes early. Ten minutes would have to suffice. The girl in front of him finally got to the register. She had a large order, she said, pulling out a notebook. Meng looked at the time. Another minute and he would have to bail.

Six Frappuccinos later, Meng ordered. A coffee. Just coffee. Nothing fancy. Just the strong stuff. He took a sip—nearly scorching his lips—and stole a glace at the time as he jogged toward the gate. He was cutting it close. But he should be fine.

Meng reached the gate and looked around. No one was there. Shouldn't there be people getting ready for the plane to arrive?

"Delayed," a business traveler said, seeing the confused expression on his face.

"Thanks," Meng said, his heart recovering. "How long is the delay?"

"An hour." The businessman returned to his *Wall Street Journal.*

Meng sipped gingerly at the piping-hot brew—he really had burned his lips, hadn't he?—and considered his next move. Should he call Cornelius? Definitely not. Buy a magazine? Go back to Starbucks for a sandwich? He hated idle time, hated not knowing exactly what he should do next.

He walked over to the arrival/departure board and checked April's flight. ARRIVED, it said. Meng drank deeply from his paper cup, burning the entire length of his throat. He swore, but not from the pain. He didn't even feel the pain. He raced back to the gate.

"You said the flight was delayed!" Meng scolded the businessman, pulling down the newspaper to expose his guilty face.

"It is!" the businessman said, infuriated.

"The flight from DC?"

"No, the flight *to* Miami!"

Meng nearly threw his coffee in the businessman's face. Sheer panic prevented him. He ran back to the arrival/departure board and checked the gate number for April's flight. It had been changed. When? When had it been changed? Why did they do things like that without warning?

He paced, a tiger in a cage. She could have just walked right by him, while he was in line, for what? Coffee? He slammed his cup into a trash can, which was full. The cup didn't make it past the lid, broke open, and splashed him on the chest.

He was losing it.

Lost it.

Yelled.

Screamed like a five-year-old.

He couldn't help it. He was boiling like a teapot, and the steam had to come out.

And then he saw her.

He couldn't believe it.

He saw her.

His fit of anger made her turn around, far down the hallway, but it was her, it was unquestionably her. But where was she going? The exit was in the other direction.

She turned. Kept walking. Meng couldn't tell whether she'd seen him or not. Probably not. She was a librarian, not an agent. She wasn't trained to note a face, to stay alert at all times, on the watch, on the prowl.

He ran after her. Not jogged, ran. Sprinted. Full speed. Cornelius had made the importance, the utter consequential magnitude of delivering April to him quite clear.

"FBI," Meng said, knocking over a little girl, who clung to her father's hand for dear life.

"Watch it, buddy!"

"F! B! I!" Meng shot back. It was simpler than an apology. The crowd ahead began splitting apart, seeing the crazed man with the badge held out like the headlight on a train.

April saw him. She was running now too. And she was surprisingly fast. But Meng knew where she was going. He pulled out his phone.

"Where are you?" Meng jumped out of the way of a concourse golf cart.

"At the gate. Xandria should be landing any minute."

"We got a runner, coming your way."

"Who?"

"The ex-wife."

"I thought that—"

"She got away."

"Does Cornelius know?"

"Yes." Meng tripped over a man with a cane. He jumped up, asking someone to please help the man as he raced off.

"And you're still alive?"

"Shut up and listen. If you come toward me, the girl will be trapped between us. Do you see her?"

"Hold on a second." Pause. "Yes. Man, she's quick!"

"Grab her." Meng hung up. He looked ahead and saw the agent, a former lumberjack before he joined the FBI, step out and catch April like a Frisbee.

Meng pulled out his gun. "Move, people!" he said, pushing the crowd aside. He put his badge away, trading it for some handcuffs. "Good to see you again, Ms. Adams."

"I just want to see August."

"And you will," Meng said, clamping the braces around her wrists behind her back. "But not yet. Besides, a family reunion just wouldn't be right unless everyone was there."

"What do you mean?"

Meng pulled April close and pressed his lips against her ear. "Charlie will be happy to see the whole family back together again, won't he?"

"Charlie? No . . . I made sure he was safe."

"There is nowhere safe. The eyes of the Dragon are everywhere," Meng said. He tightened the cuffs one click.

Two airport security officers approached the commotion, their clubs and walkie-talkies out and ready for action. "Problem here?" one of them said.

"FBI." Meng flashed his badge. He never tired of its effect on people. "We caught this one just in time."

"Is she a . . . ?"

"I know," Meng said. "She doesn't look like much. But she's as dangerous as they come."

"Really?"

"I'm surprised you guys missed this one," Meng said, maneuvering April in the direction of the exit.

The security officers looked at each other.

"Don't worry, boys," Meng said, pushing April ahead. "I'll cover you this time."

✠

The two backseats of the limo faced each other, an inconvenience for Meng, who was forced to sit in the furnace of April's harsh glare. "Stop it," he finally said.

April kept staring.

"I'm serious."

"Why are you doing this?" April asked. "Whatever it is you want, it can't be worth killing people."

"That's a pretty narrow viewpoint."

"It's *my* viewpoint, so, yes, it's very narrow."

"And that's the problem," Meng said. "You're only thinking about yourself."

"I'm thinking about my family."

"So . . . what? A few more people? Three? Four?"

April returned to staring.

Meng laughed. "In the early days, the Order of the Dragon killed hundreds, even thousands, to keep its secret safe. You. Me. We don't matter. Our lives mean nothing."

"You're wrong."

"Am I? Haven't you heard of the greater good?"

"This isn't the greater good."

Meng leaned over and opened a small, refrigerated compartment, pulling out a bottle of water. He twisted the cap, creating a sound like a cracking spine. "I think Cornelius would disagree with you."

"Cornelius can—"

Meng put his hand up. "We're here," he said as the vehicle screeched to a halt. "You can express your thoughts about Cornelius directly to his face." He opened the door and jumped out.

April followed with her hands still held securely behind her back. She tried not to fall as she exited the vehicle. A strong hand gripped her arm and pulled her off the seat.

"Meet Cornelius," Meng said.

April drew in her breath. There was something about him—the translucence of his skin, the ocean-deep embrace of his gaze, the twist of his smile—that let her know she was in the presence of evil.

"It's good to finally meet you, April."

The way he said her name made her skin crawl, like a million tiny roaches had just been unleashed in a race across her body.

"I've got a present for you," Cornelius said, fishing in his jacket pocket.

April wanted to decline the gift, wanted to scream at him, wanted to cry. But she found she could do nothing.

Cornelius held up a syringe like a boy admiring a snake he'd found in the garden. "I really should have changed the needle," he said. "But I figure, why? You all have the same blood."

He stepped forward and with one swift thrust, plunged the needle into her neck.

luminatedtwenty-twoilluminate

Twice, the plane jolted so violently that August imagined he was on an amusement-park ride. But he wasn't amused. He listened as the businessman in front of him retched into a bag. Somewhere to his right he heard a small child saying over and over *Mommy, Mommy, Mommy, Mommy.* There was a noise behind him, and August looked back just in time to see a man come staggering out of the latrine. He was swearing, and his shirt was sopping wet. August didn't bother wondering why. An irritated flight attendant assisted the man back to his seat, the two of them clutching anything in reach to steady themselves as the plane galloped like a rodeo horse through the sky.

August looked over at Xandria. She was completely calm, as if most at rest right at the center of the brewing swirl of chaos.

The captain said something over the loudspeaker, though no one could decipher it over the snarling engines and the seismic vibrations of the overhead compartments. August felt as if he were being shaken in a giant cocktail. But he was unfortunately sober and all too aware that his only relief might come in the form of a six-foot box.

Only a moment later, August felt the firmament rise up to catch the wheels of the lumbering aircraft. Then . . . *calm.* Conversations picked up from where they'd trailed off as if the crisis were only a bad dream, and now everything was back to normal. Everything was fine. Maybe even *great.*

August envied them.

"Time to pay the piper," Xandria said.

The piper she was referring to was none other than Leo Kahn, a bully who had declared the underworld his playground. August was still a little cloudy on how, exactly, Xandria would prevent Leo from killing him on the spot. "Follow my lead" was her only instruction. Not exactly the most reassuring plan, August thought, given that his life was on the line.

They waited for the plane to empty before exiting themselves. After a brief and awkward encounter with the flight attendants—who eyed them with fear, or contempt, or a mixture thereof—they left the confines of the plane forever.

"I didn't think that flight would ever end," August said.

"Who said it did?" Xandria replied.

The two of them entered the buzzing space of the airport. Like some Las Vegas impersonator's Jack Nicholson, Leo Kahn stood with three of his square-headed cronies only a few meters away. Leo was a man who took no chances. He wanted to be right there when August walked out of the tunnel. So he had purchased four one-way tickets and now, there they were.

"Just don't do anything stupid," Xandria said as she and August approached the Kahn ensemble.

"Too late for that," August said. He reached out and shook Leo's hand, which felt as weathered as a catcher's mitt. "Mr. Kahn. Good to see you. I want to introduce you to an associate of mine."

Xandria reached out her hand. Leo didn't take it. "Mr. Kahn," she said, still holding her palm open to accept his. "I'm here to make sure this transaction goes smoothly. You may not know me, but I believe you know my boss, Cornelius Hood."

Kahn's face transformed. "Cornelius!" he said, gripping her hand and giving it a firm shake. "Please pass on my best regards."

"He's in town, you know."

"Here? In New York?" Kahn asked. He seemed a bit rattled. "I didn't think he was allowed in the States."

"He's not."

"I see," Kahn said. He glanced back as if verifying his backup was still intact. "Does Cornelius have some interest in my book?" The question was aimed at August.

So the subject was going to arise sooner than later. August heard himself audibly gulp, an actual swallow, just like in the movies. "Not *exactly*."

"Yes, he does," Xandria said, stepping in. "But not the whole book."

"Not the whole book?" Kahn laughed, his men picking up the cue to join in. "What? He only wants a couple chapters?"

"Three pages."

Kahn stopped laughing. "Three pages? You serious?"

And then there they were. The three illuminated pages. Xandria fanned them out like a deck of cards before Kahn's face.

"You tore them out?" Kahn looked as if he might explode. A few parents grabbed their children's hands and darted from the area, just in case some real trouble was about to erupt among the cast of sinister characters.

"Don't worry," Xandria said. She opened the briefcase holding the Gutenberg and presented it to Kahn. "You'll still get your book."

"Great!" Kahn said, slapping his hands together. "Just what I wanted! Damaged property! You know what I give in exchange for damaged property?"

"The book is a gift." Xandria slid the case over to Kahn. "A free gift from Cornelius. Damaged or not, it's still worth more than anything else on your bookshelf."

"Then you don't know what's on my bookshelf."

Xandria took a step forward and placed a long finger under Kahn's chin. "The Order knows everything about you, down to the number of hairs on your mistress's head. Don't get cute with me. Take this deal and your debt with Cornelius is settled."

"I don't have a—"

"October 23, 1983. Moscow. Ring a bell?"

Kahn knocked Xandria's hand away from his face. He closed the lid to the briefcase and walked away, his men in silent tow.

August waited until Kahn was out of sight. "That's it? I get nothing?"

"You get your life," Xandria said. "Don't act so ungrateful." She made a motion with her hand, and two men in black suits appeared.

"Where were they when we needed them?"

"I need them now."

August caught a glimpse of guns underneath their coats.

Xandria noticed. "They're FBI. Only way to get a gun into the airport anymore. Of course, they're handy for other things too."

They seized August and spun him around, slapping a set of cuffs on his wrists. "What are you doing?" he asked.

Xandria got in his face. "Only a fool would think you wouldn't bolt at the first opportunity. But that just won't do. We still need you, August."

"For what? Just let me go."

"Now? Right before the finish line? I don't think so."

✝

The ride to the warehouse reminded August of his experience driving to the courthouse with April to sign their divorce papers. The tension boiled practically to the point of overflow, but he felt a tangible need to keep a lid on it, let the bubbles churn until the proper moment of release.

"Are we there yet?" August said. At least the bad joke made everyone else as ill at ease as he was.

"It wasn't funny the last time you asked, and it still isn't funny now," one of the agents said, pulling back his jacket just enough to reveal his gun.

"Point taken," August said. "Maybe we could all sing 'Kumbaya'?"

The agent pulled out his gun. "Can I?" he asked Xandria.

"No," she said. "I mean, you know, not *now* anyway."

The limo pulled into a warehouse driveway and stopped. Xandria got out first, followed by the two agents, leaving August to exit unaided, his hands still fastened tightly behind his back. His foot slipped on a shifting mat, and he toppled out of the vehicle, landing face-first on the pavement. One of the agents pulled him to his feet, shaking his head at the sight of August's bloodied face.

"I think I broke my nose," August said.

Without warning, the agent landed a fist in the exact location of August's misery. "Now you *know* it's broken," he said.

August's knees buckled, but the other agent caught his fall. "You should have a matching pair of ribs," he said, gunning a punch into August's abdomen.

Like vultures taking alternating picks at a carcass, the two agents thrashed August. Xandria watched for a moment before stopping them.

"That's enough!" she said. "Cornelius is coming, and I doubt he'll be impressed by you beating a man in handcuffs."

"Cornelius is *here*," a voice said. "And you're completely right."

The agents let August go. They straightened their jackets and inspected their shirts for splatters of crimson.

Cornelius walked over to August and looked down at the quivering figure on the ground. "Is this our savior?" he asked.

"I hope so," Xandria said.

"Then why are we crucifying him?" Cornelius turned to the two agents. They didn't breathe.

"Get out of here."

They swiftly left the presence of the Dragon Master.

"Help him up," Cornelius said to Xandria.

"I'm always available to help," she said, stroking her hand against his arm. She walked over to August and helped the groaning man rise to his feet. He leaned against the side of the limo. "I'm sorry that happened," she said. He didn't reply.

Cornelius approached him. "Look at me," he said.

August strained to lift his head.

"Look at me," Cornelius said again, grabbing August by the chin.

August peered into an intense glare.

"You're not going to make this easy, are you?" Cornelius reached into his pocket. "Lucky for you, I've got something that should help you be a little more cooperative. Sodium pentothal, sodium amytal, and pure adrenaline. Basically, truth serum with a kick. You won't sleep for a week. I'm told that it's a bit unstable, but it should do the trick."

August felt something sharp pierce him on the left just below his jawbone, but he didn't have the strength to fight it. A second later the pain was gone, but in its wake he felt, or imagined, a tiny flame coursing through his veins. He thought he was going to black out when suddenly the reverse happened: he was wide awake, more alert than he'd ever been in his life. His heartbeat doubled, maybe tripled. He became hyperaware of his surroundings: a fly buzzing in the distance, a bead of sweat collecting on the edge of Cornelius's hairline, a faint shadow of fear on Xandria's face. And there were voices. Hundreds of them. But where were they coming from?

"He's ready," Cornelius pronounced. "Take him inside."

✛

The warehouse was an empty shell. August heard his own footsteps reverberate between the concrete floor and the metal surround-ings, a steady *tap-tap-tap* that reminded him of the sound he heard in his head when he read Poe's "The Raven." "I sold a first edition of Edgar Allan Poe's *Tamerlane* for three hundred thousand dollars," August said.

"What are you talking about?" Xandria asked.

"I made a killing on that one," he said. "I bought it from a kid working for his mom at an antique store. He didn't know any better. He sold it to me for fifteen dollars."

"That's robbery."

"I know," August said. He felt as if some lock inside his head had been broken open, and he was scared what might come crawling out next.

They walked toward a room, which resembled a giant white gift box, in the middle of warehouse. It looked strange situated there, and August wondered if had been constructed expressly for him, specifically for this purpose.

"What is this place?"

"I'm told they used to pack pharmaceuticals here. The government bought it two years ago to facilitate an undercover operation."

"The place is empty. What kind of business were they conducting?"

"Ironically, drug deals. Cocaine mostly," Xandria said. "The business was supposed to be used by the FBI to infiltrate a crime ring. But at some point, the agents involved ceased being agents and became honest-to-goodness drug runners. I suppose the pay increase had something to do with it."

"Money is a drug too, you know."

"It's certainly more seductive. But there are things even more desirable than that. Power, for instance." Xandria glanced around to make sure they were alone. "Cornelius asked if you would consider joining the Order."

"You're crazy."

"I told him you would say that. But I also told him that once you understood the big picture, once you saw the opportunities you could have as a result, maybe you'd say yes." She got closer. "Cornelius is willing to bring you into the fold as a full-fledged member. Not some little errand boy, like the agents. You would have real power. You'd have more money than you could dream of, enough to fund thousands of expeditions looking for rare books, if that's what you desire."

"In exchange for what?"

"Your brilliance. Your passion," she said. "After tonight, the Order will enter a new age. And because of that, there will be a need for new leadership."

August turned to her. "You think you understand me," he said. "But you don't. You and me, we're not the same. I love my work; I'd be lying if I said I didn't. But I'd take back every book I've sold, every adventure I've experienced, if it meant saving my family. I can't believe it's taken this much pain to figure that out."

"Don't be such a martyr. The pain isn't over yet," Xandria said. She put her hand on the door of the inner room. "All nine of the illuminated pages are lying inside on a high-radiance table. Gutenberg's journal says the light of a full moon will reveal the ultimate truth of the illuminations. We didn't want to test the fates with a cloudy night, so we had a special table created to emulate the effect."

"You guys thought of everything, didn't you?"

"For the most part, yes," Xandria said. "But there have been some unanticipated glitches."

"Those glitches are human lives."

Xandria continued, undeterred by August's appeal to decency.

"You will be constantly monitored, so don't think you're going to get away with anything. You will have three hours to solve this riddle."

"It's not enough time."

"I think you've proven that it's more than sufficient."

"I'm going to need my handcuffs off."

"No."

"How do you expect me to do anything?"

"We've arranged for you to have help," Xandria said, opening the door.

"Dad!"

August fell to his knees, silenced by the sight of his son.

"August!"

He looked across the room at April. Despite her frazzled state, he'd never seen her look so beautiful. He tried to speak, but the words failed him. He felt the tears swell in his eyes, a dam of pent-up emotion unleashed.

"Get up," Xandria said.

August struggled to his feet and ran over to Charlie, who threw his arms around his father. April got up from her chair—arms still bound—and joined the embrace in Charlie's arms.

Xandria threw August's notebook and the Gutenberg journal onto the table. "Make sure and say your good-byes. This might be the last time you see each other alive."

The door slammed.

The countdown began.

luminatedtwenty-threeilluminat

The air was rife with questions. August, April, and Charlie all wanted to recount every second of the last few hours, compare notes, try to figure out exactly what had happened, and why. But there just wasn't time, so they focused on the immediate: how August broke his nose (*they beat me within an inch of my life,* he said), how April ripped out the last three illuminated pages (*they threatened Charlie's life,* she said), and how Charlie had come to be there at all (*they promised me candy—what?—just kidding, they kidnapped me,* he said).

"Who was that lady that brought you in here, Dad?"

"She's someone your mother would call a—"

"August!"

Charlie filled in the blank for his dad.

"Charlie! Where on earth did you hear that?" April huffed.

"Probably from me. That's where he seems to pick up all his bad habits, right?"

"That's not true. Grandma Rose has some bad habits. I saw her smoke one time."

"Your grandma does *not* smoke."

"Mom. I saw it with both my eyes."

August smirked. "I think I'm starting to like your mother more now that she smokes."

"August, stop. Charlie, I'm sure you just saw it wrong. Maybe she was lighting a candle."

"Why would she put a candle in her mouth?"

"I don't know, Charlie. But I'm sure there's a perfectly reasonable explanation."

"Mom! I'm not lying!"

"I never said you were lying."

"You made it sound like I was lying."

"No, I'm just saying maybe you don't know the whole story."

August stood up and stomped his foot. April and Charlie fell silent.

"Listen to us!" he said. "The drugs they stuck us with are making us babble, but we have to *focus*. I'm as interested as both of you are about whether Grandma Rose is a three-pack-a-day chain-smoker, but if we don't figure out this puzzle, we'll never find out."

"I'm not lying."

"Charlie!" August said.

"Sorry, Dad."

"Okay. Now we need a plan," August said. "Charlie, since you're the only one without handcuffs, you're going to be in charge of the laptop."

"All right!"

"Also, you're going to have to help us flip pages. Put that red book in front of your mom."

Charlie slid the book over to her.

"What is it?" April asked.

"Gutenberg's journal." August explained the connection between it and the illuminated pages.

"So it's real after all?"

"The binding is right. The foxing seems consistent for the age. It could easily be a contemporary with some of the incunabula I've picked up over the years."

"Incu-what?" Charlie asked.

"It's an old book," April said.

"You're the best German reader here," August said to April, which he hoped she'd take as the compliment he intended, considering that his own German wasn't too shabby. "I don't have the big picture on all this yet. We'll need to study the journal a bit more."

"I know some German!" Charlie chimed in.

"You know how to *count* in German," August said. "That's not going to help us much."

"You should be more encouraging!" April said. "He knows more than you think he does."

"I know French too!"

April seemed surprised. "Who taught you French?"

"Mrs. Laroche."

"Who is Mrs. Laroche?"

"She plays poker with Grandma Rose on Thursday afternoons."

August smiled. "This just gets better and better."

"We'll talk more about this later," April said to her son. She turned to August. "Which entries did you want me to look at?"

"Any that mention the books of the Bible linked to the illuminations," August said. He gave her the list of books in the same order Xandria had on the plane: 1 Kings, 2 Chronicles, Romans, Judges, John, Daniel, Maccabees, Luke, and Genesis.

Charlie flipped through the pages as April scanned them. His hand slipped, and the book fell open to the last page.

"What's this?" April asked, staring at a list of names scrawled there. "Twenty-one names. Original members of the Order of the Dragon." She read the list aloud.

"I'm guessing that each of those people commissioned Gutenberg to create a copy of his Bible for them," August said.

"And that's where he hid the illuminations."

"Right in their hands. But three separate copies of his Bible were needed to understand the secret meaning." August pointed to the nine illuminated pages on the table, which were laid out in a three-by-three matrix. "The pages on my right came from the copy owned by the Morgan Library. The pages in the middle came from my copy. And the pages to my left came from—"

"The Library of Congress," April said. "It's remarkable that these pages all came from Bibles originally owned by members of the Order of the Dragon."

"The best-preserved copies were the ones owned by royalty. And if the Order of the Dragon was anything, they were that. Royal. Blue-blooded through and through. Their copies of the Gutenberg would have been the best cared for in all of Europe."

"Tell us what you know so far about the illuminations," April said.

August quickly walked through his speculations about the nine images:

> the two white dog-dragons chasing the fox and the hare,
> Sigismund on the throne with the golden globe,
> Gutenberg holding the sword and journal,
> the swan-dragon devouring the blue man,
> the eagle holding Charlemagne's banner,
> Daniel, afraid of the hedgehog,
> Vlad II Dracul in his green cape,
> the ox seeming to forecast light,
> the hart, tormented by the wolf

"I don't know," April said, trying to absorb the volumes of information. "What if you're seeing things that aren't really there?"

"It's entirely possible," August said. "But it's the best I've got."

The illuminated pages glowed over the lunar light. They seemed to almost radiate a message. But what was it?

Charlie's eyes were transfixed on the pages.

"What is it?" April asked him. August turned at the concern in her voice. Charlie didn't blink for more than a minute.

"Charlie! Snap out of it!"

Charlie blinked. "I'm fine. I was . . . you know . . ."

"I do know. But that worries me. You need to stay with us, here."

"It's just . . . the pictures . . . they fit together."

August looked up from the journal. "What do you mean?"

"I was daydreaming about the animals in the pictures, and it's like they wanted to chase each other. And then I noticed how close they were to one another, not how they are now, but if you, like, stacked them on top of one another."

August scanned the illuminated pages. He was beginning to see it. "Go on."

"Can I show you?"

"Right away."

Charlie ran around to the other side of the table. He turned all the pages so that they were facing him. "Hmm," he said, stroking his chin like a professor. The gears in his head were turning faster and faster. He started rearranging the pages, flipping some over so that their images were reversed. And then he began to stack them, one by one, until all nine of the pages were on top of one another. "Wow!" he said, like he'd just opened a Christmas present.

"What is it?" August and April said in unison. They jumped up from their chairs and peered over Charlie's shoulders.

"Amazing."

"Unbelievable."

"The images are all linked."

"They were meant to go together," April said.

The collective effect of the illuminations was overwhelming. The images cascaded through the thin vellum sheets, lit by the warm glow of the table. At the top right was the ox with his banner underfoot. Next was the man being eaten by the swan, and then the lion's den. Up the left-hand side was Dracul holding the sword, then the eagle with Charlemagne's banner, and finally Sigismund on his throne. The remaining three illuminations framed the entire work: Gutenberg's ape companion climbed the vine in the left margin, the creation story filled the right margin, and at the bottom of the page, the white dog-dragons pursued the hare and the fox. The images danced and intertwined with one another, each individual story becoming richer as it intersected with another.

"Something's missing," August said, breaking the wonder of the moment. "Look at all the figures. Every animal, every person, is facing some object in the middle, some object they all seem to be admiring. But it's not there."

"What is it?"

"Xandria mentioned a tenth image."

"Another illumination?"

"No. An image from a different source. She said that it was mentioned in the journal."

April returned to her seat. "Charlie, could you help me look through this?" Charlie came to her side and flipped through the journal, helping her in the tedious search for information about the tenth image. After thirty long minutes, she spoke. "I think I may have found something, but it's not quite clear."

August looked at the passage she indicated. "What does it say?"

"Basically, it says that the tenth image is inside the journal."

"Do you see it?"

"That's the problem," April said. "There aren't any images in the journal. Charlie, flip through one more time and see if you can find any pictures."

Charlie opened the journal at page one and swiftly, but deliberately turned through the pages. "Do you want me to do it again?" he asked, reaching the end.

"You didn't see anything?"

"Nope."

"I was watching, and I didn't see anything either," April said. "What are we missing?"

August stood. "What *exactly* did the journal say?"

"That the tenth image could be found inside the journal."

"Inside?" August walked around the table. "Charlie, I want you to rip the cover off the journal."

"Mom?"

"Wait a second. What are you thinking? You can't just rip apart a book like that."

"If the pages hadn't been ripped out of the Gutenberg, we never would have understood how everything fit together." August leaned down to face his son. "Rip it."

Charlie didn't hesitate any longer, tearing the cover off the journal like he was wrestling the stubborn top off a new action-figure box. The fight was tremendous, but Charlie was the definitive victor. He slapped the whole front-to-back cover down on the table.

"Have you been working out?"

"Funny, Dad."

August leaned against the table and took a closer look at the leather cover. "I never noticed this before!"

"What is it?" Charlie asked.

"At first, I thought the design on the cover had no rhyme or reason, just a decorative flair. But now I see what it is. Do you?"

Charlie held up the cover for both him and his mother to see. April spotted it first. "A colophon! It's half of the one duplicated at the Library of Congress!"

"A what?"

"A printer's mark," August said. "Fust's colophon."

"Whose?"

"A man who helped print Gutenberg's books."

"I still don't see it," Charlie said.

"But what is it doing on the journal?" April wondered.

"Showing us where to look next? *X* marks the spot, right?"

"Someone tell me where it is!" Charlie was nearly in tears.

"Hold up the cover so it's vertical," April said, trying to calm him.

Charlie turned the leather ninety degrees.

"Now try to ignore the lines that are ornamental—the flowers and vines and boxes and circles, stuff like that—and concentrate on finding the letter in the middle. It crosses both the front and the back of the cover."

Charlie squinted hard. "I see it!" he announced. "So what's the *X* on there for?" he asked, his innocent curiosity a thankful redirect of the conversation.

"It was used by a man named Johann Fust," April said. "He gave money to Gutenberg to help him print his Bibles. The *X* is actually the Greek letter *chi*, which was the symbol Fust chose to say, 'Hey, I worked on this book.'"

"He should have used a jaguar instead."

"A jaguar would have been great!"

"Okay, sorry to derail the tangent train, but we need to move on," August said.

"You're not being fun, Dad."

"April, would you please explain to our son that our lives are in jeopardy here?"

"Why don't you tell him?"

August shot a glare at his ex-wife, then turned to Charlie. "Our lives are in jeopardy," he said.

"Dad, this isn't helping. What do we need to do next?"

"Open the cover."

Charlie turned the cover over and examined the damage where

the pages had been torn away from the spine. The gash revealed a paper of a different color. He reached inside. "There's something inside."

"Be careful. Whatever it is has been in there a long time, so it's probably pretty fragile."

Charlie slowly retracted his hand. "I'm pretending that I'm playing that game Operation, but instead of just a buzzer going off, I die if I mess up."

April's expression crumpled. "That's morbid."

"But accurate," August said.

Charlie's hand emerged, his index and middle finger tweezing a folded piece of paper. He laid the item on the table, then carefully opened it.

"The tenth image," August whispered.

"It looks like a map," Charlie said. His fingers traced the winding paths marked on the ancient page. "What are all these holes for?"

August smiled. "Place it over the illuminations," he said.

Charlie did, marveling as the illuminations lined up with the empty compartments of the map.

"I think we've solved the puzzle," August said, "but not the riddle. We have a map, but for where? And for what?"

April joined the group to study the page. "Follow the lines leading away from each illumination. Most of them lead to dead ends. But the one from Sigismund leads directly toward . . . what is that?"

At the center of the map were two circles with faint markings inside.

"Charlie, rub your fingers over the circles. Do you feel anything?"

The boy placed his fingers delicately on the page and moved

them over the marks as carefully as if he were petting a tarantula. "Yeah. Just barely. I can feel ridges."

"These images are rubbings of a coin. And I bet there's more of them," August said. He backtracked from the image of the coin to the image of the king. "I thought this was a picture of Emperor Sigismund. But I might be wrong. There's something I missed. Look at his eyes."

"One of them is missing!" they said together.

"This isn't Emperor Sigismund," August said. "This is John the One-Eyed—Jan Žižka—the greatest general of the Hussite army. *Žižka* means 'one eye.' He was so famous that after he died, they stretched his skin over a drum and beat it during their battles."

"Cool," Charlie said.

August continued. "He was Emperor Sigismund's most hated enemy, but in the illumination, Žižka sits on his throne. I'd say that implies that he now controls the power Sigismund once held."

"That would make sense if the Orphans stole the Order of the Dragon's treasure," April said. "No wonder they want it back so badly."

"But where is the treasure now?" August closed his eyes, tumbling the fragments of information in his mind. "The map needs a location to make sense."

"It has to be within the boundaries of the Holy Roman Empire," April said. "And if it has anything to do with Žižka, then there's really only one place it could be . . ."

"Tábor!" August said.

The door swung open. Two armed agents entered, looking dangerously alert. Xandria slithered in behind them. April glared.

"Tábor," she said, circling the table and looking down at the illuminated map. "Amazing. You've done an excellent job!" She clapped—a slow, mocking clap, a rhythm that matched a dirge, a death march.

"But what's hidden there?" August asked. "A few gold coins?"

"Think bigger," Xandria said. "What treasure would be worth spending centuries to find?"

August knew immediately. "The Templar treasure is just a myth."

"A myth?" Xandria laughed. "The myth is that it doesn't exist. Listen to the truth: In 1118, the Knights Templars found a secret chamber under the place where Solomon's temple once stood. Inside, they found thousands upon thousands of ancient gold coins. The Templars were elated at first, until they inspected the coins closer. They all bore the same markings, unlike any coin they knew: on one side, a woman's profile, and on the other, a five-pointed star encircled by five Hebrew letters."

"What were the letters?" August asked.

"J-R-S-L-M, the ancient Hebrew spelling for *Jerusalem*. The letters assured the Templars that the coins had been stamped in the Holy City. And the five-pointed star added even more proof."

"I thought the five-pointed star was an occult symbol," August said.

"The five-pointed star didn't have any occult connotations until the 1800s, when a man named Eliphas Lévi inverted it to create the Sigil of Baphomet, the official symbol of the Church of Satan. Before then, the five-pointed star was linked to the first five books of the Bible, known as the Pentateuch, and was used as a symbol for truth."

"So what was the truth about the woman on the coin?"

"It was beyond the Templars' comprehension. They were steeped in biblical history, and knew that no person's face had ever been printed on coins at the Temple Mount. Not even a king or queen."

"Caesar's face was on plenty of coins," August said.

"Not a temple coin," Xandria said. "Caesar's were printed in Rome. In Jerusalem, the human face was strictly forbidden. But one thing was permitted: images of heavenly beings."

"I thought the Pentateuch had pretty strict rules against that kind of thing," April said, still looking darts at Xandria.

"Idols have always been frowned upon," she explained. "But heavenly figures—not always. Think of the angels over the Ark of the Covenant, for example. Such representations were prohibited later, but not during the age of these coins."

"So we've got a coin with an angel on it," August said. "Not exactly the find of the century, wouldn't you say?"

"You're forgetting that in the Jewish tradition, angels are always male," Xandria said, meeting August's challenge.

April's eyes widened. August's jaw dropped. "Are you saying that the Jews worshiped a female deity?" he finally managed.

"Exactly."

"God's a girl?" Charlie asked.

August leaned heavily against the table.

"The Templars turned their discovery into power through blackmail," Xandria said. "They saw a system built entirely upon men. Male popes. Male cardinals. Bishops. Priests. The idea that God was female would crush a system like that. They were given enormous amounts of power. In 1139, Pope Innocent II issued a bull—the *Omne Datum Optimum*—stating that the Templars owed no taxes, could go anywhere unfettered, and were subject to no authority other than the pope. In other words, they could do anything they wanted."

"But self-preservation wasn't the only reason the pope wanted to bury the Templars' discovery," April said.

"You're right. What they found had huge implications for Jesus," Xandria said.

"What implications?" August asked.

"Mary couldn't have been impregnated by a female deity," Xandria said. "Which means the real father wasn't 'heavenly' after all, and therefore, neither was Jesus."

April just shook her head. "This is nuts."

"So why didn't they come out with the information?"

"They believed that lining their pockets served the greater good. They kept the world in the dark, but used the secret to secure their power until a time they wanted to reveal the truth. And so the Templars buried the secret and the proof, both literally and figuratively. And it's remained hidden ever since."

"Until now."

"Yes," Xandria said, admiring the illuminated map. "Until now."

April protectively stood in front of Charlie. "We don't care about your quest. We just want to go home."

"You're free to go," Xandria said, waving an arm at the door.

"No!" Charlie yelped. "If we walk out, we'll trigger the bombs!"

"Oh. Yes. I guess I forgot about the sensor chips you're implanted with," Xandria said, picking up the illuminated map and making her way to the door. Her two escorts had their guns drawn. "I suppose with minds as bright as yours, you can figure your way out of this. Or has all your brainpower been drained for the day?"

August lunged at her, in vain, stopped instantly by her bodyguards, who dropped him to the ground. He had no way to defend himself, and the agents gave him a quick set of blows.

"This isn't the last you'll see of us," August said, spitting out a tooth.

"I'm afraid it is," Xandria said. "The explosive charges have been set for a thirty-minute delay, just enough time for me and my team to clear the area." She turned, digging a heel into August's neck.

He bit his lip to keep from screaming.

She leaned down to his ear. "I hear the weather in Tábor is beautiful this time of year," she said. "Good-bye, August."

The door closed.

The lights went off.

And the room fell into complete and utter silence.

luminatedtwenty-fourilluminate

TWELVE HOURS LATER
TÁBOR, CZECH REPUBLIC

The streets of Tábor were built to confuse. That was their intended purpose. They wound this way, then that, taking sharp turns or simply dead-ending. The streets' function served their citizens many times throughout history, confounding enemy troops so completely that they often attacked themselves, disoriented, or found themselves trapped to the Hussites' advantage.

But Xandria wasn't confused. She had a map. Two, in fact. One for the streets, and another—much more precious—for *beneath* the streets.

The tunnels of Tábor were well documented, by others besides Gutenberg, but had remained essentially unseen for hundreds of years. They were just too dangerous. Most areas threatened collapse, the result of years of erosion and careless design. The main sections of the tunnel were solid enough, but its expansion had been spoiled by hasty and makeshift construction. Secret storehouses and worse (it was said that cantankerous women were often imprisoned in some of the more hidden corners) spiderwebbed beneath the city.

Xandria didn't care about the risk. She had a treasure to find.

"Where do we get into these tunnels again?" Agent Terrence Barber asked, one of the five people of the entourage stuffed into the rental van.

"Žižka Square," Xandria said. "It's named after the man who founded the city."

"It feels like we've gone back in time," Barber replied, noting the ancient beauty of the buildings and houses they passed.

"Nothing's changed here for over five hundred years," Xandria explained. "Only the Hussite army lived here, and they set up the city to be an eternal stronghold. *Tábor* means 'camp.'"

"It's the nicest camp I've ever seen," Barber said, placing his trademark aviator shades over his dark brown eyes. "Better than anything the FBI has!"

The two other agents chuckled.

"Shut up," Cornelius said from the front seat. He had been silent since they disembarked from the plane.

The agents glared at each other.

The van exited the corridor and entered a large town square buzzing with people. This was clearly the most active part of the city—its beating heart—as alive now as it ever had been.

"Look!" Agent Clyde Wynant said, pointing his bony finger out the window.

Ten eyes gazed across the square at a tall limestone statue. It was Žižka, armed for war, in eternal watch over his troops. He wore a thick coat, lined at the edges with lamb's wool. His face was sturdy and strong and singularly his, cut with a broad mustache and his legendary patch, which made his good eye—the one peering out from beneath his bell-shaped helmet—even more penetrating. In his left hand he held a broadsword, its point stuck next to his armored feet. And in his right hand, a scepter, which Žižka appeared to be aiming at a point in the ground about twenty yards away from the statue.

"That's where we're headed," Xandria said, waving toward the scepter's mark.

The van drove across the square and everyone unloaded, immediately plunging into the roles they'd been assigned. The three agents in the group—who were all wearing hard hats and one-piece gray jumpsuits—began setting up orange cones around the area. *Restricted Access,* read the tape barricade they set up around the perimeter of the cones.

A policeman approached the scene, clearly suspicious of the activity. Did they have record that such work was to be performed? Men jackhammering into the ground? Xandria caught Cornelius's eye.

Cornelius approached the policeman, launching into a heated discussion in Czech. He presented a document, which the policeman studied for a few minutes before handing it back. They shook hands. Everything was fine. The policeman waved, setting out in search of an offense more egregious than a few workers fixing a water main.

"That was close," Agent Frank Jorgenson said, wiping the sweat from his brow.

"Stop worrying. Cornelius took care of everything during the flight." Xandria watched the husky agent with a combination of amusement and frustration. He was already huffing hard, removing the rubble from the site.

The men continued ripping through the stone. It wasn't long before they dug straight into a square metal plate about two meters wide. Xandria brushed away the inch-deep layer of gray dust covering the plate, revealing an image that made her gasp. Watching over her shoulder, Jorgenson shouted, "You've got to come see this!"

Everyone gathered around. The image was unmistakable. It was the same icon that each of them wore on their medallions: a coiled dragon.

"What are you waiting for?" Cornelius boomed. "Open it up!"

Jorgenson and Wynant jammed crowbars under the lid and tried to pry it away from the ground. After they exhausted nearly all of their efforts, the plate gave way, peeling up to reveal a narrow chasm plummeting straight down into the earth. Barber uncoiled a rope and dropped it into the space. "Next stop, hell," he joked.

"Jorgenson, you go first," Cornelius said. "I don't want you slipping and falling on my head."

"Thank you, Master," the hefty man said, grabbing the rope and linking it onto his belt. He shimmied his way down into the hole, winking at Xandria as he disappeared.

Xandria went next. She dropped about ten meters before coming into a wider space. She touched down, and Jorgenson flipped on a flashlight. "It's a tunnel," he said. "Which way do we go?"

Xandria grabbed the flashlight from him and studied the illuminated map as the others landed in the room, turning her body to align it with a north heading. "This way," she said, walking in the downward direction.

The others tagged closely behind as she scurried ahead. Barber put his hand out and traced the wall with his fingers. "It's damp," he said.

Cornelius seized his arm. "Idiot! This passage probably hasn't been used for centuries. There's no telling how unstable it might be."

They pressed onward. While the tunnel was initially wide enough for any of them to stand fully upright, arms spread apart, little by little the hole was closing in on them. Before long, Xandria found herself stooped over, and not long after that, they were forced onto their hands and knees.

"Are you sure this is the right way?" Wynant asked, though as the skinniest member of the party, he had the least to worry about.

Xandria ignored the slight doubt that quickened her heart. "I'm sure," she said.

The tunnel continued its course, steadily declining and sometimes curving to such a degree that everyone agreed they were spiraling like a corkscrew farther and farther underground. Every once in a while, a tiny trickle of water would appear, its faint ripple soothing the claustrophobia that gnawed at the back of Xandria's mind.

After about thirty minutes, Xandria noticed a dark spot in the tunnel floor ahead. "I think I see something," she called from the front of the pack.

"I hope it's a McDonald's," Jorgenson said.

Xandria's hand went down on the dirt, then began to slide straight down. "Stop!" she yelled.

"What is it?"

"Hand me a rope."

Barber passed one forward. "Secure this," she instructed, handing back one end. He took out a small drill and drove an anchor into the floor, tying the rope to it.

One by one the draconists exited the tunnel high in the wall of a cavernous room. They slowly descended to the floor, unsure of their surroundings in the darkness.

"Set the flares," Cornelius said.

The three agents removed the objects from their pockets and ignited them, pitching them around the room until the space was aglow in warm reds and oranges. Xandria walked slowly across the room, listening as the ancient floorboards creaked beneath her feet. "Stay alert," she said. "I don't think this is firm ground beneath our feet."

Jorgenson bounced on his toes. A loud crack broke out from under him. He instantly stopped. "Holy—"

"Don't move!" Xandria said.

The floorboards continued to groan, like a giant dead tree about to give way to gravity.

"Walk forward, slowly," Cornelius said.

Jorgenson scooted his right foot forward. He began shifting his weight to it, dragging his other foot up behind him. The floor held. "It worked!" he said, smiling. And then the ground opened, and he was swallowed by the darkness.

"No!" Wynant screamed, running toward the hole.

Cornelius grabbed him. "What are you doing? This entire place could fall to pieces! Stay focused. We have a job to do."

Xandria took a quick survey of the room. The space was circular. If there was a ceiling, it was too high above her head to see. The walls were made of stone, ornately carved with a variety of designs, some recognizable, some strange and unfamiliar. She took the illuminated map out of her bag and unfolded it. "It's here," she said. "The treasure is right here."

"What do you mean?" Cornelius asked. "I don't see it anywhere."

Xandria cautiously crossed the floor toward him. "Have you ever heard of a Sierpinski carpet?"

"No. But I'm sure you will enlighten me," Cornelius said.

Xandria continued. "On first glace, a Sierpinski carpet just looks like a symmetrical diagram full of squares." She got closer. "But if you look closer, you begin to notice that its actually far more complicated: a square with a square cut out, with that figure repeated infinitely." She put the map in front of Cornelius's face. "I thought that this was only a representation of the entryway to the tunnel, and maybe the entire tunnel system as well. But I didn't know that it was also a representation of the treasure room itself."

"Let me see."

She turned the illuminated map so that each of the figures on the page lined up with the figures on the wall. "See!" she said. "The ox. The swan. The lion. The dog. The hare. The fox. The ape. The eagle. The king. All right here around us."

"And in the middle . . ."

"The treasure," Xandria said. "Jorgenson had the right idea, it was just that his approach was a bit too hasty." She picked up one of the flares and hurled it into the broken space in the floor.

"Is it down there?" Barber asked.

Cornelius gestured toward the hole. "Why don't you look and see?"

Barber held up his hands. "I was just asking."

Cornelius frowned. "I wasn't."

Barber accepted his master's challenge, but he wasn't about to make the same mistake as his dead comrade. He tied a rope around his waist and secured it to the wall, making a journey toward the hole that was painstakingly slow.

"Do you see anything?" Xandria asked.

Barber peeked over the edge of the splintered boards. "It's pretty far down. I can just barely see the flare."

"You're going to have to go down there," Cornelius said.

"Let me do it," Xandria said.

Barber didn't argue. He retreated from the hole and untied his rope, handing it to Xandria. "You're braver than me," he admitted.

"No," she said. "I'm just more committed." Fastened firmly, she crawled out toward the gap. She turned and dropped her legs down into the nothingness below the floor. "Do you have me?"

"I gotcha," Barber said. "I'm going to let you down just a little at a time."

Xandria gripped the rope tightly, feeling the vibration of it rubbing against the edge of the wood. Her body began to go down.

"You okay?"

"I'm fine," she called back. One meter. Two meters. Three. Four. Still, the ground seemed a long distance away. She might run out of rope before reaching the floor.

"Can you see anything?" The voice belonged to Cornelius.

"Not really," Xandria said. She looked up and watched the hole grow smaller and smaller. Good. At least she was making progress.

"We don't have much more rope," Barber said from above.

"Just get me as far as you can," Xandria said. She wasn't about to give up now.

The rope stopped.

"Is that it?"

"I'm afraid so."

She looked down at the flare on the ground below her. It was still at least six or seven meters away. If she fell wrong, she could easily break a leg. But the journey down was only half the problem. It was the journey back *up* that worried her. It would take too much time to get another rope. She tried to look around the room to see if there were any visible exits. She figured there had to be one down there somewhere. Surely they didn't just drop the treasure in from above.

"I'm going to let go!" she yelled.

"What?"

"I'm going to . . . oh, forget it," she said. She unfastened the rope from around her waist and plummeted toward the ground. As luck would have it, her fall was broken by the soft, pillowy gut of Jorgenson, whose dead body lay faceup on the floor. Xandria pushed herself off the grotesque figure, her head feeling like it had just taken a hit from an aluminum baseball bat. But she was alive. And as far as she could tell, fully intact.

"Are you okay?"

Xandria pulled out her radio, tired of fatiguing her voice. She hit a button. "I'm fine."

A moment later Barber's voice crackled through the speaker. "Forgot we had these."

"I'm glad we do," Xandria said. She tested the ground with her foot. "It's solid dirt down here, thank goodness."

"Do you see anything?"

She fished Jorgenson's flashlight out of her pocket and shone it around the room. "It's weird," she said. "The light just disappears in the distance, like it's going straight into a fog."

"Can you hear any water? Maybe there is fog down there. We saw those little trickles heading down this way in the tunnel. It's got to go somewhere."

Xandria listened. She did hear something. A rushing sound, like a waterfall. "I'm going to go take a look," she said. "Call me every minute or so to make sure I'm still alive."

"Roger that."

Xandria headed out from the island that was Jorgenson's body into the murky outer perimeter. She closed her eyes and listened for the sound again. Where was it coming from? She pivoted on her heels until she thought that her feet were pointed in the right direction.

The radio burst to life. "Cornelius wanted me to tell you to hurry up. There's no telling how unstable the environment is down here."

"Cornelius is welcome to come down here if he'd like to speed things up."

Xandria put the radio away. She could tell she was getting closer to the sound. She waved the flashlight in front of her, looking for any clues as to where it might be coming from. But once again, the beam died out only a few meters in the distance. Fog. It really was fog. She was close enough to feel it now, clinging to her skin like a ghost.

The sound of rushing water grew to a low rumble. The fog closed in, enveloping her, cutting her off completely from the light of the flare. It was just her and the flashlight now. She strode ahead, hoping her movement was in a forward direction and not in circles. The only thing that guided her was the sound, which had grown to a thunder.

Xandria felt a change in the air, but whether it was from something real, like a change in the temperature, or from something unreal, like unbridled fear, she couldn't tell. She directed the flashlight up, wondering if the actual space she was in had shifted. It had. Dimly, through the fog, she could see a ceiling not too far above her head. Too high to touch, but low enough to explain that she'd entered some kind of tunnel. She continued more confidently, feeling like she may have discovered something important.

And in fact, she had.

"Are you . . . kay?" Barber asked over the radio, his voice breaking up only slightly.

"I'm more than okay," Xandria said. "I wish you could see what I'm looking at."

"What . . . it?"

"A waterfall."

"Sorry, you were . . . up. What did . . . say?"

"A waterfall! You wouldn't believe how amazing it is!"

"You'll have to . . . later. I can . . . you."

Xandria tucked the radio away. She'd give them the full report soon enough. But first she had to take in the sight for herself.

She stood at the edge of an underground cliff. Across from her—pouring down from the shadowy heavens—was the most glorious waterfall she had ever seen. Its prodigious waves produced a roar that would have caused lions to tremble.

And then she saw the doors.

At first she thought they were too big to be doors. Positioned directly behind the waterfall, she could only catch a glimpse of them at a time, and only in fractured views, as she could only illuminate small portions with the flashlight. But the longer she looked, the more she was convinced. There were doors behind the crashing waters. Gold doors. Nearly twenty feet tall. And set in the center was an unmistakable image. Xandria pulled out the illuminated map and studied the woman's profile that adorned the impression of the coin. It was a perfect match.

✠

Agent Terrence Barber slapped the radio. "Why won't this thing work?"

"Maybe she's dead," Cornelius said, ice cold.

"Xandria? I don't think so," Barber replied. "That girl is tough. I once saw her kill a black widow spider just by staring at it."

"You're lying," Wynant chirped from across the room. He was taking pictures of the figures carved into the walls.

"Of course he's lying, you idiot," Cornelius said.

Barber smacked the radio again. "C'mon, Xandria! What's taking you so long?"

There was a burst of static from the device.

"Hello?" Barber said.

Static.

"Can you hear me?"

". . . won't believe . . . behind the water . . . I'm opening the doors now."

Barber turned to the others. "Did she say something about doors?"

Cornelius and Wynant came as quickly as safety allowed to Barber's side: Xandria had found something.

They waited for what seemed an eternity for her voice to come through again. A moment later they heard her, sounding like she was on some distant planet. ". . . so dark . . . not sure if . . . wait, I see something . . ."

"This is killing me," Wynant said.

"I'll be killing you if you don't shut up!" Barber barked.

"Sh!" Cornelius didn't have to hush them twice.

The radio fell silent again. Far below their feet they heard a disturbing boom, a distant explosion of unknown fury.

"What was that?" Wynant asked.

Cornelius and Barber tried to act calm, but neither of them succeeded. Something horrible was happening, and they had no power to stop it.

The room shook. Pieces of rock fell from the ceiling and from the walls. A section of the floor fell from its place, crashing loudly.

Xandria's voice burst through the radio. ". . . terrible . . . everything falling apart . . . I can't . . . get out now!"

The three men ran for the rope leading back to the tunnel. But it was too late. The room began to cave in, collapsing upon itself like a dead star. They were hopelessly trapped. The last words they heard were from Xandria. She said, quite simply, ". . . so beautiful . . ."

And the world went dark.

luminatedtwenty-fiveilluminate

SIX MONTHS LATER
PRAGUE, CZECH REPUBLIC

August walked into the Crowne Plaza Hotel, bought a coffee, sat down at a table, and waited. He didn't have to wait long. A man cylindrical in build squared himself on the opposing seat, tugging his gray suit into line.

"Before we speak about the Black Queen," the cylindrical man said, "I want to see the merchandise."

August smiled and stuck out his hand. "August Adams," he said. "And I presume you must be James Calendar. So good to finally make your acquaintance."

Calendar, who couldn't seem to sit still, bouncing like a small engine in his chair, took August's outstretched hand and shook it rapidly. "The merchandise?"

"You make it sound so enchanting," August said. He put his briefcase on the table and opened it. "You're not going to go running off with this, are you?"

"Oh, no, no, no . . . ," Calendar said, holding his hands up in protest, wagging his head. "You can count on me. Just let me have my book."

"Are you going to hold it with your bare hands?" August asked.

"I was . . . I thought . . ."

"Shame on you, Mr. Calendar. I hope you don't treat all your other priceless treasures with such reckless abandon!" He grinned and handed him the book. "To be honest, I really don't care if you put it in a bun and eat it. I just want what I bargained for."

"And you'll get it!" Calendar said, taking the book gingerly. He looked lovingly at the object he had been yearning for since childhood: a first-edition copy of Robert Louis Stevenson's *Treasure Island*, circa 1884.

August leaned over the book. "That's worth over thirty-five thousand dollars, I'll have you know. Very tricky to find. I was almost bludgeoned to death by a woman with a cane while trying to take it out of her hands."

"Your mother, I'm guessing?"

August laughed. "Grandmother, actually, but she'll get over it." He shut his briefcase and placed it on the floor between his feet. "Now. My information."

Calendar couldn't help but continue to admire his book. He forced his attention on August, hoping the encounter would last only a scant moment longer. "You're in luck," he said. "I have discovered through my sources that the opportunity you desire has, in fact, become available this very eve!"

August sat forward in his chair, a hand on each knee. "Tonight?"

"Yes!"

"So soon? How? Why?"

"It seems as though St. Vitus Cathedral has fallen into a bit of disrepair. So bad is the situation that the city has decided to take up the work of fixing it immediately. They transported the equipment yesterday. This morning, the workers began setting everything in position. And by tomorrow, things will be in full swing. But tonight!"

"Tonight?"

"Yes! Tonight you will be able to slip in unnoticed. The surveillance cameras were removed for the repair work. The other security devices are still active and will catch anyone who happens to try and break in. But for those people who know the proper entrances—"

"You can get me in."

"Ah, yes!" Calendar fiddled with his collar, trying to straighten it. "But why would someone like you want to pay a visit to the Black Queen?"

"This is precisely why I have paid you as handsomely as I have. No questions." August stood and placed his briefcase back on the table, opening it. "Of course, if you're not happy with the merchandise . . ."

"Oh, no, no, no," Calendar said, holding the book to his chest. "I'm more than happy." He made a motion across his mouth with his fingers: no more questions.

"Good," August said. "I'd best be going. I assume I'll find all the necessary items—maps, keys, and such—in the place we discussed?"

Calendar nodded, bobbing on his seat cushion.

August took one last sip of his coffee, set the cup down on a passing tray, and left Mr. Calendar to his fantasy adventure.

☩

Nightfall.

August loved Prague. The city surrounded him like a symphony, rich and regal and steeped in history. He wished only pleasure had brought him there—a trip to take in the sights and sounds, the cafés and the museums, and maybe a bookshop or two. But the edifice of St. Vitus Cathedral reminded him of his grim task.

He walked through the thin crowd of people milling in the courtyard of the Prague Castle complex. A couple strolled by, whispering sweetly in each other's ears. A little girl in a white dress held her father's hand, holding a red balloon by a string in the other. An elderly couple pointed at various features of the cathedral, discussing the architectural history at great length. It was an ordinary night, but a pleasant one. Nothing out of sorts. Why did August feel so ill at ease? *Maybe because you're grave-robbing,* he told himself.

Yes. That might be it.

He stole across the complex to the cathedral's southern entrance, the Golden Gate. Above the gate's three soaring archways, and behind the newly erected construction scaffolding, he spotted the famous fourteenth-century mosaic known as the *Last Judgment.* "How fitting," August said, approaching the iron gate beneath the westernmost arch.

He took a key out of his pocket. It was a bulky, crude key that would have appeared natural hanging from a dungeon-keeper's ring. He placed the key in the lock and turned. The tumblers groaned and the lock fell open. August pushed the heavy gate forward, wincing as it squealed in rusty protest. A few people glanced at him, then returned to their business. No big deal. Just someone working overtime. August adjusted the hat of his construction uniform, picked up his tool bag, and walked inside.

The first thing that captured his attention as he entered the cathedral was the aroma, faintly musty and inherently ancient, the accumulated smells of the medieval stone and wood that comprised the massive building. August crept through the corridors, keeping tightly to the path that Calendar had arranged for him on the map. *Someday I'll come back in the daylight,* he promised himself. He had never seen all the cathedral had to offer, including the tombs of several Bohemian kings, an ornate chapel dedicated to Saint Wenceslas, and, most notably, a celebrated relic: the arm of Saint Vitus. But there was one rare sight he wasn't going to miss tonight.

August stopped in the shadow of a corridor. Had he heard someone? He remained silent for a moment, listening, but nothing bent his ear. *Just the chatter of church mice,* he mused. Still, it would do him good to stay alert.

He finally reached the room he had been searching for. Calendar's map was precise to the last detail. There, on the other side, was the crypt. He approached it warily, trying to extinguish the ridiculous notions in his head. The quiet of the cathedral. The staleness of the air. The creepy, Gothic touches that filled every nook and corner. It all made for a nightmare, especially when combined with the sight before him: the grave of the Black Queen.

She was known in her lifetime by a different name: Cillei Borbála, or, more commonly, Barbara of Cejle. The daughter of

Count Herman II, she came from a long line of nobles, a commanding dynasty that continued for centuries after her departure from this life, her very blood running in the veins of Nicholas II of Russia hundreds of years later.

Her rise to prominence came with her marriage to the Holy Roman emperor Sigismund, a ruthless man who would stop at nothing to preserve his own crown, even going so far as to have his first wife and her mother kidnapped and then brutally killed. Sigismund met Barbara after her father saved Sigismund's life during a battle against the warring Turks. Barbara recognized him as the type of man she would need to collect the great forces of the land under a new banner of her own design—the Order of the Dragon.

August put his hand on the crypt. It was cold. He read an inscription carved into the stone: *Crna Kraljica. The Black Queen.* The name referred to a dark myth that had surrounded Barbara since her second death.

Yes, her second.

The story told of a powerful magician named Abra-Melin, also known as Abraham the Jew, a practitioner of magic based on his kabbalistic belief that the world was formed by the demons under the direction of angels. Sigismund knew of Abra-Melin's abilities—his creation of a spirit army to help Fredrick of Saxony, his supernatural aid in freeing the Earl of Warwick from prison, his saving of the antipope John XXIII from the Council of Constance —and employed the magus to advise him on a variety of matters, both public and private. Abra-Melin was said to have provided many extraordinary services for the emperor and his queen, but none so well known as Sigismund's final request: to raise Barbara from the dead.

It was just a legend. A gruesome fairy tale. But August found, as he prepared to remove the lid of her sarcophagus, that he couldn't dodge the image of Barbara sitting upright in her deathbed and grabbing him by the throat.

He inspected his work, the crank connected to the jack that would force the crypt open. "This is wrong on so many levels," he said aloud, his voice acting as a whistle in the dark.

He gripped the handle and began to turn. Soon he heard the grating sound of stone slipping on stone. The lid was coming free. A minute later a narrow crack emerged. He tried to shine his flashlight into the opening, but he couldn't get the right angle. He cranked some more. Half an inch. An inch. Two inches. He tried the light again. And this time, he saw something that made his heart quiver.

"Don't you know that it's bad manners to play with dead people?"

August spun. "I thought you were—"

"Dead myself?" Xandria pointed a gun at August's face. "You shouldn't believe everything you read."

"How did you get out?" he asked.

"I should ask you the same question."

"Ladies first."

Xandria lowered her gun, but kept it in a ready position. She would have plenty of time to fire a well-aimed shot if August even flinched. "Despite what you heard on the news, none of the bodies were ever recovered. They were simply too far down. The whole tunnel collapsed, making recovery an expensive endeavor, too expensive to merit digging up a few bodies no one wanted to claim. So when I escaped, I was free. More free than I had ever been, because I was *dead*."

"Did you find anything down there?"

"You know that I didn't," she said. "Otherwise I wouldn't be here. All that was left down there was an oversized souvenir, an empty room with a thousand empty vessels. The treasure must have been hidden there at one time, but I suppose it was moved after the Templars were vanquished. I escaped the same way the treasure did, through a passageway that led straight to the Kotnov Castle, or what's left of it, anyway."

"Did anyone else escape?"

"No. I went back to Žižka Square to see if I could save them. But the police had already arrived and were swarming the area. I stayed undercover for an entire month before leaving Europe."

"When did you start following me?"

"About two months ago. After returning to the States, I contacted one of the FBI agents connected to the Order, saying that I was an associate from overseas. He told me that you and your family had escaped, which at first I couldn't believe. Then he told me about Meng."

August remembered the day exactly as it had happened. Twenty minutes had expired from the clock. None of them—not he or April or even Charlie—could think of any way to escape. They'd been sealed in a box, that box was going to explode, and there was nothing they could do to stop it. With only a few moments left, they heard the door being unlocked. At first, they thought it was one of the FBI agents coming to put them out of their mental anguish. The door opened. It was an FBI agent, but his aim wasn't to kill, but to save. "Come with me, right now," Meng said. The three of them resisted at first, despite Meng's assurances that he was trying to help them. He had disabled the sensors injected into their bodies, he explained, but there was no way to deactivate the bomb, meaning that it was still about to go off. In the end, they had no choice but to follow him. Luckily, he was true to his word.

"We never would have gotten out of there if it wasn't for him," August said. "He disappeared a few days later. I still have no idea who he's working for, but it sure isn't the Order of the Dragon."

"I should have killed him while I had the chance," Xandria said. "He caused problems every step of the way, I just didn't know it. Was it Meng who figured out that the treasure was hidden here?"

August smiled. "Actually, you figured it out for me."

The gun dropped to Xandria's side.

"I couldn't help thinking that it was strange for the Order of the Dragon to have a male leader, when it acknowledged the existence of a monotheistic female deity."

Xandria didn't speak.

"Cornelius was a fraud, wasn't he?"

"As are most male leaders. How did you know?"

"I had to go back to the illuminations to figure it out. I'd seen them long enough to recall them clearly. I sketched them out and looked for any clues that I might have missed before, using the new set of criteria. At first, I didn't see anything, until—and it sounds so silly to me now—I got rid of the illuminations."

"I don't understand."

"The illuminations were there to distract from the truth," August said. "It made sense. Gutenberg was a man of letters and words; he would never hide a secret in pictures. The *initials*. That was the key. I wrote them down in the order the journal listed them: *S, M, S, A, N, A, E, L, I*. Nonsense, right? I looked up each of the occurrences in the Vulgate and discovered that the initials used for some of the illuminations were incorrect. I knew better than to assume it was a printing mistake: this was the message Gutenberg was trying to get to us."

Xandria was shaking. "What message?"

August tried to ignore the gun in her hand. "April uncovered the solution."

"April? Since when do you work together?"

"Actually, we've been getting along better than we ever did," August said. He couldn't help but grin a little.

"How sweet," Xandria ridiculed. "What did you find?"

"There was another book that Gutenberg printed while he was working on the enormous task of the Bible," August said. "Do you know what it was?"

"No. I've never heard anything about it."

"That's because he printed this other book in secret in an effort to pay his loans back to Fust. The book was called *The Sibylline Prophecies*, and it was fraught with distressing claims of the future. But the most interesting thing about the verses was the way in which the predictions were established. You didn't simply read the book. You *discovered* it."

"How?"

"The reader was supposed to take the first initial of each verse and combine them to create words. It was almost like a game."

"The first initial of each verse. I see. Just like the initials of the illuminations."

"Right. We applied the same idea to the Gutenberg initials. It wasn't easy. We didn't even know what language the result would be in . . . Latin . . . German. We weren't sure where to start. But then we remembered the map. In the center—connecting all the illuminations—was the coin with the woman's face. Based on that clue, we reduced the possibilities to a list of ancient goddesses and female royals. Eventually, we came up with a name that made sense. *Messalina.*"

"Barbara."

"Yes. Messalina was originally the wife of the Roman emperor Claudius. Our friend here"—he indicated Barbara's tomb—"was known as the Messalina of Sigismund's Holy Roman Empire."

"Emperor Sigismund was a pawn too," Xandria said. "He was nothing without Barbara. Before she came along, he was withering in his own stupidity. War was rampant. Even his allies hated him. The entire Holy Roman Empire was crumbling around him. Barbara changed all that with the Order of the Dragon."

"But she was forgotten for it, wasn't she?"

"Not by everyone. Not by me." Xandria paced, waving the gun. "You see, some people would look at her and say that she didn't achieve what she wanted because ultimately she didn't get credit for it. But credit can often equal death. I was happy to work from the shadows and allow Cornelius to take the credit, as well as the blame."

"So you were happy to sit by and watch the draconists idolize him?"

"Until the time was right."

"For what?"

"To fulfill the destiny Barbara was never able to attain," Xandria said. "The treasure will make it possible. Once it's in my hands, the Order will fall completely under my command. And that's just the beginning."

"Well, I hate to burst your bubble," August said. He reached into the crypt. "May I?"

Xandria nodded, lifting the barrel of her gun.

"The crypt of the Black Queen was the only place the treasure would have been hidden, given her history with the Order of the Dragon. The myth of her undeadness was probably added later to keep curious souls at bay. Who would dare disturb her grave?"

"You, apparently."

"You're right about that," August said. "I'm just too much of a fool to let a ghost keep me away from a fortune." August pulled out a single gold coin. "You were also right about the inscription," he said, holding it up. "It does indicate that the coin was made in Jerusalem. But you were wrong about the five-pointed star and the woman."

"What do you mean?"

"Archaeology has come a long way from the time of the Templars," August said. "The woman on the coin is a female deity, but not the one you or Barbara thought she was." He held up the side of the coin featuring the woman's profile. "Do you know who this is?"

Xandria glared, but didn't speak.

"The five-pointed star on the opposite side of the coin only makes it easier to prove," August said. "It's not even a star at all. It's a pentagon, surrounded by five rays. The pentagon was the shape of a temple built by Solomon. Maybe you should have read one of those Bibles you stole. The story is right there in 2 Kings."

"Get to the point."

August extended the coin to her. "Xandria, meet Ashtoreth."

"Lies," Xandria said. She raised her gun. "Lies!"

"It's not your fault," August said. "It's the Templars'. They found the Mount of Olives where Solomon's temple was built, but it seems they excavated the wrong location. They may have been good knights, but they were poor archaeologists. In spite of the Israelites' spotty history of faithfulness to Yahweh, no one knew any better, so the Templars were able to pull off the biggest blackmail job in world history. But all that ends tonight, because now you know the truth."

Xandria leveled her gun, and August imagined the laser-sight pinpricking his forehead. She was shaking.

August raised his hands. "Maybe we can work something out."

"I don't think so. I guess this was the one thing Gutenberg didn't see coming."

"No," a voice said. "This was."

Xandria turned. There was a loud crack, and she fell backward, striking her head against the stone wall. The gun fell out of her hand and clattered to the floor. August raced over and picked it up. He pointed it at her, but there was no reason for it. She was out cold.

"You were supposed to be here half an hour ago!" he said, taking a roll of wire out of the tool bag and wrapping it around Xandria's wrists and feet.

"Sorry," April said, shaking the pain out of her hand. "Charlie wanted me to read him a bedtime story before I left him with Grandma Rose."

"Isn't he a little old for that?"

"I still can talk him into it sometimes," April said, massaging her knuckles.

"You shouldn't baby him."

"I'm his mother. I can do whatever I please." She walked over to the crypt and peered inside. "Charlie will be happy to hear that we actually found the treasure."

August joined her. "Shall we?"

The two of them cranked aside the lid of the crypt and listened as it rumbled away. August climbed up, then extended a hand to pull up April. The two of them looked down on a shimmering ripple of gold. There were thousands of coins. Maybe *millions*. It was hard to imagine all the pains that had taken place to keep the treasure—and its lie—hidden. Wars had been waged. Lives had been lost. The magnitude of the discovery hadn't even begun to take effect.

August beamed. "It's beautiful, isn't it?"

"I think it will look better in a museum," April said. "The Smithsonian, maybe."

"But you know," August said, scooping up a handful of coins, "it may not be a bad idea to keep a few tiny mementos."

"I don't think so," April said, taking his hand and emptying it of the bounty. "If I know you, those would be on eBay in an hour."

"What are you talking about?" August said. "I've changed my ways."

"Some things never change."

He smiled. "Some things do."

illuminatedepilogueilluminatedil

CHRISTMAS
CHICAGO, ILLINOIS

Dalton Richards heard a knock at the door. "Who could be arriving so early?" he asked his wife. She was too busy to venture a guess. They had guests arriving in thirty minutes—grand-parents, aunts, and uncles—pretty much everybody they were related to.

"Just go ahead and answer it!" she said, running by with a plate of cookies.

Dalton opened the door.

"Is there a Clayton Richards at this address?" a deliveryman inquired.

"Yes. That's my son," Dalton said. "Don't you guys take today off?"

"Used to," the deliveryman said. His name tag announced him as *Wilson*. "Mind if I come in? It's getting pretty bad out there."

Wilson entered. Dalton wasn't sure whether to offer him something warm to drink. It would mean bothering his wife, and that was the last thing he wanted to do. Her glare was worse than a kick in the shin. "So," Dalton said, making pointless conversation. "You're here to deliver something to Clayton?"

"Yep. Sure am. Well, actually, no."

"No?"

"Well, it's sort of hard to explain."

"I don't follow."

"What's going on, Dad?" Clayton bounded down the stairs. "I heard someone say my name."

Dalton rubbed his son's head. "This is Wilson. He has a delivery for you."

"Oh, boy!" Clayton said. "Is it from Santa?" he asked his father, giving a wink.

"Actually, I don't know who it's from," Dalton said. He turned to Wilson with a puzzled expression on his face.

Wilson looked at his digital board. "It's from a Mr. Adams . . . a Mr. August Adams."

Dalton was still confused. "I don't think I know of anyone by that name. Do you, Clayton?"

The boy tapped his head, Pooh Bear-style. "I can't remember," he said.

"Where do I sign?" Dalton asked. "No point in sending someone away with a gift on Christmas Day. I'm sure we'll figure it out."

"Maybe it's from Santa after all," Clayton said.

Dalton scribbled his name on the digital signature pad. "Maybe you're right!" He handed the board back to Wilson. "So where is this mysterious package?"

"That's the weird part," Wilson said.

"It's not with you?"

"No. It's at the zoo."

"The zoo?" Dalton laughed. "Why did you leave a package for my son at the zoo?"

"This might be presumptuous of me to say," Wilson said. "But I don't think you would have had enough room for it here at your house."

"I beg your pardon?" Dalton said.

Wilson looked at Clayton. "In two weeks, go to the zoo. Look for the signs pointing to a new display. When you find it, you'll see your name on a little bronze plaque next to the glass."

"Listen, I'm sorry," Dalton said, escorting Wilson toward the door. "We've got guests coming in only a few minutes, and I'm afraid I'm going to have to ask you to leave."

"Suit yourself," Wilson said, stepping out into the cold. He called back into the house at Clayton. "Merry Christmas!"

Dalton shut the door. "What was all that about?" he asked Clayton before scurrying off to join his wife in the last-minute Christmas cleanup.

Clayton grinned. He knew exactly what was going on.

His tiger shark had arrived.

further mysteries

This book is a journey we experienced together. With the characters as your guides, you unraveled the secrets the same way I did—piece by piece, puzzle by puzzle. And now you have the opportunity to engage the story in a whole new way, because this is only the beginning of the mystery.

But before we move forward, I need to share with you the roots of this book. I wish I could say that I dreamed it all up. That would certainly be less alarming, to tell you that none of it was true.

Years ago I saw a show on A&E proclaiming Gutenberg "Man of the Millennium." Man of the Millennium? Really? I was shocked. From my memory, Gutenberg was a footnote in my high school history book. So who was this guy? I hunted everywhere for articles about him, stumbling across one in particular that made my eyes bulge. It turned out that his famous Bible was worth—could this be right?—nearly $100 million dollars. (You probably thought I made that up!) As they say, truth is stranger than fiction, but this wasn't even close to the strangeness I would later uncover.

Gutenberg was a man of mystery. His birthdate was—at best—a guess. Sizeable chunks of his life were an abyss, completely void of information. The few facts that did exist seemed to suggest a larger story, something far more disturbing going on behind the curtain. But what was it? That was the question that drove me.

Delving deeper into the murky waters of Gutenberg's history, I uncovered conspiracy after conspiracy, secret society after secret society. I realized that finding an end to the multitude of rabbit holes meant focusing my attention on two opposing forces that circled Gutenberg's life.

THE ORDER OF THE DRAGON. Any clandestine club crazy enough to call themselves by that name had to be at the top of my list. Again, stuff like this is too good to be made-up. The Order was real. (And, if the Web sites are true, it still exists today!) They were vicious, well organized, and determined to vanquish anyone in their path. Which led me to their most hated enemy . . .

THE ORPHANS. Started by John Huss and later led by the illustrious general Žižka, they were equally motivated to battle, though by a completely different set of ideals, a combination of factors both political and religious. Their headquarters—the city of Tábor—was an enigma as well, with its maze of underground tunnels and hidden passageways. How great was all this!? It was like *Lost* and *24* and Lord of the Rings all rolled into one!

Each new day of research and writing took me deeper into the medieval labyrinth. I must admit that a certain amount of paranoia eventually set in. It all seems a bit silly now, but I remember the late nights, feeling my heart quicken, imagining Dracula-shaped specters from the past creeping up behind me and slitting my throat for shedding light on their nefarious plans. Like I said—silly. (Okay, I just glanced over my shoulder and noticed a man in a black suit, staring at me. And was that a dragon medallion around his neck?)

This book is a work of fiction. But its strangest ideas are built upon a firm foundation of historicity. I'll warn you, if you begin to dig into the facts of this story for yourself, and if you possess the same obsessive soul I have, you may find yourself in the back recesses of some forgotten library, blowing dust off books and glancing over your shoulder in fear! But whatever happens, please let me know what you find. As I said, this is a journey we're on together. I've pointed out the edges of the path – but it's up to you to pick up your torch and voyage into the darkness that lies ahead.

Free soundtrack for *Illuminated* available at
www.mattbronleewe.com

acknowledgments

Although this book was written in what could best be described as the solitary confinement of my mind, it was by no means created alone. There is a long list of contributors, co-conspirators, inspirers, mentors, and enablers, only a small portion of which can be mentioned here.

To my little family, I owe the world. They are my world. Karin, thanks for putting up with the strange hours and last-minute trips and general zaniness that became our life. I promise nothing but more for the future! Your love sustains me through the hard times, and makes the good times even more golden. Thanks for being my first reader, my first editor, my first everything. I am so lucky to have you! George, Cole, and Grace—my little chiplings, my little fire breathers and life givers and heart-warmers—all my love and devotion. This new journey would mean nothing if I could not share it with you.

Beyond the obvious contribution of my existence, I must thank my amazing parents—Tom and Bev Bronleewe (also known as Dad and Mom!). You are a beacon of light in a dark-filled world. Words cannot express my gratitude.

There are a few people who are responsible (I say "responsible" for those of you who would like to know who to blame for releasing this novel upon an unsuspecting public) for giving me the opportunity to fulfill a dream. Charlie Peacock was the first person to listen to my notion that I fancied myself a writer and not laugh. Rather, he kindly opened the doors to the wonderful world of book publishing for me. Charlie, I cannot thank you enough. The result of Charlie's efforts was to be connected with the legendary Don Pape, whose mind has the ability to swallow new worlds whole. Don, thank you for letting me be one of the few privileged enough to be represented by you. Lee Hough, thank you for picking up the torch from Don and carrying it onward. Your wisdom and insight are a welcome shelter in the storm that is the creative life. I look very much forward to working more with you and the brilliant people at Alive Communications.

I hold deep appreciation and admiration for my publishing family at Thomas Nelson. Allen Arnold, thanks first and foremost for getting it, for giving me (and my crazy ideas) a place to call home. You're an absolute genius, and I feel lucky to call you both publisher and friend. Mike Hyatt, thanks for the taking the time to encourage me, even when I was just a twinkle in Thomas Nelson's eye. Amanda Bostic, thanks for your ceaseless enthusiasm and creative focus. I fear I would be lost in the creative woods were it not for you lighting the path ahead! Jennifer Deshler, thanks for your undying fervor and amazing ability to dream big. To my other friends and supporters there—Ami McConnell, Natalie Hanemann, Lisa Young, Mark Ross, Heather Adams, Carrie Wagner, and so many more!

The research for this novel was extensive, and could never have been accomplished without the diligent eyes and mind of Casey Mask. Thanks for going above and beyond what was asked of you.

Thanks to the kind people at Greenville College, the Huntington Library in California, the Morgan Library in New York, and the exquisite Library of Congress in Washington, D.C.

This novel grew by leaps and bounds in the deft hands of Erin Healy, whose title as "editor" falls well short of the importance it includes. World-changer, idea-exploder . . . these seem like better titles (though probably less professional sounding!) Thanks for pushing, pushing, and then pushing some more for the absolute best.

I must thank my manager, Dave Steunebrink, for not batting an eye the day I told him, "I'm writing a book." I think if I said, "I'm building a rocket and flying to the moon," he would simply say, "Awesome. How can I help?" He's simply the BEST, and I don't have enough fingers and toes to count the number of times he has blessed me with his grin. I also must thank Lani Crump, who balances budgets and calendars and a million other things, and contributes daily to my madness. Keep those fresh ideas coming!

To my writer-friends, who humble me with their abilities: Ted Dekker, Robert Liparulo, Chris Well, Allan Heinberg, Eric Wilson, Sigmund Brouwer, Reed Arvin, Xan Hood, Tom Davis, and so many others: thank you, thank you, thank you. Art would be meaningless without community.

I wish I could go on. This book would double in length if I were allowed to finish this list. Wait! My sisters, Emily (Pardy) and Erin (Stansbury), and their respective families; my good friend Jeremy Bose; the Swansons; the Duvalls; more Bronleewes; and so many others! This is too unfair. To everyone that I can't thank in writing, I hope to in person!

Before parting, I must give thanks to the Great Writer, the Magnificent Creator, my loving and inspiring heavenly Father, without whom nothing would be possible.